The Queen's Captain

A Ransom-Family Novel

Thomas R. Lawrence

Also by Thomas R. Lawrence

Delta Days, Tales of the Mississippi Delta

Cow College, Tales of Mississippi State College

will d…a life in science

My Magic Year

Jake's Revenge

Thomas R. Lawrence

The Queen's Captain

A Ransom-Family Novel

Thomas R. Lawrence

Thomas R. Lawrence

For my brother, Steve

Front Porch Press, LLC
Publishers
4881 Canada Road
Lakeland, Tennessee 38002

Front Porch Press Logo Is a Registered
Trademark of
Front Porch Press, LLC
© 2014
Thomas R. Lawrence
All Rights Reserved

Library of Congress Cataloging-in-Publication Data
ISBN Print 978-0-9839216-9-1
ISBN e-Pub 978-0-9978114-0-7
© 2017 by Tom Lawrence
All Rights Reserved

ACKNOWLEDGMENTS

Special Thanks to the Following:

My companion, Clista Haley, provides the balanced and loving environment that enables me to spend the needed time to pursue my passion for writing. Her support, encouragement, and honest feedback were essential in helping me accomplish the result that I endeavored to deliver in *The Queen's Captain*.

My business partner, Deborah Fagan Carpenter, served the essential role of first editor. She suggested rewrites, designed the cover, formatted the book, and performed the final production.

I am blessed to have Maggie Lee as my final editor. Maggie is meticulous and thorough, and any errors or mistakes are mine, not hers.

Writing the book was the easy part.

Thomas R. Lawrence

INTRODUCTION

The inspiration for a novel about the Ransom family was found in a short story that I wrote in 2010. The piece was set during the Reconstruction period following the War Between the States, and the central character for the narrative was based on a direct descendant of Miles Stuart Ransom, the protagonist of *The Queen's Captain*. That short story was chosen for publication by a respected journal of Southern literature, and it was the first of my writings to be published. I still get a tingle up my spine when I remember it.

The Ransom family continued to appear from time to time in my short stories, and the Will Ransom character in *Jake's Revenge* is the modern-day family member. In 2016, my brother, Steve, suggested that I use them as characters for a full-length historical novel. *The Queen's Captain* is the first in a series of books chronicling the lives and adventures of the Ransom family in the New World. Set during Queen Anne's War in 1710, the story introduces and follows Captain Miles Stuart Ransom, of the Royal Navy, as he recovers from battle wounds and makes the decision to seek his fortune in Colonial America.

1 THE QUEEN'S CAPTAIN

The late summer sun warmed the air as the 74-gun ship of the line, *HMS Dragon,* docked at Boston's busy waterfront. Royal Marine Captain Miles Stuart Ransom leaned against the rail of the ship and took a puff on the tightly rolled cylinder of tobacco leaves. The *Dragon* had made a short visit to Kingston, Jamaica, and Miles had purchased a case of the little smokes that the Spanish called cigarros.

Ransom had picked up the cigar habit during a visit to Havana, Cuba, in 1703, when he discovered the Montoya family's products, and he tried to keep a supply on hand. Acquisition of the quality smokes had become a challenge since Britain decided to declare war on France and Spain. Fortunately, Jamaica was a hotbed of privateers preying on Spanish ships, and there were plenty of Spanish goods for sale.

Miles Ransom commanded the Royal Marine detachment on the *Dragon* and could have cared less who ended up on the Spanish throne. The fact that Queen Anne cared was enough for him. He'd fight the French, the Spanish, or anyone else who crossed the Queen. He'd been an officer in the Royal Navy since he was 13 years old, when his father, the Earl of Conway, had purchased his commission.

It never occurred to Miles to question the concept of primogeniture that gave the family title to the oldest son, sent the next son into the military, and consigned the youngest to the church. The truth was that he'd rather be a soldier than a Peer, and, while he considered himself a member of the Church of England, he never gave a thought to a career as a clergyman.

While it may have been true that his brother David would become the sixth Earl of Conway, Miles's father had not left him penniless. The family financial affairs had been administered by the Dalhousie Merchant Bank in Bordeaux since the first earl had won his fortune fighting with Henry V at Agincourt. Percy, the first earl, had understood the risk of owning wealth in a monarchy and had wisely kept most of his liquid assets offshore. The Dalhousies had been merchant bankers since before William's victory at Hastings and had offices worldwide.

On the day that Ransom's father had delivered him to the Royal Navy at Portsmouth, the earl had deposited 10,000 Spanish gold doubloons into Miles's account with the Dalhousies. Miles's father told him that if he allowed the Dalhousies to manage his inheritance, then he would never be dependent on his meager military pay. Miles had followed his father's advice and become a very wealthy man. His account with the Dalhousie firm stood at £175,000.

Captain Ransom was a wealthy man but limited in formal education. The series of family tutors had taught Miles to read, write, and perform basic math. His older brother, David, attended the university at Oxford, and his younger brother had studied religion at a seminary in Rome. Miles, on the other hand, entered the Navy at such a tender age that he was forced to educate himself.

Over the years, Miles had accumulated a reasonably decent library, which he kept at his family home. When at sea, he always had several books to read. Ransom finished his cigar and tossed the butt overboard, just as a midshipman came running up and with a salute stammered, "Sir, the captain requests your presence in his cabin."

Ransom returned the salute and made his way below. As Miles knocked on the captain's cabin hatch, a deep voice called out, "Enter."

Miles opened the hatch and bent his six-foot frame as he went through. The captain of *HMS Dragon*, Sir William Darcy, stood beside his desk in full uniform. He adjusted his sword and said, "We'll be receiving a special visitor this morning, and I want all officers to attend a meeting in the wardroom at six bells on the forenoon watch. This gathering will be especially important to you and your officers. It is very likely that we will be the flagship for a fleet attacking Port Royal in French North America, and there may be the need for you and your officers to lead a contingent during an amphibious operation."

"Do we know when we'll sail?"

"Not yet, but I suspect we'll find out later this morning. Ransom, I've grown to depend on you, and I know you will discharge your duties in the best traditions of the Royal Navy."

Ransom stood to attention and replied, "Aye aye, sir. I'll not let you down."

"I'm sure you won't."

Ransom saluted the captain and closed the hatch behind him. When Miles regained the deck, he looked about and saw his second in command, First Lieutenant Robert Gaines, keeping watch. Gaines stood to attention when Ransom approached, and Miles said, "Stand down, Bob; it seems that we might see a little action. Sir William just gave me a heads-up for us to attend a meeting this morning. We may be the flagship of a fleet attacking the French, and he mentioned a possible amphibious operation, as well."

Gaines relaxed and replied, "God knows we've drilled our men enough in launching such an action. I doubt that any Marine company in the Royal Navy could match us."

"Yes, we've pushed them hard, and they should perform well if the situation demands. We'll need to have all hands prepared to receive our visitors by six bells. Make sure they are in full uniform to man the rails. I'll relieve you here and complete your watch; you go and take care of the men."

Ransom stood to the starboard side of the foredeck and watched the busy Boston waterfront. He reached into his tunic pocket, pulled out another cigar, and bit the end off. He was preparing to light it when a voice said, "How about it, Ransom; those things come like dead men, one to the box?"

Miles turned toward the voice and said, "No, sir.

Would you like one?"

Lieutenant Commander Lloyd Sparks, the *Dragon*'s executive officer, grinned and said, "Don't mind if I do. If I know you as well as I think I do, you loaded up while we were in Kingston."

Ransom pulled another cigar from his tunic and handed it to Sparks. Sparks bit the end off and waited for Ransom to light the smoke. Sparks took a deep puff, exhaled it, and said, "I saw you coming up from below; did Sir William give you the news?"

"He did, in as much as he told me that the *Dragon* might be the flagship of a fleet attacking the French."

"There's no maybe about it. I've seen the orders. Sir William is being promoted to commodore and will lead the fleet. I've been promoted to commander and will captain the *Dragon*."

Ransom snapped to attention and said, "Congratulations, Commander—a well-deserved promotion for both you and Sir William."

"Oh, before I forget it, the orders included the appointment of a marine officer to be in command over all of the fleet's marine companies."

"That's interesting; to whom will I be answering?"

"To yourself. Congratulations, Major Ransom."

"Pardon me, sir, but are you certain about this? I'm junior to most marine captains in the Navy, and it's highly unlikely that I would be promoted over men with more seniority."

"How old are you, Ransom?"

"I just turned 25 in August."

"Then you are probably the youngest major in the entire Navy. Doesn't hurt that Sir William and your father were classmates, does it?"

"I hope that isn't the only reason for my promotion."

"No, I'm sure your father's position on the House of Lords committee of the Admiralty came into play, as well."

Ransom stiffened and replied, "Sir, I hope the performance of my duties has been satisfactory."

"Oh, relax, Miles. You've been an outstanding officer, and Sir William and I agreed to your promotion."

Ransom took a pull on his cigar and said, "Thank you, Lloyd. I don't want to jump over half the Navy if I haven't earned it."

"Well, you certainly have, but you are going to have to live with the fact that you're among the richest officers in the service and the son of an influential Peer."

"I suppose you're right. I'll just have to handle it. Did our orders mention a promotion for Lieutenant Gaines?"

"No, but since he's under your command, I suppose you can promote him, if it pleases you."

"It does please me. Robert is an excellent officer who cares for his men. I'll tend to his promotion right away."

"You do realize that you are no longer under the command of the captain of the *Dragon* but are on the commodore's staff, don't you?"

"Does that mean you'll be buying your own cigars from now on?"

"No, but it does mean that I'll be responsible for your food and lodging. Try not to piss me off, and I'll see that you get a pleasing berth."

"Rank doth have its privileges."

"Indeed, it does."

When the bell sounded the end of the watch, Ransom went below to change into his dress uniform. When he stooped through the hatch, he saw a new red dress jacket, complete with the shoulder board and the single crown of a major. There was a dress hat sitting on top of the jacket with a note.

Major Ransom,

Congratulations on your well-deserved promotion. Please accept these gifts as an indication of my personal and professional esteem.

William Darcy, KBE
Commodore, RN

Miles looked at the label in the coat and recognized his tailors on Bond Street. Sir William had known about this promotion well before they left Portsmouth. Miles took off his captain's jacket, put on a clean white shirt, and then pulled on a freshly blackened pair of boots. When he donned the new coat, it fit perfectly; apparently, his tailor was involved in the conspiracy.

Once Major Ransom was satisfied with his new uniform, he removed the captain's insignia from his old coat and made his way to Lieutenant Gaines's cabin. He tapped on the hatch, and, as he pushed it open, he saw Robert Gaines standing in his underwear. Gaines grimaced and said, "Damn, Miles.

I need to get into uniform to welcome our guests."

"That's why I'm here. I didn't want you to be improperly dressed."

"You're joking, right? I've been dressing without your help for a long time, and I don't need to stand for your inspection."

"Careful, Captain Gaines; you're bordering on insubordination."

Gaines turned to look at Miles and said, "Did you just call me 'Captain'?"

"I did, and you should be more respectful when addressing field-grade officers."

Gaines looked at the insignia of rank on Miles's shoulder and snapped to attention. Miles grinned and said, "I thought you might like to have these."

Without comment, he handed Gaines the captain's shoulder boards.

Gaines took the boards and looked at them with disbelief.

"Miles, is this official?"

"It is, and, since you are in command of the flagship's Marine Company, I'll leave you to your duties. I need to visit with the commodore."

Miles shook Gaines's hand, withdrew through the hatch, and walked to the commodore's cabin. Two of his marines stood guarding the door and snapped to attention as he approached. Ransom nodded and smiled as he entered the hatch. Sir William and Sparks were bending over a map in a broad discussion. When the commodore saw Ransom, he looked up and said, "Ah, Major, I see you found your new uniform. Come and join us as we plot our course to New France."

"Yes, sir, and thank you for your kind note and the uniform."

"You are welcome. Come and give us your opinion."

Lloyd Sparks moved to the side and gave Miles room near the desk. Spread across its mahogany top was a Royal Navy chart of French North America. Sir William used a pen as a pointer and put the tip on Port Royal, the capital of French Acadia. He tapped the pen three times and said, "This will be our objective."

The three men studied the chart for several minutes, and they clearly saw the danger of attacking Port Royal by sea. The narrow opening to the Straits of Digby would make it perilous to bring the huge ships of the line in from the Bay of Fundy. The attack would have to take place without their massive cannons.

Miles saw this right away, but he wasn't a naval officer, so he deferred to Commander Sparks. The commodore asked, "What do the two of you think?"

Sparks glanced at Miles and then replied, "There is no way we can bring the ships of the line through the Straits of Digby and risk having them trapped. The Straits could hold a single ship and bottle up the whole fleet."

Sir William looked at Miles. "And you, Major?"

"I completely agree with the commander. It would be asking for disaster to risk our ships of the line."

Sir William took another look at the chart and said, "Within the hour, General Francis Nicholson and his staff will come aboard to brief us on his grand strategy. I wanted to make sure of my position before the meeting."

"Will the other officers of the fleet be present?"

"Not at this meeting, but I intend to call a captains' meeting this evening, and, naturally, both of you will attend. Lloyd, you as captain of the *Dragon*, and you, Miles, as commander over all of the fleet marines, are important participants."

Sparks thought for a moment and then asked, "Sir

William, do we know the makeup of the fleet?"

"Yes, in addition to the *Dragon* and *Falmouth*, the *Feversham* and the *Lowestoft* just arrived from New York. *HMS Chester* is stationed here in Boston, so it will also be part of the fleet. In addition to these warships, there are two bomb barges and 36 transports."

Miles paused. He then asked, "Sir William, are you familiar with General Nicholson?"

"Francis Nicholson has served as a soldier and colonial administrator since 1685, and he's currently carrying a commission as major general. In the past, he was governor of Maryland and Virginia, and he and his patron, Samuel Vetch, are current favorites at Queen Anne's court. Nicholson is more politician than military leader."

Miles decided to keep his thoughts to himself and let the morning play out. His father had mentioned Nicholson as someone not to be trusted, but the man clearly had the confidence of the Queen. Like him or not, he was going to be leading this operation.

There was a knock on the hatch, and a midshipman said, "Sir William, the general's carriage is approaching."

The commodore sighed and said, "Well, gentlemen, shall we go greet our illustrious leader?"

When they gained topside, the crew—in dress uniform—was formed up along the rails. Commander Sparks moved to the gangplank and stood at attention as Major General Francis Nicholson and his staff boarded the ship. The general was resplendent in full dress uniform, as were the three officers trailing behind him. After saluting the general, Sparks led him to Sir William, who also saluted him and suggested that they retire to the commodore's cabin.

Miles fell in behind the staff officers, one of whom he noted wore the uniform of a major in the Royal Marines. From the grizzled look of him, Miles decided that the oldest and the youngest majors in the Royal Marines might be on the same ship.

Once inside the commodore's cabin, Sir William offered the general a seat at a small table and indicated that Sparks should join them. Another officer with the insignia of a full captain took the last seat. Miles and the other two members of the general's staff stood along the walls of the cabin. When all were comfortable, Sir William said, "General Nicholson, it is my honor to represent the Royal Navy on your future operations. My men and my ships are at your service."

Nicholson was a tall man with a lean, sharp, clean-shaven face, and he wore a dark-brown wig that flowed below the stiff collar of his uniform. He signaled to the Navy captain and said, "Captain Reed, would you provide the commodore with a copy of my orders?"

The officer reached inside his tunic, removed a folded paper, and handed it to Sir William. Sir William read the paper and asked, "General, may I share this with my officers?"

Nicholson nodded and replied, "You may."

Sir William passed the note to Sparks, who read it and said, "Major Ransom," as he extended the note to Miles.

Miles read:

I, Anne, by the Grace of God, Queen of the United Kingdom of England, Scotland, and Wales, on this day, August 15, in the tenth year of our reign do proclaim:

To all loyal subjects of my realm, I make the following appoint of Major General Francis Nicholson as

"General and Commander in Chief of all and sundry the Forces, to be employed in the expedition dispatched to capture and occupy Port Royal in French Acadia."

Anne R

May 22, 1710

When Miles had finished reading the commission, he handed it back to Sparks but thought, "Well, that didn't leave much open to debate. Nicholson is firmly in command."

Sir William handed the commission across the table to Reed without comment. Reed folded it and put it back into the tunic. He then said, "Commodore, I know you are interested in what part you will play in my plans, so let's cut to the chase. You and your ships will support my landings at Port Royal. Your heavy cannons will be our artillery."

A cloud passed over Sir William's face, and he replied, "I believe it is too risky to bring ships of the line through the Straits of Digby. We can give you two bomb barges to provide supporting fire."

"Commodore, did you not understand my orders from the Queen? You will deploy your ships as I direct, and you will follow my orders promptly and willingly. Are we clear on this?"

"I have already considered the risk of having the fleet trapped in the Bay of Digby, but I have been assured that the nearest enemy fleet is south of Hispaniola. I refuse to have five men-of-war sitting idly by while Major Holmes's brave marines assault the fort at Port Royal. You will do as I order, or I will replace you with Captain Reed," Nicholson said pointing to the naval officer sitting at the table.

Sir William turned crimson, and Miles thought he might explode. In an earlier day, he might have slapped Nicholson with his gauntlet and challenged him to pistols or swords, but he regained control and said, "I am quite clear. Is there anything else you want to tell me?"

"Just this. Major Holmes will be commanding all of the Royal Marines in the fleet, and your major here will be his subordinate. He will report to Major Holmes when ordered. Is that clear, as well?"

"Perfectly."

"Good, I'm glad we've come to an understanding. Now, we must return to my headquarters to complete our work. We sail on the 29th."

Nicholson rose, and he and his entourage marched to the deck. Without ceremony, they trooped down the gangway and departed in their carriage. Sir William, Sparks, and Miles were left standing on the deck watching their commander disappear.

2 THE QUEEN'S CAPTAIN

Once Nicholson's carriage was out of sight, Sir William muttered through clinched teeth, "To my cabin."

Sparks and Miles dutifully followed Darcy and stood at attention until he snapped, "Stand down and have a seat."

The two officers sat and watched Sir William pace back and forth with his hands behind his back. Finally, he stopped the pacing, leaned across his desk, and growled, "Ransom, do you have any of those foul-smelling cigars you love so much?"

Miles took a cigar out of his tunic, stood, and offered it to the commodore. Darcy bit the end off and spit it on the deck. Miles lit it for him. Sir William took a deep puff and blurted, "Damn, Ransom. You and Commander Sparks could join me."

Miles handed a cigar to Sparks and lit one for himself. The three of them smoked for several minutes until Sir William said, "Gentlemen, what you witnessed this morning should never have happened. A professional military man would have presented his orders in private. He would never humiliate a fellow officer in public. I have been in the Royal Navy for nearly 30 years, and I never expected to be treated so disrespectfully."

Miles and Sparks sat silently as Sir William continued, "I regret that you had to witness this, but I hope you can put it out of your minds. I will follow the orders given to me by the officer the Queen appointed. I'll expect nothing less of you. Let there never be a mention of this unfortunate episode in the future."

Lloyd Sparks stood and said, "Of course — we'll honor your request and execute our duties to the best of our abilities. There is only one thing that I will ask of you. You must enter this morning's meeting into the ship's log, state your concern about the Straits of Digby, and allow Major Ransom and me to countersign the log."

Sir William thought for a moment and then replied, "Yes, Commander, that is exactly the proper thing to do. I will have the yeoman prepare the entry for your signatures. I thank both of you for your discretion in this matter. Captain Sparks, I'll hold a captains' meeting at two bells on the first dog watch. We'll meet in the wardroom. Please see that your executive officer is present, and, of course, I want Major Ransom to be included. Now, I'd like some private time to prepare."

Sparks asked Miles to come to his cabin and, when the hatch was closed, he said, "I agree with Sir William. No professional would have acted as Nicholson did."

"No, of course, you're both right, and I don't think that ass-kissing captain behaved any better. He should have protested Nicholson's threats. Do you know anything about him?"

Sparks thought for a moment and then replied, "Dixon Reed, wasn't it? No, the name is not at all familiar to me."

"Nor to me. I suspect we'll have to keep a close eye on him."

"How about the marine major? I believe his name was Holmes. Do you know him?"

"No, but some of my noncommissioned officers have been around a lot longer than I. I'll have Bob make inquiries. Holmes must be close to 40 or 45, and he looks like he's seen a lot of action."

"I'm surprised that you didn't protest his appointment as commander of the fleet's Royal Marines. You hold the same rank."

"We may both be majors, but, unless he was promoted in the carriage on the way here, he most surely has the seniority."

"Aye, there's that for sure. I hope he proves to be competent."

"As do I. I know you have business to attend to so I'll allow you to do so. I'd like to go to Boston to see if I can find lodgings."

"Why? Don't you plan to remain in your cabin on board?"

"Yes, I'll still use it when we're no longer in port, but I'd like to be out from under Bob's feet while he gets his sea legs in his new command. It will go more quickly if I'm not around all the time."

"Well, don't forget to be here for the captains' meeting. Today would not be the day to irritate Sir William; he's in the mood to keelhaul someone."

"I think I'll send him a box of cigars before I go. It'll give him something to chew on besides your sorry ass."

"Any help along those lines will be appreciated."

Miles left the cabin and went to his. He removed the dress uniform and put on the white pants and blue coat used for regular duty. He removed a box of cigars from the case in his locker and left to find Captain Gaines. He found Gaines sitting at his desk in his cabin. Miles tapped on the hatch and said, "Bob, I'll be going ashore until the first dog watch. While I'm gone, I'd like for you to do two things for me."

"Of course," Gaines replied.

Miles handed the cigars to Gaines and said, "First, I'd like you to have one of the midshipmen deliver these to Sir William's cabin with my regards. Second, check around with the senior enlisted men and see if we have anyone who has served under a marine officer named Richard Holmes. Holmes is currently a major and will be commanding the fleet's Royal Marines."

"I thought Sir William had appointed you to that position."

"He was overruled by General Nicholson, who brought Holmes with him."

"What will be your role?"

"He has yet to let me know, but I'll be happy to serve under him."

Gaines gave a quizzical look and replied, "As you

say. I'll check to see if any of the men have served with him. I'll let you know when you return."

"Thanks, Bob. I'll be back in time for the captains' meeting at two bells."

Miles closed the hatch behind him and climbed to the main deck. He saluted the ensign and made his way down the gangway to the dock. He saw a hansom cab waiting nearby and signaled the cabby to pick him up. He gave the cabby an address, sat back, and took in the busy sights of Boston Harbor.

Miles could see the rest of the fleet anchored in the harbor, as there was only room for the flagship to dock. He could see the naval ensigns waving in the wind, and it sent a shiver of pride down his spine. Boston was a little bit of England, and he felt at home here.

The cab made its way up from the harbor and stopped at 210 Hanover Street. Miles instructed the driver to wait, and he stepped onto the cobbled street. There was a small brass plaque proclaiming 210 to be the offices of the Dalhousie Merchant Bank, and Miles tapped on the door. When it opened, a tall, lean young man with a slight French accent said, "Good afternoon. I am Philippe Dalhousie. How may I be of service?"

Miles reached inside his tunic, produced an envelope,

handed it to the man, and replied, "My name is Miles Ransom, and this is a letter of introduction from your firm's London office."

The young man smiled and said, "Welcome, Major Ransom. Please follow me."

Philippe turned and walked through the small lobby into a private office with "Manager" painted on the door. Motioning for Miles to have a seat, he sat behind the desk, opened the letter, and read it carefully. Then he said, "You have come very highly recommended, Major. What can the Dalhousie Boston office do for you?"

"I serve on *HMS Dragon,* currently berthed in the harbor, and we will be based here for the foreseeable future. When in port, it is my custom to take rooms in the city rather than remain on board. I would like your assistance in locating such accommodations."

Philippe Dalhousie paused for a moment and then asked, "Do you wish to rent these rooms?"

"I'd prefer to buy, if it's practical, but I'm willing to rent if nothing can be found to buy."

"Tell me what would be ideal for you."

"I wish to buy a commercial building with a business on the street and rooms on the upper floors. I always like to own a lodging that has a paying tenant, as well."

"I take it you've done this before."

"Yes, I own such buildings in Paris, Bordeaux, and Rome."

"Major, I feel compelled to remark that many of your holdings are in countries presently in a state of war with Great Britain. How do you maintain your properties in hostile lands?"

"I have a long-term relationship with your firm. Dalhousie takes care of my holdings regardless of the current political or military situation."

Again, Philippe smiled and replied, "And it will be our pleasure to arrange such a place in Boston. Your letter of introduction includes a letter of credit for £25,000 sterling. Would you like to draw on it now?"

"No, I currently have sufficient funds, but I would like to use the letter to purchase a property if one is available."

"How long will you be in port?"

"We have no present plans to return to sea. I can be reached on board the *Dragon* if you find something you think I might be interested in."

"I'll begin to look for such a property immediately,

but, in the meantime, if you wish to lodge in the city, I might suggest the Henry House Tavern and Inn on Queen Street. It has clean rooms, a convivial atmosphere, and excellent food."

"Alright, I believe I'll take your advice and rent a room at the Henry House if there is a vacancy."

Philippe took a pen and began writing on the back of a small white card. When he finished, he handed the card to Miles and said, "Give this to Josiah Adams."

Miles looked at the engraved card and read it.

Philippe de Moyne Dalhousie
Dalhousie Merchant Bankers
210 Hanover Street
Boston, Massachusetts

London — Lisbon — Amsterdam

Miles turned the card over and saw a handwritten note:

Josiah, please extend all possible
courtesies to my good friend
Major Miles S. Ransom,
HMS Dragon.

Miles put the card in his tunic and said, "May I address you as Philippe?"

"Please do," Philippe replied.

"And please feel free to call me Miles. Thank you for the introduction. I couldn't help but notice that there is no mention of offices in any French or Spanish location, yet the headquarters of your firm is in Bordeaux."

Philippe smiled and said, "As the saying goes, we must react to the exigencies of war. With the world in constant turmoil and considering that we have offices across the globe, we find it necessary to have new cards printed on a regular basis. A minor inconvenience compared to the main tragedy of the current conflict."

Miles frowned and asked, "Just what might that be?"

Philippe saw the frown and said, "I must confess to a personal issue. I have developed an insatiable need for high-quality cigars from Cuba. All of the tobacco shops in Boston have been sold out for the past two years."

"You mean you haven't had a smoke in two years?"

"No, local smugglers bring in cigars, but they are of lower quality, and I fear I'm beginning to like the damn things."

"Well, I might be able to brighten your day," Miles said, as he reached into his tunic and removed two of his Cuban cigars. He handed one to Philippe and said, "Try this out. If you like it, then I'll send you a box."

They bit the ends off and lit the cigars. Philippe took a long puff and held the smoke in for several seconds before exhaling it and sighing, "You are right about brightening my day. This is the best cigar I've tasted for too long a time."

"It will be my pleasure to see that you have an ample supply. I recently bought several cases in Jamaica. Please let me hear from you regarding the purchase of a building, if one can be found."

"Miles, I'd like to ask a question before you leave."

Miles took a long puff on his cigar and said, "Of course — please feel free to do so."

"I'm not seeking specifics, but I'm interested in your opinion of the war. We at Dalhousie are responsible for our clients' financial affairs, and, as such, we have an interest in wars and their outcomes."

"I'm afraid that I have little to contribute. I've been in two major battles since the war began in 1701. When I was a lieutenant of marines aboard *HMS Specter*, we were part of the fleet laying siege to Gibraltar in 1704, and we supported the invasion troops, but there was no significant naval action. Since then, I have served on several different vessels, all of which provided escort to supply ships or protected vital sea lanes. I was aboard *HMS Spitfire* in action off Lisbon in 1708, but neither of these engagements allowed me a view of the overall course of the war."

"I see. Well, thank you, but we'll always be interested if you think of something."

"Philippe, we both know that my father is in a much better position to have an opinion than I, and we both know he's a longtime client of the firm."

"Yes, and I'm sure someone in our London office has posed the question to Lord Conway."

"Now, I'd like to turn the tables and ask you the same question."

Philippe grinned and said, "That's fair enough. The way we read the tea leaves tells us that when the whole thing is over, nothing much will have changed. Who sits on the throne of Spain isn't essential. Spain is being reduced to a has-been in Europe and will find her colonies under constant pressure in the future.

"The English will increase their influence in North

America, mostly at the expense of France, but the French will be able to retain their grip on French North America. The balance of power will not change as a result of the present conflict. Overall, the war has been good for the British Colonies around the world, and especially so here in New England."

Miles thought for a moment and then replied, "I suspect you're right on all of those observations. England is a trading island. The overall economic health of the realm depends on trade, and we have strengthened our grip on that commerce as a result of the war. The Royal Navy has become the instrument of an expansionist government in London."

"Does that bother you?"

"Not in the least. I serve the Queen and her ministers. The Royal Navy is always the pointed end of the Royal Lance."

The men visited for a few more minutes, and then Miles pulled his watch from his tunic, clicking it open. He checked the time and said, "If I'm going to try to secure a room at the Henry House, I must be on my way. I've enjoyed talking to you, and I hope to see you again soon."

"I, too, enjoyed our visit, and I'll be looking forward

to the next. I'll keep you informed on my search for a commercial building."

Philippe saw Miles to the door and shook his hand as Miles climbed into the cab. When he entered the cab, Miles told the driver to go to the Henry House Tavern and Inn on Queen Street. It turned out that the inn was only three blocks away. When they arrived, Miles stood beside the cab and addressed the cabby: "I'll only be a minute or two, and then I'll need to return to the docks. Please wait here."

The cabby touched the brim of his cap with his whip and said, "Yes, sir. I'll be here until you return."

Miles entered the front door of the three-story townhouse and found himself in a brightly lit tavern. There was a large, red-faced man — with a white apron wrapped around his sizable girth — wiping the copper-topped bar. He looked up and said, "Welcome, stranger. You have found a home away from home."

Miles returned the man's smile and replied, "Indeed, I hope I have."

Ransom handed Philippe's card to the man and watched as he turned it over and read Philippe's message. The bear of a man walked around the end of the bar. Miles realized that he must have been close to six and a half feet tall, and probably weighed over 20 stones. At just six feet, Miles was tall in his own right, but this giant towered over him. The titan stuck out his hand to Miles, introduced himself as Josiah Adams, and then roared, "Any friend of Philippe Dalhousie is a friend of mine! How can I be of service, Major?"

"I am in need of lodgings until I can find a permanent home in the city. Have you anything available?"

"It so happens that we're fully booked at present, but I have a small set of rooms on the third floor that I keep for special guests. A friend of Philippe's certainly qualifies as special. Would you like to see those quarters?"

"Yes, I certainly would."

Adams turned toward the kitchen and bellowed, "Annie, I need you out front!"

A stunning, redheaded young woman, wearing the dress of a barmaid, came out of the kitchen, wiping her hands on a dishcloth stuck in her apron. She smiled and said, "Well, Papa, you bellowed, so here I am."

Josiah Adams's face broke into a huge grin, and he said, "Major Ransom, this fetching creature is my daughter, Annie, the apple of my eye. Annie, this is

Major Miles Ransom, and I'd like you to show him the rooms on the third floor."

Annie looked at Miles with sparkling green eyes, curtsied, and replied, "Major Ransom, if you'll follow me."

Completely captivated by this exquisite young woman, Miles was certain that if she led the way, he would follow Annie Adams through the gates of hell. Instead, she led him to the third floor and into a two-room suite that offered a writing desk and a comfortable chair in one of the rooms, and a large bedstead covered with quilts in the other. She looked at him quizzically and asked, "Do you have any questions? The rent is two bob a night, and that includes breakfast and maid service. The loo is out back and is kept quite clean. I ought to know this since I am the maid and loo cleaner. Mum does the cooking and runs the kitchen. Pa runs the tavern while drinking half a keg of ale every day."

Miles had a hard time taking his eyes off the enchanting girl and was nearly speechless, but he finally managed to blurt out, "It's precisely what I need!"

"Good, then let's go down, and you and Pa can work it out."

When they were back in the tavern, Annie curtsied

again and said, "It was good to meet you, Major Ransom. Welcome to the Henry House." She then disappeared back into the kitchen.

Miles stood, watching the drape she had gone behind, until Adams cleared his throat and said, "Well, what did you think?"

When he finally came to, Miles replied, "You're right; she's a lovely girl."

"I was referring to the rooms," growled Adams.

Miles put the image of Annie Adams in the back of his mind and hastily replied, "Ah, yes, yes, the rooms are perfect. I'll take them until I find a building of my own. Annie explained the rent and amenities, and two bob a night is acceptable." Miles reached into his tunic, took a gold sovereign out, and handed it to Adams. "Put this on my account, and let me know when more is needed. I'll have my bags delivered sometime later today, and I'll plan on spending the night here."

Josiah Adams put the sovereign in his apron pocket and replied, "I'll see that your bags are taken to your rooms, and let me give you a key to the front door, in case you need to come in after closing time."

Miles bade Adams goodbye, returned to the waiting

cab, and, as he got in, instructed the driver to return him to *HMS Dragon*.

3 THE QUEEN'S CAPTAIN

The cabby parked next to the ship, and, as Miles got out, he looked at the man in the driver's seat and said, "Tell me your name."

The cabby touched his cap and replied, "I'm called Johnny, sir, Johnny Cochrane."

"Well, Johnny, you seem to know your way around Boston. How'd you like to have a regular fare?"

"You mean every day?"

"Yes. How much do you make in a day?"

"On a good day, I've done five shillings."

"Would you be interested in working for me when my ship is in port?"

"Well, guv, what would you expect?"

"I'd want you to be here from the ringing of the church bells at seven until I retire for the evening."

"Seven days a week?"

"Aye, every day, including Sundays."

"Would I be allowed to take other fares?"

"Only if I have released you for a period."

"I see. And what might you want to pay me for this?"

"If you have seven good days, then you'd be making 35 shillings. I'd propose to pay you £2 a week."

The cabby scratched his head and then replied, "When would you want me to start?"

"You started at seven this morning."

"Aye, guv. I'll be here if you need me."

Miles climbed the gangplank, saluted the colors, and went to his cabin to prepare for the captains' meeting. He knew that the visiting captains would be in dress uniform, so he changed back into his. He was putting on his boots when Bob Gaines tapped on his hatch. Miles motioned for Gaines to enter.

"What can I do for you, Bob?"

"The cigars were taken to Sir William as you requested, and I checked with the noncommissioned officers about Holmes. Sergeant Trent served with him aboard *HMS Fury* when Holmes was a lieutenant."

"What did he say about him?"

"That he was a fair man, a good officer, and brave under fire. His only other comment was that Holmes loved his wine and rum."

"We'd never hold that against a man, now would we?"

"No, sir, we certainly wouldn't."

Miles brushed his boots and stood.

"Thanks, Bob. I'll have to be off to the wardroom. Don't want to keep Sir William waiting. Have all of the fleet's captains come aboard?"

"All but the *Chester* and I saw his cutter approaching when I came below."

"I'll be keeping rooms in town while we're in port, but I'd like to see you for a moment after the meeting."

"Aye aye, Major. I'll be on deck."

Miles made his way to the wardroom and found it filled with the fleet's captains and their staffs. He was the only marine officer, but he took a seat against the wall with the other staff officers. Sir William stood, and all quieted. He looked the room over and then said, "Gentlemen, thank you for being prompt. I wanted to relay the fleet's orders in person. Major General Francis Nicholson has been commissioned by the Queen to lead an expedition to capture Port Royal, the capital of French Acadia. As most of you know, there have been earlier attempts to take it, and all have ended in failure.

"General Nicholson has a force of 2,000 regulars, 400 Royal Marines, and 3,000 militia and native warriors. We are to secure the Straits of Digby, escort the troop transports into the Bay of Digby, and provide any support needed to reduce the fortress at Port Royal. Orders were prepared for each of you, and you should have read them before coming on board. Does anyone have a question or comment?"

Captain Isaac Boyd of *HMS Chester* stood and said, "As I understand my instructions, I am to sail on the morning tide, secure the entrance to the Straits, and then await the arrival of the rest of the fleet. Shall I conduct a reconnaissance of the bay, as well?"

"No, Captain Boyd. Lay off the Straits and prevent any sail from entering or leaving. I do not want you trapped in the bay."

"Aye aye, sir," replied Boyd.

An elderly captain stood and asked, "Do we have any intelligence concerning the French and Spanish fleets?"

"General Nicholson has assured me that both are no closer than Hispaniola, but we will keep patrols to be sure that they do not appear unexpectedly," Sir William replied.

The captain then asked, "Am I to understand that we will be expected to provide direct fire support to the Army?"

"Yes, that is General Nicholson's plan."

"Are you suggesting that the fleet's men-of-war enter the Straits and operate in the Bay of Digby?"

"Aye. Again, this is the general's plan."

The older man looked across the table at Sir William. "I feel compelled to suggest that this might put the fleet in danger of being trapped in the bay."

"I have already protested this to the general, but he gave me a direct order to bring our ships into the bay to provide direct fire support to his army. Based on this directive, we will comply."

There was a murmuring among the captains, but, soon, quiet returned to the wardroom. Sir William invited the captains to his cabin for dinner and suggested that the others join the *Dragon*'s officers in the wardroom.

Miles accompanied them and took a seat next to an older lieutenant from *HMS Falcon*. Miles introduced himself and allowed the steward to pour him a flagon of wine. The lieutenant also requested wine and then introduced himself as Ronald Vest, executive officer on the *Falcon.* He took a sip of his wine and said, "No disrespect intended, but surely you must be the youngest marine major in the Royal Navy."

"None was taken, and I suspect you are right. I've been a major for almost 12 hours."

"Sir William must have total confidence in your abilities, Major Ransom."

"Please, address me as Miles, and, yes, one hopes that he does."

"Well, Miles it will be, and I'm Ron. Will you command the fleet's marines during the upcoming action?"

"It is my understanding that while I'll command the fleet's marines, I'll be under the overall command of a Major Richard Holmes, an officer on Nicholson's staff."

"So, you'll be working for Tricky Dick Holmes, which

should be a challenge."

"I assume you've served with the major."

"I have. I was a midshipman on *HMS Fury* when Holmes was a lieutenant. Dick Holmes was as brave a man as I ever saw. He led a boarding party that saved the ship during an engagement with Moorish pirates. He was a worthy officer when he was sober. Unfortunately, he was rarely sober."

Miles sipped on his wine while dinner was served and thought about Holmes. Ron Vest was the second man to give the major a mixed review. Miles decided to wait until he had a chance to get to know the person before passing judgment on his competence. After dinner, Miles pulled two cigars from his tunic and offered one to Vest. They both lit up. Vest took a puff and said, "We sail for the Bay of Fundy in a week's time. Will you sail on the *Dragon*?"

"I assume so, but I haven't met with Holmes as of yet. He may have other plans for me."

"You would be welcome aboard the *Falcon* should you choose. It seems that we'll be leading the fleet into the Bay of Digby, the pointed end of Nicholson's stick, so to speak."

The men chatted for a few more minutes until a

midshipman came and announced that the captains were preparing to return to their ships. Vest stood, shook Miles's hand, and said, "It's been good to meet you. Thanks for the smoke. Be sure to keep a close eye on your Major Holmes, and don't forget my invitation to sail with the *Falcon*."

Miles assured him that he would do both. He watched as the captains and their staffs boarded their cutters and faded into the night. Miles returned to his cabin and changed into a regular uniform, packed a small leather bag with some personal items, and climbed back on deck.

Miles saw Bob Gaines on the foredeck and asked, "Bob, are you standing a watch?"

"No, I don't have the watch until morning."

"I'm planning on spending the night in the rooms I've arranged to rent, but I'll be back on board in the morning. My rooms are in the Henry House Tavern and Inn. If anyone is looking for me, then you'll know where to send him or her."

"Miles, I know you want to give me room to establish my authority, but you don't have to move off the ship."

"I prefer being ashore. I do this whenever my ship posts to a new port. After I get settled in, I'll have

Lloyd and you as my guests for dinner."

"How do you plan to get there? There's a cab on the dock, but he's not for hire. I've seen him turn down several fares."

"I'll bet I can convince him to take me. See you in the morning."

Miles took his bag down the gangway, spoke briefly with Johnny Cochrane, and got in the cab with a wave to Gaines. When they arrived at the Henry House, Miles climbed out and handed Johnny two crowns.

"Here's your first week's wages, Johnny. Be here by seven o'clock in the morning to pick me up, but I think we've completed our work for the day."

Cochrane shoved the coins in his pocket and hit the brim of his hat with his whip. "Goodnight, Major. I'll be here at seven."

Miles found the inn door still open and walked into the tavern. Josiah Adams was wiping the bar top when he saw Miles coming in. He bellowed, "Evening, Major. Just closing down, but I'll pull you an ale if you like."

"No thanks, Josiah. I've had a bit too much already, but let me buy you one."

"I'll never turn down a free pint. Have a seat, and I'll join you."

Adams poured a pint of ale and settled his colossal frame into a chair opposite Miles. Miles was amazed at the natural grace of the big man, and he also saw that the 20 stones were mostly muscle not fat.

When Adams got comfortable and took a drink of his ale, Miles lit a cigar and asked, "Tell me, Josiah. How'd you become an innkeeper in Boston?"

"My great-great-grandfather, Henry, sailed from Somerset and settled near Braintree in 1632. All of my folks have been either tradesmen or craftsmen. I was my father's first son, and he apprenticed me to a cobbler in 1683 when I was 13. My father died in 1702, and I had to care for my mother and younger brother, Jonathan. I didn't much like the cobbler's life, and, when Jonathan was old enough to take over the family farm, I decided to try my hand at innkeeping."

"Is your brother still in Braintree?"

"Aye, Jonathan is now 21 and a first-rate farmer. He's a bright young man, and I saw to it that he got an education before I left. How about you, Major? What brought you to the Bay Colony?"

"My father is an earl and a member of the House of Lords, but I'm not the oldest son. I joined the Royal

Navy in 1698 as a midshipman, and I go where the Queen sends me. Boston is her latest port. How do you like inn keeping?"

"Very much. Martha and I, along with a lot of help from Annie, have been able to make a go of it, but we may have just done too well."

Miles asked, "How can that be?"

Adams took a long drink of his ale and replied, "We don't own the property, but we have a 10-year lease. The lease states that in the event of the lessee's or the lessor's death, the agreement would be voided. That didn't bother me much three years ago when I signed it. Mr. Goldstone, the owner, was in his fifties, and I figured he'd outlive the term of the lease."

"I take it that didn't happen," Miles said.

"No, just a month ago, he passed away, and his heir is insisting that we sign a new lease, doubling the payments."

"What are you going to do?"

"Haven't figured that out yet, but I know for sure we can't run this place if the rent doubles. I'm looking for another location, but we've established a reputation for good food and clean facilities. It will be hard to start over again."

"When do you have to decide?"

"He's given me until October 20 to give him an answer."

"How old is the heir?"

"Young lad, no more than 30 — a barrister over on Hanover Street."

"Josiah, have you told your wife and daughter about this?"

"Not yet. I've been hoping to work something out, but I'll have to say something to the two of them soon. We'll have 30 days to vacate if I don't sign the new lease."

"Hold off a day or two. I know someone who might be able to help you. Let me talk to him, and I'll get back to you."

Josiah looked at Miles with a flicker of hope and said, "I'll keep it to myself until the 20th, and maybe a miracle will happen."

"Maybe it will," Miles replied. "They've been known to before. Now, I need to get some sleep. Put the ale on my bill, and I'll see you in the morning."

"Will you have breakfast with us?"

"Yes, but may I have it in my rooms?"

"It will be there at seven if that's acceptable."

"I'll be expecting it at seven. Good night, Josiah. I'll get back to you after I've had a chance to talk to a friend."

"Aye, and thank you, Major."

The next morning, Miles had bread, cheese, and coffee in his room. He also found Johnny Cochrane waiting, as agreed. Soon, Johnny parked in his spot on the dock, and Miles climbed aboard the *Dragon*. He went below to his cabin and made sure his uniform was proper. He was giving his boots a final brush when there was a knock on his hatch. He said, "Enter."

One of the midshipmen stood in the passageway and handed Miles a folded note. He thanked the young man, broke the seal, opened it, and read:

September 22, 1710

Miles S. Ransom, Maj. HMRMC
HMS Dragon

Major Ransom,

The pleasure of your presence is requested for dinner at the Sherman House on the evening of September 22, at one bell on the first dog watch.

Richard O. Holmes, Maj. HMRMC
Headquarters, Fort Hill, Boston

Miles read the note and thought, "It appears that I will finally meet the mysterious Major Holmes and see what he has in store for me; I shall look forward to attending with great anticipation."

Miles sat down at the small desk in his cabin and pulled a sheet of white paper from the center drawer. He unscrewed the cap on his inkwell, dipped a quill, and wrote:

September 22, 1710

Richard O. Holmes, Maj. HMRMC
Headquarters, Fort Hill, Boston

Major Holmes,

It is with great pleasure that I accept your kind invitation of September 22.

Miles S. Ransom, Maj. HMRMC
HMS Dragon

Miles folded the note, sealed it with a drop of red sealing wax, and took it to the wardroom. He handed the note to a midshipman and said, "Mr. Forbes, take this letter to the cab parked on the dock. Tell the driver that Major Ransom wishes him to deliver it at once and that he should then return to his station."

The young man scurried on his way. Miles left the wardroom and knocked on Commander Sparks' hatch. He waited for several moments and then tried again. Once satisfied that Lloyd was elsewhere, Miles climbed to the main deck. Lloyd Sparks was standing on the quarterdeck talking to one of his junior officers. Miles waited until the officer was dismissed, climbed beside Sparks, and said, "Good morning, Lloyd. Is all well?"

"Much better than yesterday, I'm pleased to say. I've already met with Sir William, and your cigars must have worked their magic. He's in a more positive frame of mind."

"Glad I could be of service. What's on the schedule for today?"

"We're devoting this morning to cleaning the ship and preparing for sailing on the 29th. The balance of the day will center on gun training. Captain Gaines is drilling his marines on repelling boarders. What are your plans?"

"I have none, but I suspect all *that* is about to end this evening. I was summoned to dinner with Major Holmes, and I expect he'll give me my orders."

"Sir William is holding an inspection tour of the transports today, and he's ordered me to accompany him. I hope to God the captains of those floating hellholes have at least cleaned them since the troops went ashore. Sir William regards a troop transport in the same light that he views a slaver."

"So far, the best thing about my promotion has been that no one seems to need me to do anything. I have some personal business to attend to before someone figures that out."

Miles heard the cab come down the cobblestone street, and he watched as Cochrane expertly backed it into his spot. Sparks observed the attention Miles paid the cab and said, "Now, it makes sense. You've bought that cab, haven't you?"

"Bought may be overstating it, but I have engaged the cab full time for as long as we're in port."

"I should have guessed that when he refused to take my executive officer to town this morning. Must be nice to be rich."

"It has its moments. I need to go see a man about a building, so I'll be bidding you good day."

Sparks laughed and said, "Good day to you, as well. When will you return?"

"I'll be back on board by two bells on the afternoon

watch. I'll have to dress for dinner."

Miles saluted the colors, walked down the gangplank to the waiting cab, and said to Johnny, "Take me to 210 Hanover, Mr. Cochrane."

"Aye, sir, and I delivered your note to the army headquarters."

"Excellent," Miles replied and settled into the coach for the short drive to Hanover Street.

When Miles rapped on the door, Philippe opened it with a smile and said, "Good to see you, Miles. You're just the man I'm looking for.

4 THE QUEEN'S CAPTAIN

"I'm looking for you, as well, but, please, go first," Miles replied.

Philippe led him into his office and offered Miles a seat and a cup of tea. Miles sat by the fireplace and said, "No tea, thank you. I find tea bland, so I've developed a preference for coffee. Hazards of foreign service, I guess."

Philippe chuckled and said, "Coffee will be no problem; no self-respecting Frenchman would touch a cup of tea."

Summoning a young man from the outer office, Philippe requested two cups of coffee. Once the hot beverages were served, Philippe began, "Yesterday, you mentioned buying a commercial building with accommodations for a suite of rooms."

"Yes, and that's why I'm here this morning, but I've interrupted you. I apologize. Please go on."

"Did you go to the Henry House as I suggested?"

"I did, and I've engaged a two-room suite while I look for something to buy."

"Were the accommodations satisfactory?"

"Yes, very much so, and I've grown fond of the proprietor, Mr. Adams."

"Well, it might be possible to buy the Henry House. Just this morning, I met with the owner of the property, and he may be willing to sell."

"That's interesting because he just doubled the rent and gave Josiah 30 days to accept or to vacate the property."

"That IS interesting; he gave me a financial projection showing steady rental income for the past three years, but no mention of an increase. The price he's asking was based on those numbers, and it's quite a bit higher than the surrounding properties."

"What's he asking?"

"He mentioned £500."

"And you think that's too much? What should the price be?"

Philippe thought for a moment and then said, "More in the range of £350."

"Can you arrange a meeting with the owner?"

"I'm sure I can."

"He's not a Dalhousie client, is he?"

"No, he's not."

"Do you think you could do a little snooping to see what kind of business reputation he has?"

"Again, I'm sure I can."

"I'd like for you to see what you can find out about him and arrange a meeting as soon as you know something."

"Give me a day or two, and I'll send you word at the Henry House when I've achieved both."

Miles took a sip of his coffee and said, "Now, let's have a smoke."

Once their cigars were lit, Miles said, "Philippe, are there other Dalhousie offices in North America?"

"I'm sure you're familiar with our Montreal office. All the firm's affairs in North America are managed from there. We've had an office in Charlestown in the

Carolina Colony since 1701, and one in Mexico City since 1645.

"In 1702, d'Iberville and de Bienville were sent by the King of France to establish the colony of Louisiana, and my younger brother, Jean, accompanied them. He has opened an office in Mobile, the capital of French Louisiana. So as of today, we have four North American offices. Why do you ask?"

"Just curious. I never know where the Queen will send me next."

"I can't help but notice all the activity going on in the harbor. I suspect your visit to Boston will soon be ending."

"I can't comment on that; there are likely French agents observing the same activity," Miles replied.

"If they are, then I would be willing to bet that they assume you're planning another attempt to take Port Royal. Francis Nicholson and Samuel Vetch failed in their effort to take Montreal last summer. Nicholson felt that he'd been betrayed by Vetch when the fleet never came to his support. Nicholson has been begging the Queen to give her assent for an attack on Port Royal. My point is that if an attack on Port Royal is imminent, then you can expect the French to be ready."

"Point taken, and I agree. Seldom are military plans kept secret, and we have to press on as best we can. In the meantime, I'll be looking forward to meeting with young Mr. Goldstone."

"Miles, whatever happens, please be careful. We take the welfare of our clients very seriously. I'll contact you as soon as I arrange a meeting with Goldstone."

Miles bade Philippe adieu and instructed Johnny to drive to the ship. Once on board, Miles sent a midshipman to seek an audience with Sir William. The lad returned and said that the commodore would receive the major in his cabin. Miles went below and knocked on the commodore's hatch. Sir William opened it and said, "Major Ransom, how can I be of service?"

"Thank you for seeing me, Sir William. I won't take but a moment of your time."

Sir William sat down at his desk and motioned for Miles to have a seat. The commodore smiled and asked, "So, what do you need?"

"I need your guidance. I have been invited to dine tonight with Major Holmes, and I'm unclear as to exactly what my duties are."

"I would think it very clear. You are in command of

the fleet marines and subordinate to Holmes, who also commands the marine detachment brought by Nicholson. I would think that you've been invited to dinner to receive your orders. Nicholson promoted Holmes to lieutenant colonel this morning, and Holmes, in turn, promoted one of his captains to major. This should establish a clear chain of command."

"Thank you, Sir William. I was unaware of these developments. There is another issue I'd like to bring to your attention, if I may."

"And that is?"

"I believe I know why Nicholson acted as he did."

"We agreed to put that business behind us, but go on."

"Last summer, Nicholson and his friend Samuel Vetch planned an attack on Montreal. Nicholson had command of the ground forces, and Vetch was to accompany a Royal Navy fleet in support. Vetch never showed up, and Nicholson sustained heavy losses. I suspect he intends to keep the Navy on a short leash this time."

"Yes, I'm familiar with those events, but it is no excuse for his actions toward me. I'll execute my orders faithfully, but I'll never forgive the man. I thank you for your concern, but we must move on."

"Aye aye, sir. Thank you for seeing me."

"You're welcome. Now, go and tend to your duties."

Miles left Sir William's cabin and walked to the wardroom, where he found Captain Gaines dipping a piece of hardtack into a cup of tea. He took a seat and said, "Damn, Robert. You don't have to eat that crap while we're in port."

Gaines grinned and replied, "I happen to like it. Want some?"

"I think not," Miles said and motioned to a steward.

"Please bring me some fresh bread and a slice of Stilton."

When the food arrived, Miles went to the coffee urn, poured a cup, returned to the table, and said, "Bob, it seems that Nicholson has promoted Holmes to lieutenant colonel, and Holmes, in turn, has promoted one of his captains to major. He has invited me to dinner tonight, when, I assume, I'll receive my orders."

"Well, the good news is that you have seniority on the new major."

"I have a feeling that's not going to matter much. Holmes will decide who does what, and I'll obey his orders. I just wanted you to know what's going on."

"Thanks, but I'm sure it will all work out."

"As am I. Are you certain you don't want some of this Stilton?"

The men sat and ate while visiting about shipboard scuttlebutt until the ship's bell sounded, indicating the start of the afternoon watch. Gaines stood and said, "Well, I've got the watch, so I'll see you later. Let me know how your dinner goes."

"I will. I'll tell you first thing in the morning."

Miles finished eating and went to his cabin to catch a nap before he dressed for dinner with Holmes. Years of service had taught him to eat and sleep at every opportunity, as the occasion might not present itself later. He stripped to his undergarments, climbed into his bunk, set his mental alarm for two hours, and fell into a deep sleep.

Awakened in time to hear the ship's bell ring out four times, Miles went to his washbasin, lathered up, and shaved. Miles did not like facial hair and made every effort to remain clean-shaven. He put on his dress uniform and climbed to the deck, where he saw Lloyd Sparks standing on the quarterdeck looking out on the harbor. Miles stood beside him and said, "Well, Commander, what have you spied?"

"Hello, Miles. I'm watching the clouds build up to our southeast. Going to be a blow tonight, I suspect."

Miles looked to the southeast and saw the dark shape of a line of thunderclouds on the horizon and replied, "Aye, it appears that way. What will you do?"

"Since we are securely tied to this wharf and prepared for foul weather, we'll be alright. The ships in the harbor will have to lower sea anchors to hold their positions. We don't need them thrashing about into each other."

"How is the provisioning going?"

"We'll have everything but the powder and shot aboard tomorrow. We'll do that on the 29th."

"How are you making it with Sir William?"

"He keeps to his cabin and leaves the *Dragon* to me. Frankly, I think the incident with Nicholson broke his spirit. I hope he can recover before we sail."

"I had a visit with him this morning, and he did seem a bit subdued. He's an excellent officer, and I'm sure he'll rise to the occasion."

"Let's hope so. At this point, he's allowing the captains to operate on their own, but there's not much to do until we sail. Do you know your orders yet?"

"I'm on my way to dine with Holmes, and I expect to find out at dinner. I'll let you know as soon as I do."

"Bob Gaines is doing a masterful job with our marines; they're at the top of their form."

"I knew Bob would do well. He's a professional and will rise in rank."

"Does it bother you that there is no Royal Marine officer above the rank of lieutenant colonel in the entire Navy?"

"Not so much. I was quite young when I joined. Position never seemed important, and, now, I'm not entirely confident that I'll make a career in the Marines."

"I never thought you'd leave the service. What's brought this on?"

"Nothing in particular. I'm just trying to decide what kind of life I want. I have the advantage of personal means, so I have options that other officers don't."

"I can see what you're thinking, but, for me, I know I want a naval career, and I hope to reach flag rank before I retire."

"Lloyd, you are an excellent officer, and I'm quite sure you'll go far in the service. I, on the other hand, may have reached my potential as an officer. But, I don't have to decide now; I'm still a young man. At any rate, I'll deal with all of that after Port Royal."

Sparks said, "Speaking of Port Royal, do you have any idea why we want to capture it?"

"I've given that some thought, and the best I can come up with is a three-part answer. First, we're at war with France, and Nicholson is a professional soldier. He, therefore, needs to have an army and attack some French possession.

"Second, Nicholson is an avid supporter of these colonies. He led the military contingent during the short-lived Dominion of New England under Sir Edmund Andros, and he fully understands the strategic importance of Acadia or Nova Scotia as we know it. Nova Scotia is the key to the Bay of Fundy, which controls significant fishing banks.

"The last thing is Nicholson's embarrassment over last year's failure at Montreal. He wants to redeem his reputation. The Queen has given her approval to his scheme, and you and I are the instruments he will use to make it happen."

"Seems like a lot of blood, sweat, and tears to assuage

a man's ego."

"Lloyd, the way I see it, is this. When we chose a life in the Navy, we accepted that we would be fighting other men's fights. Frankly, I don't much give a damn which man or cause he's pushing. I'd just as soon fight the French and Spanish as the Hottentots. Our honor and reputation depend on how well we fight these battles."

"I know you're right. Leave the strategy to the courtiers and concentrate on the tactics."

"Aye, that is our task."

Miles was still thinking about his conversation with Sparks as he rode to his dinner meeting and didn't notice that the cab had stopped until Johnny opened the door and said, "Major, we've arrived at the Sherman House."

Miles put his thoughts aside, told Johnny to wait, and entered the front door. The foyer of the Sherman House was ablaze with candles and oil lamps. Miles was greeted by a tall man of African descent and dressed in black. Miles told the man that he was a guest of Colonel Holmes, and the man ushered him to a private room. When Miles entered, he saw a table set for three, and the two seated men rose to their feet.

"Ah, Major Ransom, thank you for joining us."

Raising his hand toward the other man, Holmes said, "This is Major Amos Clark. Amos, this is Major Miles Ransom of *HMS Dragon*."

All three men shook hands and sat down. There was a bottle of claret on the table. The waiter poured three full glasses and then said, "Gentlemen, tonight's dinner is clam chowder, baked cod, and cherry tarts. I will await your signal to begin serving."

Holmes smiled and replied, "Excellent, Toby. We'll visit awhile before we dine."

Holmes turned to Miles and said, "Miles, I know you have been concerned about the chain of command and as to just what your duties will be. General Nicholson had to accept our plans before I made them known, and, today, he approved my ideas. As you can see, I've been promoted to lieutenant colonel and placed in command of all Royal Marines, those in the fleet and those serving with the Army.

"Major Clark will be in command of the marine unit attached to the Army and will report to me. You will be in command of the fleet marines, and you will also report to me. Do you have any questions?"

"Aye, sir. As you know, the fleet marines on each ship are under the direct command of the vessel's captain, and, as their commander, my responsibilities are limited to training and equipping each contingent. I have no tactical control over them. Is this in keeping with your understanding of my role?"

"Aye, that is what I expect."

"Am I to remain aboard the *Dragon*?"

"Aye, you should be on the flagship, but I must warn you that you will be under my command. Do you see a problem with that?"

"Sir William is a stickler for naval traditions and may not be comfortable with the situation; however, the captain of the *Dragon* will be alright with it, and he and I work together well."

"I wouldn't worry too much about Darcy; he won't be a problem."

Miles thought, "Now that's a strange thing to say. The commander of the fleet could have a serious problem with this plan, and I don't want to be caught in the middle. I'll just bide my time and see what develops."

Miles took a sip of his wine and said, "I want to thank you for the clarification. I'll await further orders."

"You're welcome. It's always best to have a personal understanding of what's expected. Now, let's talk about the plan to take Port Royal, and Amos's role in doing so. Amos has been with me since our days on

HMS Fury and has experience in amphibious operations. He and his marines will be on four of the transports, and he will lead the ashore directive in support of the regulars and the militia."

Miles thought for a moment and asked, "Isn't it unusual for marines to serve as foot soldiers?"

"Unusual, yes, but not unprecedented. The marines under Amos have been training for amphibious operations for over a year. I believe it will be the future for the Royal Marines. The duties of your command will remain as usual — support and protect their ships."

Miles considered what Holmes had said and replied, "The fleet will be within range of the fort's guns if we are to attempt to reduce them. We will have to accept damage and casualties. What do you plan on the ground?"

Holmes unrolled a map of the Bay of Fundy, pointed to the Bay of Digby, and said, "The entrance to the Bay of Digby is almost a mile wide, and the shipping channel is well charted. Sir William and *HMS Dragon* will be posted to guard this entrance, and the balance of the fleet, under the command of Reed, will sail into position between Goat Island and the French fort just north of the city."

Miles looked intently at the map and finally asked, "Do the French have batteries on Goat Island?"

"We aren't certain," replied Holmes. "However, if they do, then we'll reduce them before taking our ships in."

"If I hear you clearly, Sir William is to be relieved as commander of the fleet. Is that so?"

"*Relieved* is too harsh. He will merely detach the fleet under the command of Reed until the fortress is secured."

"I have served under Sir William for several years, and I doubt that he will accept this order."

"What Darcy will or won't do is of no concern to us. The decision is final, and Reed will be in command."

"If I'm to be effective, then I will need to be aboard one of the ships in the bay. I've received an invitation to join the *Falcon,* so I'll move aboard her as soon as possible."

"Yes, that sounds reasonable," Holmes said.

There was a flash of lightning and a loud clap of thunder that rattled the china and crystal and lit up the street outside. Soon, a driving rain was beating against the windows, and Holmes took the distraction as an opportunity to shift the conversation away from the forthcoming operation to old friends and shared experiences. The meal was served as the precipitation pelted down, and, by the time the coffee and brandy came, Miles offered each officer a cigar.

The trio sat, sipped brandy, and enjoyed the smoke until the hall clock struck midnight. Holmes and Clark had rooms in the Sherman House. Holmes took the last of his cigar and said, "Gentlemen, I'm glad we had this opportunity to get to know one another and to establish a clear picture of our responsibilities. The fleet will continue provisioning and will depart on September 29. Miles, if you transfer to the *Falcon,* then I am going to suggest to Reed that she be sent ahead to secure Goat Island. If so, then be prepared to land a force of marines."

"How soon should we sail?"

"That will be up to Reed, but at least two days before the fleet, I would suppose. Orders will be given to the *Falcon*'s captain."

The three men stood and bid each other good night. Holmes and Clark retreated to their rooms, and the rain began to slacken as Johnny took Miles to the Henry House.

Thomas R. Lawrence

5 THE QUEEN'S CAPTAIN

The next morning, Miles boarded the *Dragon* just as the sun peeked over the Atlantic. He found Lloyd Sparks and Bob Gaines having tea in the wardroom, and, after pouring a mug of coffee, Miles joined them. Gaines smiled and said, "Good morning! You seem to have survived your dinner with the colonel."

"I did, and—I have to admit—I found him very professional and very sober."

"Did he tell you what your role will be in the expedition to Nova Scotia?"

Miles decided not to mention the relief of Sir William or the responsibility of the Dragon—best to just let these things run their natural course. No sense in being the bearer of bad news just to show you're in on the scuttlebutt. Let the chain of command do its job.

"Not only that, but he told me something that will affect us all. The fleet will move into the bay and provide direct fire support to the Army. As for my orders, I am to transfer to *HMS Falcon* and assume command of the fleet marines."

"Did he explain why he wanted you on the *Falcon*?"

"Not really—just that he felt the *Falcon* a better fit than the flagship."

Bob Gaines laughed and said, "Well, I guess I'll get your cabin by default."

"So it would seem. I'll be moving to the *Falcon* as soon as the orders are issued."

Lloyd Sparks sat quietly while the exchange between Miles and Gaines took place, and Lloyd finally said, "I'm getting the feeling that the *Dragon* is somehow being shifted out of the main thrust. Did you pick up on this at dinner last night?"

Miles thought for a moment before answering and then said, "Lloyd, I'm going to ask that you allow me to evade that question. If there is anything I know, then you will be brought into the loop very shortly, and I don't want to betray a confidence or lie to you."

Sparks looked Miles in the eye and said, "I understand. I'll find out in due course, and, in the meantime, you must do what you think best."

"This is a case where I must put my personal feelings aside and follow my orders. I'd like to discuss all of this with the two of you once everything is out in the open."

Lloyd Sparks stood and adjusted his uniform. He was unmistakably miffed and said stiffly, "I must get about the business of the ship. I wish you the best in your new assignment and look forward to seeing you soon."

After Sparks had left, Bob Gaines said, "Don't worry, Miles; Lloyd will get over it. He's a solid officer, and he'll realize that he put you in a difficult situation, which, by the way, I thought you handled correctly."

"I know that Sir William has been Lloyd's mentor, and, of course, he is protective of the commodore. I, too, feel strongly that Sir William has been treated poorly, but this happens from time to time and goes with command and responsibility."

"Sir William is old navy," Gaines replied. "He's having some difficulty with the modern concepts of expediency and compromise."

"I agree, and the next couple of weeks will be very challenging for him. He'll need all of the moral support we can muster. I suppose I should have my gear transferred to the Henry House and let Lloyd have some time to regroup. Would you have my trunks moved to the cab that is waiting on the wharf?"

"Of course — let me know when you're ready, and I'll send a detail."

Miles left the wardroom and began packing his two sea chests. He was always amazed at just how little he had in the way of worldly goods: uniforms, a couple of sets of civilian clothing, a few books, and his personal grooming gear. He took special care of a matched set of long flintlock pistols made by the Italian gunsmith Pito Fiorentino. They had been a gift from his father when he joined the Royal Navy.

Miles packed the boxed pistols carefully in his sea chest and checked around the cabin to be sure he had everything. It took him less than 15 minutes, after which he sent a midshipman to fetch the marine detail. They moved his chest to the cab, and he asked permission to climb to the quarterdeck.

Captain Lloyd Sparks granted Miles permission and stood flinty-eyed as Miles approached. Miles extended his hand and said, "Captain Sparks, I've enjoyed serving under you and hope we can maintain our personal and professional relationship."

Sparks took his hand and said, "Thank you, Major Ransom. I, too, have enjoyed our service together. I'm sure our paths will cross in the future, both personally and professionally. I wish you the best of luck."

Miles came to attention and saluted Sparks, who returned the salute. Miles then said, "I request permission to leave the ship, sir."

"Permission granted," Sparks replied.

Miles saluted him once more and pivoted toward the ensign, saluted again, and walked down the gangway just as Johnny and the marine detachment stowed his chest on the top of the cab. Miles climbed aboard and told Johnny to take him to the Henry House Tavern and Inn.

When the cab pulled in front of the Henry House, Miles climbed out and instructed Johnny to wait. He found Josiah behind the bar and asked, "Is there anyone to help me with a couple of chests?"

Josiah smiled and said, "I'll be glad to take care of them, and you have two pieces of mail that came this morning."

Josiah slid two sealed notes across the bar. Miles saw that one was from Philippe Dalhousie, and the other was from Colonel Holmes. Miles opened the one from Holmes first and found formal orders to board *HMS Falcon* and to assume command of the fleet marines.

Miles then opened the note from Philippe and learned that a meeting had been set up with Goldstone for four o'clock at the Dalhousie offices. Folding both, Miles put them in his pocket and said, "There will be no need to move my chests. I've been ordered to board *HMS Falcon.*"

"Does that mean you will be leaving us?"

"No, I'll continue to keep my rooms, but my gear will be aboard the *Falcon*. Do you have a minute to discuss some business?"

Josiah looked puzzled and asked, "Of course — what do you have in mind?"

"After our earlier conversation, I've been thinking we might do well in business together. I'm meeting with the owner of this building at four o'clock this afternoon, and I intend to make an offer to buy it. If I'm successful, then I will, naturally, become your landlord. I'm willing to renew your old lease for ten years, with a ten-year extension, if you want, or I'm prepared to enter into a partnership with you."

Josiah was stunned. Finally, he asked, "What would be the terms of the partnership?"

"I thought we could form a simple alliance with each owning 50 percent. I'd put up the building and £100 of working capital, and you would agree to manage the property. I would require the use of my rooms when in Boston."

"What would the rent be?"

"There would be no rent. I would receive my 50 percent of the profits on a quarterly basis."

Josiah thought for a moment and then said, "I believe the profits generated could be substantial. Suppose I wanted to expand or invest in another property?"

"I would hope we could do so under our partnership, but you'd be free to act on your own if you so choose."

"You will be at sea most of the time. Who would look after your interests?"

"That will be you. I believe you to be a gentleman and totally trustworthy. The Dalhousie firm manages my affairs, and you and Philippe can tend to my interests."

"Major Ransom, I don't know what to say. I never imagined such an opportunity would come my way."

Miles extended his hand and said, "Just shake on it, and I'll have the papers drawn up if I'm successful in acquiring the property."

They shook hands. Miles said, "Now, I must go to the *Falcon*. I'll meet with Goldstone this afternoon and have an answer by this evening. We'll talk again."

When Miles returned to the cab, Johnny was losing the straps that held the chest down. Miles said, "Tie them back and take me to the harbor."

The *Falcon* was one of the ships moored in the harbor, and Miles found the pier serving her. He asked Johnny to wait for further instructions. There was a young midshipman in charge of the *Falcon's* boat detail, and Miles requested to be taken to the ship. The ship had her floating gangway down, and Miles stepped up on it, facing the officer of the day. Miles requested permission to come aboard, stating his name, rank, and purpose. Permission was granted. Miles saluted the ensign and climbed the stairs.

Once on deck, Miles asked the officer to direct him to Lieutenant Vest. A midshipman was assigned to escort him to the lieutenant's quarters, where Miles tapped on the hatch and waited. Ron Vest opened the door. He recognized Miles at once and said, "Major Ransom, I've been expecting you. We received a copy of your orders just this morning. Come, Captain Lowry is in his cabin awaiting your arrival."

Vest dismissed the midshipman and led Miles aft to the captain's cabin. The hatch was open, and Andrew Lowry was seated at his desk without his uniform jacket. He looked up, saw them coming, stood with a broad smile and an outstretched hand, and said, "Ah, Major Ransom, Ron has told me to expect you. Welcome aboard *HMS Falcon*. Has Ron shown you to your cabin?"

Miles was taken aback by the casual but warm welcome. He had not had the opportunity to present himself formally to the captain, and it was a little unsettling. He came to attention and said, "Major Miles Ransom reporting for duty, sir."

"Yes, yes—glad to have you, Ransom. We don't stand on ceremony on the *Falcon*. Do we, Ron?"

"No, sir; we're fairly relaxed. I haven't had a chance to show Miles to his cabin."

"Well, do so and give him an opportunity to get settled. When he's ready, both of you should join me for the noon meal."

"Aye aye, sir," Vest replied and led Miles back into the passageway to a small cabin near midship. Ron pushed open the hatch and said, "I regret that this is the only cabin available. I suppose you could pull rank and force Captain Allen, commander of our marine detachment, to trade, but I'll leave that up to you."

"No, this will be adequate. I don't want to disturb the routine of the ship. I'll only be on board when we are at sea; otherwise, I have rooms at the Henry House on Queen Street."

"Will you want to meet with Captain Allen today?"

"No, I think not. There'll be plenty of time to meet all my marine officers before we sail. I'll have my chests brought on board and be ready to dine with you and the captain."

"I'll instruct a midshipman to take a detail to get your trunks. Are they still on the *Dragon*?"

"No, they're in a cab on the dock. Have the midshipman instruct the driver to help them unload."

"Fine. While the men are fetching your chests, join me in the wardroom for a cup of tea."

"I hope you keep coffee as well as tea," Miles said with a smile.

"We do. I prefer it to tea, but many officers think it too common."

"To each his own," Miles replied.

Miles poured a cup of coffee, sat down across from Vest, and said, "Ron, the captain seems a bit unorthodox in his approach to naval traditions. I'm surprised Sir William has tolerated it."

"The *Falcon* has not served under Sir William prior to last week. Captain Lowry might allow a certain relaxation, but he is meticulous when others are aboard."

"How do the men respond to this 'relaxation'?"

"Captain Lowry is a stickler for the crew's welfare; they are well fed and healthy. He will not tolerate insubordination in any form. The men respect him and work hard to please him. All in all, his system seems to work. The only complainer is Captain Allen, our marine commander; he feels uncomfortable with the captain's attitude and does not allow his men any reduction in military courtesy."

Miles didn't reply, but he thought, "I may have to agree with Captain Allen. I've always believed that familiarity breeds contempt. I don't think it's fair to the men in the long run, but this isn't my fight, and, as long as it doesn't affect my marines, I'll say nothing."

Miles decided to change the subject and asked Vest, "Where has the *Falcon* served before this assignment?"

"We were on the East Indian Station in 1708, supporting the expansion of the reorganized East India Company. I noticed the change in Captain

Lowry while we supported the Dutch in Asia. I think he wanted our men to be better treated than the Dutch."

"Did the *Falcon* see action in India?"

"Nothing involving ship-to-ship combat, but we escorted the merchant ships, both British and Dutch. So, to answer the question that you'd really like to ask, no — the ship and its crew have not faced an enemy ship at close range."

"No offense intended, Lieutenant, but, yes — that is exactly my question. Until you have experienced that brutal one-on-one combat, you don't know how the crew will respond."

"I agree, but it's my belief that our men would perform in the best traditions of the service."

"I'm sure they would. I hope it doesn't prove necessary during our impending operation."

A midshipman entered the wardroom and reported to Vest: "Sir, the major's chests are secured in his cabin. May I be of additional service?"

"No, Danny, that will be all for now."

Vest stood and said, "I'll give you a little time to sort your cabin out, and we'll join Captain Lowry in his cabin."

Miles stood and replied, "Thank you for the orientation. I'll meet you in the captain's cabin."

Miles found his sea chests stacked on the floor near his bunk and began to unpack them and put away the contents. He hung his uniforms in the small space provided and placed his book on the diminutive desk. He left his pistols in their case and put both of the chests beneath the bunk. Then, he squared his uniform, walked to the captain's cabin, and tapped on the closed hatch.

Captain Andrew Lowry called out, "Enter."

When Miles stepped through the hatch, he saw Ron Vest and a Royal Marine captain standing near the captain's desk. Lowry smiled and said, "Major Ransom, I believe you know Lieutenant Vest, and this is the *Falcon*'s marine commander, Captain Thomas Allen."

Allen was a short, swarthy man with black hair and piercing, dark eyes. He stood and extended his hand.

"Major Ransom, welcome aboard. I've been anxious to meet you. I'd have to say you're much younger than I expected."

Miles didn't respond to the age comment but said, "I'm pleased to meet you, as well. I plan to call a commanders' meeting on Friday of this week, if Captain Lowry will allow me the wardroom."

Lowry indicated the table, which was set with four places across the cabin, and said, "You may certainly have the wardroom. Just let Ron know when. Now, gentlemen, let us share a meal."

Two stewards appeared, as if by magic, and began serving the food and filling the wine glasses. As the meal progressed, Lowry talked about the upcoming operation and the *Falcon*'s role. He pointed out that the *Falcon* would leave Boston on the morning tide of September 27 and join *HMS Chester* off the Straits of Digby, where she would conduct a reconnaissance of the Bay of Digby and Goat Island.

Miles asked, "Have you received formal orders for this?"

"Yes, they came from General Nicholson and Captain Reed just this morning."

"Was there any mention of the role of *HMS Dragon*?"

"Yes, the *Dragon* will sail with the rest of the fleet on September 29 and relieve *HMS Chester*. The *Dragon* will be responsible for securing the Straits during the attack on Port Royal, and the *Chester* will rejoin the fleet for the bombardment of the fort."

Miles thought, "Orders must have arrived shortly

after I left the *Dragon*. I can only imagine Sir William's reaction to finding his ship assigned to sentry duty. I'll be surprised if he doesn't resign over this."

Captain Allen had been listening attentively and interjected, "Major, have you determined exactly what you will expect from the marines on each of the fleet's ships?"

"I plan to cover that in the meeting on Friday, but I can say that the first responsibility of each ship's marines will be the safety of their ship. I will never issue an order that contradicts that fact."

Lowry nodded and said, "Major Ransom has to walk a tightrope in this regard. The marines posted to each of the ships are still under the direct command of that ship's officers. The major will have to coordinate another activity with each ship."

"It sounds like your role is mainly to see to the rationing and welfare of the fleet's marines and not an operational command position," commented Allen.

Lowry said, "We'll just have to see how things develop, Captain. I'm sure all will be made clear before we launch the attack on Port Royal."

The meal ended without any further discussion of Miles's role, and, after they bid the captain goodbye,

Miles and Ron Vest returned to the wardroom, where Vest said, "I realize that Allen seemed a little cheeky, but I believe he's genuinely interested in understanding his chain of command. He's a good officer and can be depended on to do his duty."

"No offense taken. I'm as confused as he about what I'm supposed to do. In the absence of orders to the contrary, I intend to support each of the ship's marines as a unique unit and to work intimately with each ship's officers."

"I think you'll find most captains willing to work with you in that manner. I did notice Allen's comment regarding your tender age."

"Yeah, I get that a lot. Can't blame a man who has served for years before attaining a promotion for being a little resentful of a 25-year-old field-grade officer. I just have to live with it."

"I think you can handle it. I'll have the wardroom set aside for your use on Friday morning at four bells on the morning watch, if that works for you."

"That's fine; I'll need some coffee and tea. I'm ordering each of the ship's marine commanders to attend, so there will be six officers present. The *Chester* is on station off Digby."

Reaching inside his jacket, Miles pulled out two of his

cigars and offered one to Vest. Vest shook his head and said, "No, thank you. I've decided never to smoke tobacco again. I cannot see how it can be good for your lungs."

"It probably isn't, but smoking does give one a sense of ease and comfort."

"The same can be said of spirits taken in moderation."

"True, and I have to admit to a liking for both. I'll be going ashore to attend to some personal business and won't return today. I can be reached at the Henry House, if you need to find me."

Vest stood and replied, "I need to return to duty, so I assume that I'll see you tomorrow."

"Yes, I'll come aboard for a time tomorrow afternoon, and, Ron, thanks for the support. I'll need all I can get."

"Glad to help. See you tomorrow."

Miles left the *Falcon* shortly afterward and told Johnny to take him to the Dalhousie offices.

Thomas R. Lawrence

6 THE QUEEN'S CAPTAIN

The clock in the tower of the North Church rang three times as the carriage turned onto Hanover Street. Johnny stopped in front of the Dalhousie offices, and Miles stepped down.

"I should only be an hour or so. See if you can find a spot nearby to wait. I'll blow this whistle if I can't see you."

Miles held up a silver whistle and blew into it. Johnny touched his hat with his whip and said, "Aye, Major. I'll be within hearing distance. Just give me a toot."

Philippe met Miles at the front door and led him back to his office. He asked the clerk to bring a fresh pot of coffee and motioned for Miles to have a seat. When the clerk finished serving the coffee, Philippe said, "As you requested, I did some digging on our young Mr. Goldstone. I found some interesting facts."

Miles took a sip of coffee and said, "Such as?"

"It seems Goldstone has a bit of a gambling problem. He ran through all of the cash left by his late father and is putting all of the real property up for sale. He has mortgaged everything he owns, and the bank is close to beginning foreclosure proceedings. Essentially, he is bankrupt."

"Does he have a mortgage on the Henry House?"

"He does, to the tune of £250."

"I can see why he's asking £500; he needs the cash."

"I took the liberty of purchasing his gambling debts. I bought the £500 debt at a 75-percent discount, for a price of £125. I thought it might come in handy in our negotiations."

"Yes, I think it might," Miles replied.

"Are we still expecting him by four o'clock?"

"Yes. In fact, I see him coming in now. I think we'll let him sit in the lobby while we finish our coffee. Don't want to seem too anxious."

Miles and Philippe finished their coffee, and Philippe

signaled to his clerk to show Mr. Goldstone in to the office. The young man was dressed in the height of London fashion. He had a sable cloak thrown over his shoulder, and he carried a silver-headed cane. When Goldstone entered the office, Philippe offered him the chair opposite Miles and began, "Mr. Goldstone, thank you for joining us this afternoon. As we discussed, I believe you have several pieces of property that you wish to sell."

"Yes. I have placed a small part of my holdings on the market. I intend to upgrade my holdings with the proceeds."

"I see. Then, may we assume you are selling some of the less desirable properties?"

"No, not at all! I have quite an extensive real-estate portfolio, and I am simply selling some of the prime income-producing properties while the market is right. I'll use the proceeds to acquire less desirable locations and bring them up to market rents."

"Do you have a list of these properties you wish to divest?"

Goldstone handed Philippe a folded sheet of paper. Philippe took it and opened it. He studied the contents for a moment and then said, "I see five parcels on your list and your asking price beside each."

"Yes, and the prices are not negotiable. I expect an all-specie sale, and I will offer no financing."

"There is one parcel in which Major Ransom has a particular interest: the Henry House of Queen Street. I see you are asking £500 for it."

"That is correct, and, as I said, the price is all specie and not negotiable."

"I understand," Philippe replied. He then turned to Miles and asked, "Major Ransom, do you have any questions?"

"No, I'm willing to pay Mr. Goldstone's asking price of £500."

"Very well—do we have an agreement, Mr. Goldstone?"

"Yes, I agree."

"Is the property free and clear of debt?"

"There is a small mortgage, which I will pay off with the proceeds of the sale."

"Then, we will use this as part of our payment," Philippe said as he slid the gambling note across his desk.

Goldstone unfolded the note, and a look of dismay

crossed his face. He said, "No, this will not work for me. I must have specie."

"Is this not your personal note for £500?"

"It is, but I cannot honor it for this transaction."

"May I ask why not?"

"I need to raise specie to pay off my debts."

"Isn't this note part of your problem?"

"Yes, but I also owe the bank. I'm going to lose everything if I can't pay them off."

"How much do you owe the bank?"

"Including the mortgage on the Queen Street property, £2,000."

Philippe looked again at the list of properties and their asking prices. He then said to Goldstone, "Mr. Goldstone, would you allow me a moment alone with my client?"

"Of course — I'll step into the lobby until you signal for my return."

Goldstone left the office, and Philippe said, "Miles, Goldstone is offering all five pieces of property for £3,000. There is a £2,000 mortgage on them, and a fair price would be £2,400. I suggest that we offer him his note and £200 for the lot. That would make our buying price the £125 we paid for his IOU, the £200 in specie to him, plus the mortgage payoff of £2,000, for a total of £2,325. We could go up another £75 if we need to and still be at a fair market value."

"Let's make the offer," Miles replied.

Philippe signaled for Goldstone to return, and, when he was seated, they laid out the offer to him.

"No, I cannot do this. I must have more," Goldstone said.

"Before you make a hasty decision, I suggest you think through the consequences," warned Philippe.

"To what consequences are you referring?"

"If you leave this office without agreeing to these very generous terms, then I will be forced to demand full payment of your £500 note, which I now own."

"You can demand all you want. I don't have the specie and cannot pay you."

"Again, think about the consequences. If I present this note to the General Court as in default, then the banks will immediately foreclose, and you will lose everything and go to debtors' prison. I will then buy all of your property at auction. Your options are only two. Accept our offer and walk away debt-free with £200 in your pocket, or go to prison. It will be your choice."

Goldstone turned pale, and beads of sweat popped out on his forehead. Finally, he said, "Is there no way you could offer more?"

Philippe looked at Miles and raised his eyebrows. Miles paused for a moment and then said, "Mr. Goldstone, I suspect any monies that you leave here with will soon be in the hands of your gambling friends. I don't like the thought of wasting my money. If I could be confident that you will not gamble it away, then I would be willing to offer an additional £75 in specie."

Philippe joined in and said, "Mr. Goldstone, £275 is a tidy sum. It should allow you to find gainful employment and form the basis for your financial recovery. I suggest that you accept Major Ransom's generous proposal before he tires of this matter and withdraws the offer."

Goldstone sat quietly for a moment. He then replied, "Given my limited options, I will accept the major's offer, on one condition."

Miles asked, "And that is?"

"That Mr. Dalhousie agrees to be my banker and financial advisor. If I'm going to become productive, then I'm going to need a firm hand to guide me."

Philippe thought for a moment and said, "Mr. Goldstone, I will do as you wish, but you will have to settle for a modest living allowance, and I must approve any other expenditures. Is this agreeable to you?"

"Yes, I believe we can do business."

"Very well. If you will have a seat in the outer office, then I will have all of the papers drawn up within the hour."

Goldstone left the office. Miles smiled at Philippe and said, "It appears that I've become a rather large property owner here in Boston."

"So it would seem. I hope you are comfortable with the outcome."

"Oh, yes, comfortable and pleased. Of course, I'll place the management of all the parcels in your capable hands, with the exception of the Henry House. I'll need you to draw up a partnership agreement between Josiah Adams and myself concerning that location."

Miles outlined the terms of the partnership settled on by Josiah and himself. Then, Philippe summoned his clerk and gave him instructions to draw up both agreements. When the clerk withdrew, Miles said, "Why don't we invite the young Mr. Goldstone to share in a glass of sherry and a cigar?"

"Certainly — he has had a difficult day, and he might appreciate some support."

Miles and Philippe tried to encourage Lucien Goldstone while the paperwork was being prepared. After a glass or two of sherry and one of Miles's cigars, Goldstone began to perk up. The clerk brought the papers in, and, after signing them, Lucien thanked Miles and Philippe for bailing him out and left the building. When he was gone, Philippe suggested that Miles join him for dinner.

Miles declined, explaining that he wanted to take the partnership agreement over to Josiah and complete the transaction. Philippe smiled and said, "Perhaps we can dine together when you return from Port Royal. I have prepared a list of the properties, their locations, costs, and projected incomes. Take a look before you go."

Miles took the paper and read the following:

Private Residence   19 North Square
£175   Income £20
Henry House Tavern and Inn   211 Queen Street

£350   Unknown
Warehouse and Wharf   Battery Street   £675
     Income £80
Livery Stable and Blacksmith   201 Chestnut Street
£800   Income £200
Ship Chandler   Rowe's Wharf   £400
     Income £100

Miles looked the paper over and then asked, "Is the residence on North Square rented?"

"It is. The silversmith, John Coney, has his shop on the ground floor and his residence on the upper floor."

"Good. I see the rents will earn 20 percent, plus my share of the Henry House profits—that's a sound return."

"I agree. I think we made a good deal today."

"Indeed, we did," Miles replied. He gathered the papers together and bade Philippe a good evening. Miles had Johnny take him to the Henry House, where Miles was greeted at the door by Annie Adams, who curtsied and said, "Major Ransom, my father has shared the news about our new partnership, and I wish to thank you for your confidence."

Miles replied, "You're welcome. I look forward to a long and profitable partnership."

Miles looked at the intelligent young woman and saw, again, what a beauty she was. Not only was she beautiful, but she filled out the peasant blouse in all of the right places. He smiled and asked, "Tell me, Annie, how old are you?"

Annie cut her deep green eyes and said demurely, "I'll be 17 in November."

Miles nodded and said, "Is your father about?"

"He's in the kitchen with Mama. Shall I go fetch him?"

"Please. We have business to attend to."

Josiah came from the kitchen, holding a wine bottle and two glasses. He joined Miles at one of the tables and poured each of them a glass of claret. Miles raised his glass and said, "To our partnership — I was successful in acquiring the title to the Henry House."

The men raised their glasses and took sips. Miles swirled the wine in the glass and said, "Josiah, this is a very nice claret. Do we have more?"

"We have a cellar full. I buy this from a Portuguese trader from Rhode Island who brings it in from the Valpacos region. They have been making red wine since the Roman occupation."

"Do we serve it as our house wine?"

"No, but it has developed a loyal following among our wealthier clientele. We try to offer quality food and beverages at reasonable prices."

"I should think that would be the formula for a successful establishment."

"It has been so far, that and the fact that I do not cater to the hard drinkers. We serve a local ale at a premium price. Speaking of food and drink, Mrs. Adams has prepared a lobster dinner to celebrate our partnership."

"That sounds delicious. Do I have time to freshen up a bit?"

"By all means — Martha will put the langouste in the oven when you return."

Miles thought for a moment about mentioning his personal interest in Annie but decided it could wait until after Port Royal. He went to his rooms and changed from his uniform into a pair of black woolen pants and an open-necked white shirt. He washed his hands and face, combed his hair, and then returned to the dining area.

Martha Adams and Annie had set a table for two with white linen and the inn's best china. Josiah was sitting with a glass of wine and his pipe. He stood when

Miles approached, and Miles said, "Keep your seat, Josiah. We are friends and business partners; we needn't stand on formality. Before we dine, let's finish the paperwork for our partnership."

Miles placed the agreement on the table and said, "Here is the completed contract. Please read over it and be sure it is to your satisfaction."

Josiah carefully read it and then said, "Miles, there is one thing that I didn't understand."

Miles looked puzzled and asked, "What might that be?"

"If I'm reading this right, then you are putting the title to the Henry House and £100 into our partnership."

"Yes, that is as we agreed."

"It's far more than I originally understood. By putting up the title, you have given me a half interest in the Henry House. I thought that you intended only to provide the use of the inn and that you'd retain ownership."

"No, that was never my intention. Are you comfortable with this arrangement?"

"Comfortable to be gifted half interest in a very

valuable piece of property? Of course I am — but I think it is too generous on your part."

"Generosity doesn't enter into it. I want a long-term partnership, and I wish you to have the exact position as I. That makes our interests equal."

Josiah looked at Miles and said, "Miles, I think this is the beginning of a long and profitable partnership."

"As do I. Now, let's have a go at those lobsters."

Martha and Annie served the steaming crustaceans baked "fisherman's style." There was a corn pudding and fresh greens, as well. They finished the bottle of claret, and, after the meal, Annie served a snifter of brandy. Miles took a sip and said, "This brandy is quite good. Is it from Portugal, as well?"

"It is. It's called Madeira and comes from the same region as the claret."

"We should continue to offer both," Miles replied.

They sipped on the Madeira, and Miles lit a cigar while Josiah puffed on his pipe. When the brandy was gone, Miles stood and said, "I best be to bed. My ship sails on Saturday, and I've much to do. I'll bid you a good evening, Josiah."

"Good evening to you, Miles. Will you have breakfast?"

"Coffee and some bread will be ample. Can you have it sent to my rooms?"

"Of course — what time would you like it?"

"Six would be perfect. I want to be aboard the *Falcon* by eight."

Miles went to the kitchen, thanked Martha and Annie for the meal, and headed up to his room. He stripped out of his clothes and took care of his toilette. He then slipped naked into the big featherbed. Miles had just fallen asleep, when he heard the door to his bedroom creak open. He rose up on one elbow and saw Annie standing in the moonlight, wrapped in a woolen cloak.

Miles was about to say something when she placed her finger to her lips and shook her head. She dropped the cloak to the floor and stood naked in the moonlight. She was stunning. Her long, red hair reached to her waist, and her ample breasts stood firm. She walked across the room and slipped into bed. He took her in his arms, and they joined together.

Near dawn, Annie slid out of bed, wrapped the cloak around her, and left Miles deep in sleep.

There was a gentle knock on his door, and Annie

eased it open, carrying a tray with bread, cheese, and fresh hot coffee. He pulled the quilt across his body. She grinned and said, "Major, I think it is a bit late to worry about modesty. I hope you slept well."

Miles began to stammer, trying to regain his composure. Annie teased, "You were sleeping like a baby when I left a couple of hours ago. Something must have agreed with you."

Annie pushed the door closed with her foot and placed the tray on his desk. She took two steps and jumped into his bed, giggling. Miles took her in his arms and kissed her passionately. She reached beneath the quilt, took him in her hand, and began to stroke him. When he was fully erect, she lifted her skirts and placed him into her. He moaned with satisfaction. Eventually, she stood and straightened her dress.

Smiling, Annie said, "I hope you've enjoyed your breakfast so far. Now, I must be on with my chores."

Annie turned to leave, but Miles grabbed her wrist and pulled her to him. He said, "You and I have some serious talking to do, Miss Adams."

"I was beginning to wonder if you could actually speak. Maybe we can have our talk this evening, if my father doesn't object."

Miles nodded in agreement, and Annie flounced out of the room. Miles sat down on the edge of the bed and noticed a small bloodstain on the sheets. He thought, "Oh, great. I've deflowered my new partner's daughter before the agreement is a day old. The strange part of this whole business is that I can't get her off my mind. She has bedazzled me completely, and we will indeed have a talk this evening."

Miles dressed in a fresh uniform and finished the pot of coffee before going downstairs to face Josiah. Josiah was not in the room, and Miles decided to wait until the evening to broach the whole business. Johnny had arrived, so Miles instructed him to go to the *Falcon*.

7 THE QUEEN'S CAPTAIN

The *Falcon*'s bell rang out three times as Miles boarded the ship and went straight to his cabin to check his uniform. He sat for a moment to gather his thoughts about this morning's meeting with his officers, but all he could think of was Annie Adams. Every time he closed his eyes, he saw her face, and every time he saw her face, he became aroused. He thought, "Damn, with these tight breeches I can't go around with a hard-on all day, and I can't keep myself covered with my hat either. I better let thoughts of Miss Adams go until tonight."

Miles was not a complete boy when it came to women and their charms. He'd had the usual number of sexual liaisons with barmaids and whores — and one blissful summer in Rome with a countess, 15 years his senior. Up to this point, he'd managed to avoid falling for any of them, but he might have met his match in Annie Adams. He pushed her from his mind and walked to the wardroom.

The stewards were busy setting up the room for his meeting. The main table would give everyone a seat, and he would sit at the head. He checked the coffee and noticed that the cooks had baked some muffins, as well. He was about to pour a cup when Captain Tom Allen came ducking through the hatch. When he saw Miles, he came to attention and said, "Good morning, Major. Reporting as ordered."

Miles smiled and replied, "Good morning, Captain. Please, have some coffee or tea and one of these hot muffins."

Allen nodded in response and poured hot water over a strainer full of tea. He brought the steaming mug to the table, and Miles indicated that he should sit just to Miles's right. Once Tom was settled in, Miles said, "I'm glad we'll have a chance to visit before the other officers arrive. I'd like your opinion about each of them, if you have no objection."

"I'll be glad to offer my professional assessment, but I'd prefer not to provide a personal appraisal of a fellow officer."

"As you wish—then, your professional assessment?"

"As you realize, none of the ships in the fleet have served together recently. I was a lieutenant aboard the *Lowestoft* before my promotion. Captain Bruce Williams was my recommendation to replace me, so, obviously, I think highly of his merits. It is my understanding that General Nicholson and Captain Reed will be aboard *Lowestoft,* making it, for all practical purposes, the fleet's flagship. *HMS Dragon* will be assigned sentry duty guarding the Straits of Digby. I don't envy Bruce."

"Why do you say that?"

"I believe it will be difficult for him to know exactly from whom he is to take orders. Officially, he answers to you, but you're on another ship. He must also answer to Captain Benton, the *Lowestoft*'s captain, and, then, there are two high-ranking marine officers on board, Lieutenant Colonel Holmes and Major Clark — plenty of chiefs and few Indians."

Miles thought for a moment and then said, "I can see what you mean. What about the other officers?"

"I'm afraid that I can't be of much help. This will be the first meeting of all marine officers, and I just don't know the others."

Miles smiled and said, "Thanks, Tom; I've heard what you said about a tangled chain of command. I'll try to make it as workable as possible."

Allen took a bite of his muffin and said, "You're welcome, sir; I'll always try to be helpful."

The men were chatting about places where they'd served and people they knew when Miles heard the other officers coming aboard. The first to arrive was Bob Gaines of *HMS Dragon*. He beamed when he saw Miles and snapped to attention: "Captain Robert Gaines, *HMS Dragon*, reporting as ordered, sir!"

Miles grinned and said, "Good morning, Bob. I'd like you to meet Captain Tom Allen of *HMS Falcon*. Tom, this is Bob Gaines. Bob replaced me when I was promoted."

Bruce Williams of *HMS Lowestoft* came through the hatch, and introductions were made all around. When everyone had a tea or coffee, Miles stood and began, "Gentlemen, I am pleased to have the opportunity to meet each of you. We're about to embark on a mission to take the capital of French Acadia, and each of our ships will play a major role in this objective. Captain Louis Crane, of *HMS Chester*, could not attend due to the *Chester*'s deployment guarding the entrance to the Bay of Digby. I'll visit him on the *Chester* once the fleet arrives off Digby.

"The traditional role of marines on Her Majesty's ships has been threefold: first, to maintain order and discipline on our ships; second, to man the tops and give covering fire during close combat, and, third, to be available for amphibious landings when needed. Nothing has changed. These are still our primary duties, but the command structure of this expedition requires special attention.

"There is a contingent of Royal Marines who will be supporting the ground forces, and they are under the direct command of Major Amos Clark. Major Clark will be under the command of Lieutenant Colonel Richard Holmes, and I am assuming that both Clark and Holmes will sail aboard *HMS Lowestoft*.

"While I am subordinate to Lieutenant Colonel Holmes, each of you remains at the command of your ship's captain. His orders will always be your first responsibility. My role is to coordinate our efforts, and you will never receive an order from me that has not been agreed to by your ship's captain. I will give you written orders to this effect and will provide copies to both Major Clark and Colonel Holmes. Are there any questions?"

Bruce Williams raised his hand and asked, "Major, in the event of ship-to-ship combat, we have been trained to use our own initiative to protect our ships. Will that remain our prerogative?"

"Yes, the safety of our ships will always be our first concern. Unless otherwise ordered, you may use your initiative."

Bob Gaines said, "Major, as you know, we have encountered difficulty getting supplies and rations promptly. Will you be able to expedite these matters?"

"Yes, Bob, I'm aware of this, and I'll do all I can to speed things up. We all know the Royal Marines will always have to make do with the Navy's hand-me-downs, but I'll certainly try to improve this. In fact, this is just the sort of task that I should be doing. Providing support to the men under my command is foremost on my agenda, and I urge each of you to bring such items to my attention."

There were no other questions, so Miles dismissed the officers to return to their ships. When they had all left, he turned to Tom Allen and said, "Tom, are there any needs on the *Falcon* that I can help you with?"

"Aye, sir. We haven't been issued grappling hooks or pikes to use during ship-to-ship combat, and the other matter is that one of our men has an abscessed tooth, but there is currently no surgeon on board."

"Thank you, Tom. I'll address both of these issues with Captain Lowry this morning—with the abscessed tooth being the most urgent. We sail on

Saturday, but I'll try to resolve them before then."

"Thank you, Major Ransom. The men should be fully equipped and in good health. If you have no objection, then I'll be returning to my duties."

"No, there's nothing else. You're dismissed, but I'll be back to you regarding these pending issues."

Tom Allen left through the hatch, and Miles grabbed the remaining muffin. He ate it on his way to Captain Lowry's cabin. Miles tapped on the hatch, and Lowry called out, "Enter."

When Miles stepped in the cabin, he found Lowry sitting in his shirtsleeves at his sea desk with a quill pen in his hand. Lowry looked up and said, "Ah, Ransom, have a seat. Did your meeting go well?"

"Aye, it went very well, but there are some issues that need to be addressed."

"And how can I help resolve them?"

"First, I'd like your permission to have one of our marines sent to the flagship to have the surgeon attend to an abscessed tooth."

"Of course — permission granted. I'm contracting with a local surgeon to sail with us, but he won't be on board until tomorrow. Is there anything else?"

"Yes, sir. Captain Allen informs me that his men don't have grappling hooks or pikes for close combat. I'd like to find a supply."

"Yes, Captain Allen requested both some time ago, and I've had a requisition in for over a month. Please do anything you can to get them before we sail. In fact, while you're at it, see if you can address the lack of provisions, as well."

"Aye, sir. Thank you for your permission. I'll see what I can do."

Miles knew when to take a broad permission to go get the job done. He figured that he could accomplish a lot and then argue that he thought the agreement covered his actions.

Miles left Lowry's cabin and sent a midshipman to find Tom Allen. Allen met him in the passageway, and Miles ordered him to send the marine with the bad tooth to the flagship. Then, Miles returned to his cabin, grabbed his hat, hurried into the cutter, and ordered the midshipman to take him to the dock. Johnny was waiting, and Miles instructed him to go to Dalhousie Merchant Bank. Philippe was in his office when Miles knocked on the doorframe.

"Good morning, Miles. I didn't expect to see you today. What can I do for you?"

"Have the tenants of the properties we bought yesterday received notice of the change of ownership?"

"Yes, they were notified late yesterday, but there is only one tenant, John Coney, who leases the building on North Square. All of the others are managers who work for you."

"Are you sure?"

"Absolutely. You have managers in all four locations. Why do you ask?"

"I have to admit—I didn't understand that not only did I buy the real property, but I purchased the operating businesses, as well. We made a great deal with Mr. Goldstone!"

"Yes, I believe we did. Now that you know you own a livery stable, a blacksmith shop, a ship chandler, and a public wharf, what can I do for you?"

"I assume your firm will be responsible for the actual management of all of this?"

"Yes, that was our agreement."

"Wonderful. I need to do some business with the ship chandler."

"That will be Seymour's Ship Chandlers. It's on Rowe's Wharf. What do you need?"

"I need grappling hooks and pikes, and I need them by tomorrow. I also need a reliable source of provisions for my men."

Philippe asked, "Is your carriage outside?"

Miles nodded, and Philippe replied, "Well, let's go meet your managers."

Miles and Philippe climbed into the carriage, and Miles gave Johnny the address. Soon, they pulled in front of the offices of Seymour's Ship Chandlers and walked through the front door. They were greeted by a clerk who, working by lamplight, was filling out a ledger. He smiled and said, "Gentlemen, how may we help you?"

Philippe replied, "I am Philippe Dalhousie, and this is Major Miles Ransom. We'd like to visit with Hiram Seymour, if we may."

The man put down his quill, wiped the ink off his fingers onto the stained apron around his waist, and extended his hand.

"Major Ransom, I'm Hiram Seymour, and I'm glad that you have come by. I've been anxious to meet you."

Miles shook his hand and replied, "I, too, am pleased. Mr. Dalhousie will be your direct contact as we move forward, but I have a need for your assistance on a matter of some urgency."

"I'll do whatever I can to help you. What do you require?"

"I'm in command of the Royal Marine companies on Her Majesty's fleet in the harbor. I'm sure you are aware of our presence."

"Of course — I can name every ship in Boston harbor, and I know most of their captains. We don't have the contract to provision the Royal Navy, but I have provided hard-to-find items in the past."

Miles was curious and asked, "Why do we not have the Navy contract?"

"I'm afraid that one of our less honorable competitors has served the Navy for the past 10 years. We will not agree to provide the low-quality goods the Navy is buying. But on the other hand, we dominate the commercial fleet's needs. What is it that you'd like to procure?"

"A dozen grappling hooks and chains — they should be hefty enough to use in boarding a ship during close combat. We also require 20 pikes with iron heads to be used to repel a boarding party. These are our immediate needs, and I'm afraid we must have them on board *HMS Falcon* before we sail on Saturday morning."

Seymour put his hand to his chin and thought for a moment. He then replied, "The grappling hooks and chains we carry in stock, and I'm sure we have a dozen or more on hand, but the pikes are another matter altogether. We can supply the oak shafts, which we have in 12-foot lengths, but we have no stock of pike heads. You would have to get them through a local smithy, and I can recommend the best in Boston, but I doubt that even he could meet your Saturday deadline."

"It seems that I also own a blacksmith. Whom were you going to suggest?"

"We do all of our business with Peacock's. The smithy is housed in Nelson's Livery Stable on Chestnut Street. If anyone can do it, Peacock can. Ask for Terrence Peacock and tell him that I sent you."

"I have a list of the provisions I need, and I'd like them to be delivered to *HMS Falcon*, along with the hooks. Send the oak pike shafts to Mr. Peacock as soon as you can, and please bill my personal account for the order."

"Yes, sir, Major Ransom. Is there anything else you

need?"

"Just one more thing. See what you can do about stocking a couple of cases of Montoya cigars. They're made in Cuba, but I'm guessing that you might have a way to find some."

"I'll look into it right away. Just let me know if I may be of further service."

Miles and Philippe went directly to Peacock's smithy, where they found Terrence Peacock eager to please his new owner. Terrence readily agreed to have the pikes on board the *Falcon* before it sailed. Anxious to understand just what he had purchased and whom he and Philippe would be dealing with, Miles visited for a short time with Peacock and Ben Nelson, the manager of the livery stable.

As they drove away, Miles said, "From what I've seen so far, I believe we have exceptional management in all of the businesses we purchased. You should have no trouble overseeing them."

Philippe nodded in agreement and said, "I've heard that the late Mr. Goldstone was a hardworking and fair man. It seems that he has chosen good people to run his holdings. I'll design a profit-sharing program for each of them for your approval."

"Excellent, I want to give them every incentive to succeed."

Miles dropped Philippe back at his office and then instructed Johnny to take him to the Henry House. The sun was beginning to sag in the western sky, and, for the first time, Miles felt just the hint of a chill as he watched the wind scatter the leaves. Johnny stopped in front of the Henry House, and Miles told him to wait within whistle range.

Josiah was sweeping the floor when Miles came in the tavern. Josiah stopped and leaned against the broom handle. He grinned and said, "Can't say that I expected to see you so early in the afternoon. Would you like an ale or a cup of coffee?"

"No, but there is something I'd like to discuss with you."

Josiah propped the broom against the wall and pulled a chair back at a nearby table. "Have a seat and tell me what's on your mind."

Miles took a seat, cleared his throat, and said, "Josiah, I will always be truthful and direct with you. I have developed a personal interest in Annie, and I would like your permission to court her. Before you answer, please know that I'm acutely aware of your affection for Annie, and I'll not be offended if you say no."

"Say no? Hardly! I'm honored that an earl's son has an interest in my daughter. In fact, I'm extremely flattered and proud for Annie."

"I can pledge to you that my interests are entirely honorable, and you may be assured that I will treat Annie with the utmost respect."

"Has Annie given any indication of mutual interest?"

Miles paused and thought, "No, unless you count climbing naked into my bed last night."

Miles replied, "Not at all. She has been completely proper. I hope to change that if I can."

"Miles, you have my full permission. Annie is getting along in years, and I was beginning to fear that she would become a spinster. She is headstrong and independent. Many men find her challenging."

"Well, I admire those traits and view them as attractive," Miles replied.

"Do you plan to begin your suit right away?"

"No, my ship sails on Saturday's morning tide. I believe it better to wait until we return."

"Well, that'll be just fine. Again, let me say that I support your pursuit entirely. Will you be dining with us this evening?"

"No, I must be aboard *HMS Falcon* beginning tonight. Johnny will be back tomorrow to gather my personal belongings to take them to the pier. I would ask that you tell Annie of our conversation and assure her that I'll return once the expedition is complete."

"I'll do just that, and I suspect she will be flattered and excited."

As he stood, Miles said, "Thank you, Josiah. I'll leave now for the *Falcon* and bid you goodbye."

"Goodbye and Godspeed, Miles. Be as careful as you can."

Miles turned and walked through the inn's door, breathing a sigh of relief. He thought, "Miles, you coward — you're afraid to spend the night in your own bed for fear of Annie's crawling in it, and yet that's all you can think about. You'd better get your mind on the French if you ever want to be in that bed again."

Johnny dropped him at the pier, where Miles took the cutter out to the *Falcon*. He boarded and went straight to his cabin.

8 THE QUEEN'S CAPTAIN

After arranging his personal gear in the cabin, Miles went in search of Ron Vest. He found him on deck supervising the loading of shot and powder. The transfer of ammunition to the magazine was one of the most dangerous operations on a ship. Miles had been a midshipman when careless handling had caused a keg of powder to explode on the deck of *HMS Lancer*. The ship was heavily damaged, and over 30 men were killed. He hesitated before approaching Vest.

Ron noticed Miles standing by the open hatch and said, "You might as well come on over, Major; the blast would get you where you're standing anyway."

Miles grinned as he walked toward Vest, who was perched by a rail and was looking down at the munitions barge that was carrying its cargo of death and destruction. Miles reached for the rigging, pulled himself on the rail beside Vest, and replied, "Didn't want to distract you. I was aboard the *Lancer* when she was wrecked."

"I remember well when that happened. Were you injured?"

"No, I was on the lower gun deck supervising the repair of one of the cannons, and we all managed to get topside without casualties. It scared the hell out of me though. I'd never seen such carnage, even in battle."

"I'm here for the sake of appearances. The actual work is being done by our chief armorer and his men. They handle powder and shot daily, and they certainly know what they're doing."

"I agree. This is something better left to the professionals, but I understand that you need to demonstrate an officer's confidence in the operation."

"Well, now that you're here, what can I do for you?"

"Sometime tomorrow, grappling hooks and pikes will be delivered to our marines. I'll alert Captain Allen to be on hand to take them aboard, but I wanted to give you a heads-up."

"We've been looking for this stuff for over a month, so it's about time those idiot quartermasters sent them. How'd you know they were coming?"

"I arranged it, along with some extra rations for the crew and my men. The rations will be delivered along with the hooks and pikes, and I'll appreciate it if you treat this as a regular delivery until I choose to let Captain Lowry know that he owes me £113. I believe I might have asked his permission in a general sort of way, but, now that it's done, I may still have to beg forgiveness. However, the much-needed equipment will be here when we sail."

"I'm beginning to see why the Royal Marines have such a shady reputation among the upper ranks in the Navy."

"Just doing my job. Besides, what's the worst that can happen?"

"Aside from having you walk the plank, I suppose he could refuse to pay for it."

"I don't think I'll get the plank, and I can live with it if he refuses to pay me. I won't like it, but I can handle it."

"It must be nice to be rich. £113 would wipe out my savings."

"Yes, wealth surely has its advantages, but I still have to play by the same rules, like any other officer."

"We're all equal, but an earl's son might be just a little

more equal than the rest of us."

Miles chuckled and jumped to the deck. He saluted Vest and climbed back down the hatch, just as the bell sounded the change of watch. If rank came with privileges, then not having to stand watch was one of the most pleasant of perquisites. Miles stopped by the wardroom and picked up some bread and cheese and headed to his cabin.

Once out of his uniform and in his nightshirt, Miles took the bread and cheese to his desk and ate while he wrote in his journal. Most of what he wrote concerned Miss Annie Adams, and he began to wish he'd spent the night at the Henry House. He doused the lamp and thought about her until he fell asleep.

Miles awoke early to the sound of the anchor cable's being reeled in, so he quickly did his morning rituals and dressed in a shipboard uniform. As he strode down the corridor, he stuck his head into the wardroom, where Ron Vest was eating breakfast. Miles poured a cup of coffee, took a fresh loaf of bread, and sat across from Ron.

"What's going on topside? I heard the men raising the anchor."

"We're changing positions in readiness for sailing on tomorrow's morning tide."

"Will we still be operating the cutter back to the wharf?"

"Aye, we're expecting a surgeon to come on board this afternoon, and Captain Lowry has an appointment with Nicholson at noon."

"What's that about?"

"We have no idea, but we can hope we'll still sail tomorrow."

"If they want a look at Goat Island, then we'd better. Even Nicholson and Reed wouldn't send the fleet in until we know it's not hiding batteries."

"Whatever is decided will be well above my pay grade, so I'll just wait and see."

"I'm going to Boston this morning. Is there anything we need?"

"Just make sure you have an ample supply of those Cuban cigars."

"You can rest easy; I never leave home without them. I'll see you when I return this afternoon."

Miles went back to his cabin, donned his uniform coat and hat, and took the cutter to the wharf. Johnny was waiting in his usual spot, and Miles told him to go to the Henry House. Miles had decided he didn't want to leave without saying goodbye to Annie Adams.

When Miles walked into the inn, Annie was mopping the floor, her thick, shiny hair tied up in a bandana. When she saw him, she broke into a broad smile and leaned on the mop with one hip extended. Miles felt an erection coming on and dropped his hat to hide it. Annie giggled and said, "Why, Major Ransom, are you glad to see me?"

"Yes, in fact, it is you I came to see."

"I thought maybe you needed to conspire further with my father about my social life."

"No, he and I have already agreed to our courtship."

"And you didn't think to involve me in those discussions?"

Miles blushed and replied, "I have to admit that I thought we'd reached an understanding the night before last."

"That we did, but it doesn't give you the right to talk about my future without consulting me."

Miles moved within arm's reach and said, "Miss Adams, I apologize if I've offended you, and I can assure you that it won't happen again."

Annie was just about to counter when Miles swept

her into his arms and kissed her hungrily. At first, she stiffened, but then she grabbed the back of his head and buried her tongue in his mouth. He pulled her close and cupped her shapely bottom in his hands, as he felt her grasp his manhood. The back door of the inn slammed shut, and they heard Josiah and Martha come in from the garden.

The young lovers hastily pulled apart. Annie straightened her skirts, and Miles returned his hat to its strategic position. When the Adams couple came into the room, Annie and Miles were standing, giving the appearance of being in casual conversation. Josiah saw them, and he bellowed, "Miles, I'm glad you came by before the fleet sails! Martha made her clam chowder this morning, and we're about to enjoy a bowl. Please join us!"

Miles kept his hat in place and replied, "That sounds good. Afterward, with your permission, I'd like to take Annie for a ride in my carriage."

Annie grinned and said, "Why, Major Ransom, I'd love to go for a ride in your carriage, but I have my chores."

Martha quickly broke in and said, "Nonsense, Annie! You may certainly accompany the major. I'll tend to your chores. We all know that the fleet sails into harm's way tomorrow."

Annie lowered her flashing green eyes and replied, "Yes, then a carriage ride would be lovely, but I'd prefer a horse ride in the countryside. You do ride, don't you, Major?"

"I do reasonably well for a seaman, and, yes, I believe we can arrange a ride."

Josiah broke in and said, "Annie, before you continue to organize this outing to your satisfaction, you might wonder where the horses will be coming from, my girl!"

Miles shook his head and replied, "I don't think that will be a problem, as it seems I own a livery stable."

While Annie changed clothes, Miles joined Annie's parents for a bowl of the best clam chowder he'd ever tasted. As they ate, Josiah said, "Miles, I know you must realize that you have to be careful. Boston is full of French agents. In fact, I've got my doubts about your friend, Dalhousie. After all, his is a French company based in Bordeaux."

"I, too, suspect Philippe is gathering intelligence, but I'm pretty sure it's for his firm's use, not the French military's. The Dalhousies have managed to survive for nearly a thousand years by deftly playing politics. They would much rather know what the Crown's intentions are if we are successful in taking Port Royal than how we plan to do it. Making money is how they manage to stay in business."

Josiah lit his pipe and said, "You're probably right, and what does it matter? Everyone in Boston is aware of the exact makeup of our forces and that the fleet will sail on Monday. There's no doubt that the French know you're coming their way."

"Knowing about it and stopping us will be two different things. According to our intelligence reports, we'll outnumber Port Royal's defenders four to one. They have no naval vessels that are capable of standing up to a man-of-war, and we have four of those. The *Falcon* will go ahead of the fleet — we sail on tomorrow's morning tide."

"For Annie's sake, try to take care of yourself. I've never seen her in such a state."

They were just finishing the chowder, when Annie came down, dressed in full riding habit. When Miles looked surprised, she playfully responded, "Well, I told you that I ride. What'd you expect? Lady Godiva?"

The image of Annie as Lady Godiva flashed across Miles's mind, and he had to reposition his hat, once again, before saying, "Somehow, I expect that I'm in for quite a riding lesson."

Annie smiled and said, "That could be, Major Ransom. Why don't we go find out?"

Miles helped Annie into the carriage and instructed Johnny to take them to Nelson's Livery on Chestnut. When they arrived, Miles suggested that Annie wait in the carriage while he arranged for mounts. She frowned at him but agreed. He found Ben Nelson and told him his plans. Nelson replied, "Yes, Major, we have several good horses. I have a high-spirited stallion that I think you'll enjoy and a gentler mare for the young lady."

"Do you have two spirited mounts? I suspect the young lady is going to be able to handle whatever we choose."

"I have a new stallion that I just purchased—he's supposed to be the fastest horse in New England. I bought him for stud, but I've never ridden him. If you think you can handle him, then the lady could take Diablo, and you can ride Satan's Fury."

"I have a hunch we'll want to let Miss Adams decide which she wishes to ride. Can you suggest a route of several hours? I'm not familiar with the surrounding area."

"Yes, there are good roads to the south of Boston, and

a ride to Braintree would take no more than an hour at a brisk walk. You should be back well before dark."

"Would you mind sketching a map for me?"

"Of course, and, by the way, are you armed?"

"Well, I have my sword in the carriage, but I hadn't planned to carry it."

"You should, and I'll give you a shotgun to take in the saddle case. These are troubled times, and I'd want nothing to happen to you and Josiah's daughter."

Miles returned to the carriage and helped Annie down. He then put on his sword and scabbard. He led Annie to the stable door, where a groom was holding the reins of two prominent stallions. Miles said, "You can have your choice of mounts. The roan stallion is Satan's Fury, and he just arrived. No one here has ridden him yet. The black one is Diablo, and, of course, there are gentler, less spirited mounts, if you'd prefer."

Annie walked around the two stallions, stood close to the roan, and gently whispered in his ear. The big horse nuzzled her and all but sighed. Annie grinned and said, "I'll ride Satan's Fury if you think you can handle Diablo."

As a child, Miles had been trained to ride to the hunt.

He was an excellent horseman and thought, "Okay, Miss Adams, let's just see how you ride."

The groom led the horses back into the stable and began saddling them. Annie noticed that he was putting a lady's saddle on Satan's Fury and said, "If you please, I'd prefer a regular saddle."

The young groom looked at Miles with a confused expression. Miles rolled his eyes but said, "You heard Miss Adams. A regular saddle will suffice."

Once the saddles were ready, the groom held the reins, and Annie swung up onto the saddle with ease. She noticed the shotgun in Miles's saddle holster but said nothing. Miles led the way as they rode to the intersection of Chestnut and Charles, where he turned south. He took a look at the map, folded it, and placed it in his pocket.

Soon, Miles and Annie were on a well-traveled road and passed a sign pointing south to Braintree. They continued at a brisk walk. The warm weather of Indian summer made Miles remove his officer's jacket and tie it behind his saddle. They rode in silence, passing well-kept farms on both sides of the road. Finally, Annie leaned across her saddle and asked, "Are we going to Braintree?"

"Yes, that will be our turning point."

"Well, I know a shortcut just up ahead that will save us 30 minutes at this pace. My Uncle Jonathan lives in Braintree, and I'd like for you to meet him."

"I'd enjoy that. Why don't you lead the way?"

Annie pointed to a side trail that veered to the east into a dense forest of hardwoods. The trail was just wide enough for two riders, and the sun was dimmed by the canopy of leaves. They rode deeper into the trees until they saw a clearing just ahead of them. However, as they were about to enter the clearing, they were halted by three mounted men, cradling rifles, blocking their way.

Miles touched Annie on the arm and signaled that they should stop. He eased his horse ahead and shouted, "What business have you?"

A bearded man, dressed in homespun and wearing a slouch hat, shouted back, "This is a toll road, and we're collecting the fees."

Miles stalled for time and asked, "What is the toll?"

The man laughed and said, "Now, that depends on how much you got."

Miles was reaching for the shotgun when Annie whispered, "Follow me."

Annie spurred the big roan and turned to the left in a giant bound. Miles had no choice but to follow. The two stallions reached full speed before the three men could react. The bearded man pulled up his rifle and got off a shot, just as the two riders disappeared into the woods. The trio spurred their horses and began pursuing Miles and Annie.

Annie leaned close to Satan's mane and led them through the dense forest, but Miles could hear their pursuers crashing behind them. His first instinct was to attack. Running from a fight went against everything he believed in, but Annie's safety made a difference, and so he followed her. Soon, they raced out of the woods into fields lined with stone walls. When they broke into the open, Annie spurred Satan into another gear. Miles looked ahead and saw a four-foot-high stone barrier looming in the distance.

Annie took the wall at full gallop, expertly leaning forward as the racing stallion cleared the hurdle by at least three feet. Two shots rang out as Miles jumped the wall, and he and Annie raced toward a farmhouse in the distance. Miles turned in his saddle and saw the three men stop and head back toward the woods.

When Annie reached the farmhouse, she slowed to a walk and allowed Miles to catch up. When he reached her, he said, "Annie, I'm so sorry that I put you in danger. I'll be more responsible in the future."

Annie turned in her saddle and said, "Miles, you truly must stop believing you can control everything. I chose the path through the woods, and I thought we handled the situation just fine. In fact, you have to admit that it was exciting."

"Annie, my love, getting shot at is usually thrilling, but I experience enough peril on the job. I will admit that it gave us a chance to find out just what Satan and Diablo can do. Let me also acknowledge that you kept a level head and got us out of a tight spot."

"Thank you for saying so; I felt it would be better to run than have you kill a couple of them with your shotgun and sword. You'd have a hard time sailing in the morning if you had."

They resumed their journey and rode side by side, chatting about their adventure until Annie pointed ahead and said, "That's my Uncle Jonathan's farm. He's Father's younger brother, and he just turned 21."

Annie and Miles turned their horses toward a brown, wooden, two-story house built in the saltbox style. A handsome young man was chopping wood in the side yard, and he broke into a wide grin when he saw Annie. He dropped the ax and walked to meet her.

Annie dismounted, gave him an enthusiastic hug, and said, "Oh, Jonathan, it is so good to see you. I want you to meet my soon-to-be husband, Major Miles Ransom of the Royal Marines."

Miles was so stunned by Annie's declaration of their nuptials that he just sat on his horse open-mouthed. Annie looked at him and laughed, "Soon to be if he doesn't panic and run for his ship."

Miles managed to recover and get down from Diablo. Jonathan Adams chuckled and said, "Annie is an acquired taste, but, if what she says is true, you're about to embark on the adventure of your life. If Annie were not so old and not my niece, then I'd give you a run for your money."

Miles shook his hand and replied, "I've known her for less than a week, and it's certainly been an adventure so far."

Annie glared at Jonathan and said, "Old? I'm four years younger than you."

"Yes, and seemingly headed for a life of spinsterhood unless Major Ransom does indeed rescue you. Can I invite you in for a cup of tea?"

"Jonathan, you couldn't boil water without scorching it. I'll prepare the tea while you visit with Miles."

Annie went into the house. Jonathan turned to Miles and said, "Congratulations. Annie will make you an exceptional wife. When do you plan to be married?"

"Honestly, I don't know. Annie hasn't told me yet. It'll have to be after I return from Port Royal."

"Oh, then you're part of Nicholson's fleet?"

"Yes, I command the Royal Marines who are sailing with the fleet."

"Major, no offense meant, but aren't you a little young to hold such high rank? I'm a lieutenant in the militia, and everyone thinks I'm too young for the position."

Miles smiled and replied, "I get that question a lot, and I certainly don't take offense. I've been in the Royal Navy since I was 13, but, even at that, I've obtained rank beyond my years."

Annie came to the door and called out, "Tea's served — well, tea *and* coffee. Miles is the only Englishman who hates tea."

Thomas R. Lawrence

9 THE QUEEN'S CAPTAIN

Jonathan and Miles followed Annie to the kitchen, where she took a black iron kettle from a hook over the fire and poured steaming water into a coffee pot. She then poured water into two mugs containing tea strainers and said, "The tea and coffee will be ready in a minute or two. Jonathan, I've looked high and low for something to eat, and there's nothing. What's keeping you alive?"

"I have an arrangement with Widow Carson down the road. I eat with her and pay for all of the food. It helps her, and I get good home-cooked meals."

Annie grinned and asked, "Are meals *all* you get from the widow?"

Jonathan shot back, "Yes, she's in her sixties and

weighs at least ten stone."

Annie shrugged her shoulders and drank her tea. Miles decided to change the subject and said, "Annie and I had a bit of excitement on the ride over," and he went on to tell about the attempted holdup in the woods.

"I'm glad you were able to escape unharmed. It's a shame when our citizens have to fear such scoundrels," said Jonathan.

Miles asked, "Do you have any idea who they were?"

"If I had to guess, I'd say it was old Bart Hopkins and his two sons. They live on the other side of those woods and are well-known troublemakers. I think you ought to tell the authorities about this."

"No, I have to leave in the morning, and there's no sense starting something that I can't finish. If it weren't for sailing, then I'd tend to this myself."

"I'm sure you would. The chances are that they'll soon have to answer to the law. It is intolerable to have this in our community. I'm running for selectman in November, and, if I'm elected, I'll put a stop to them."

Annie set her teacup down and said, "Jonathan, what a busy boy you are! You're a farmer; you're serving in the militia; and now you're getting into politics. I doubt you'll ever marry."

"There's plenty of time for that. I want to get established before I even think of marriage. A man doesn't reach his prime until his thirties."

Annie said, "Oh, I see. Talk about a double standard. You'll still be in your prime at 30, but I'm approaching spinsterhood at 17."

"Annie, I didn't say life was fair. I just tell it as it is."

"As it is according to Jonathan Adams, you mean?"

"Of course."

Annie shook her head and turned to Miles. "Have you ever seen such a muleheaded man in your life?"

Miles recognized a losing situation and said, "I think we'd better start back to Boston before it gets too late. We'll take the long way back; your short-cuts are a bit too exciting. Jonathan, I'm glad to have met you, and I'm sure we'll have the opportunity to get to know each other better. I'll return to Boston after my mission is complete."

Jonathan stood, extended his hand, and said, "I'll be looking forward to that. I wish our fleet a short and triumphant engagement with the French—and for your safe return."

Miles and Jonathan shook hands, and the three of them walked to the tethered horses. Miles helped Annie into her saddle and swung up on Diablo. Jonathan patted the black horse and said, "Major, these are two fine animals. Do you own them?"

"In a roundabout way, I guess I do. I own a livery stable, and the stable owns them."

"Well, they are magnificent mounts," he said. Jonathan gave the horse a slap on his rump and added, "I hope we meet again."

The sun was dropping into the west, and shadows were growing long as they rode at a brisk walk. After riding and making idle chatter for about 10 minutes, Miles said, "Annie, I think we better talk about something before we get back. You've told Jonathan that we plan to get married, and I agree with that, but I would like to formally ask you to marry me and then ask Josiah for your hand. I think we owe this to each other, as well as your parents. So, Annie Adams, would you be my wife?"

"Yes, Miles Ransom, I will be your wife."

Miles rode in joyful silence for a few minutes and then said, "Annie, you've made me a jubilant man, and, after I return from Port Royal, we'll have a proper courtship and marriage."

Annie smiled and said, "Miles, I love you dearly, and I'll be waiting on the wharf for your return. I guess I'll have to make all of the plans while you're gone."

"I'll leave it in your hands. Whatever you decide will be splendid."

They rode and talked about how their life would be, and, finally, Annie asked, "Will you be in your rooms tonight?"

"No, I must return to the *Falcon*. We'll sail at sunrise."

"I don't suppose there's any way I can slip aboard, is there?"

Miles laughed and said, "I wish there were, but no — the Navy is pretty strict about such things."

"Then, we'll wait until you return."

The couple soon found themselves back in the city and made their way to the livery stable. Miles helped Annie down and into the waiting carriage. He then led the horses to the stable door, where he was met by Ben Nelson. Ben asked, "How was your ride?"

"Uneventful and enjoyable. I'm afraid we may have to share Satan with Miss Adams. She rode him well."

"Sir, you're the owner of this establishment, so whatever you say is how it'll be."

"No, Ben. You and I will make all of the major decisions together. You're the man on the scene, and I'll never second-guess you. When I return, we'll have a chance to work all of this out. In the meantime, if you need anything, then just call Philippe Dalhousie."

"I will, and, Major, be careful."

"I will, Ben. See you upon our return to Boston."

The sun had set behind the horizon, and winter darkness fell all at once. The street lamps were being lit, and Miles could hear the ship bells sounding in the harbor. Miles helped Annie into the carriage and instructed Johnny to return to the Henry House. When they climbed down, Miles held Annie's hand and felt a flush build in his lower regions. He smiled to himself and thought, "Glad I brought my hat; I guess I better keep it handy."

Miles and Annie entered the inn and found Josiah and Martha sitting at the kitchen table, reading by an oil lamp.

When Josiah saw them enter the room, he asked, "How was your ride?"

"Exciting and informative…we were attacked by armed robbers; we spent some time with your brother, Jonathan; and I asked Annie to be my bride. All in all, an entertaining afternoon."

Martha smiled, saying, "And did Annie accept your proposal? With Annie, one never knows!"

"Oh, mother," Annie chided. "Of course I accepted, but Miles insists on asking Papa for my hand."

Miles looked at Josiah and said, "Mr. Adams, I wish to have your permission and blessing. I have asked your daughter, Annie, to be my wife."

"You have both my permission and my blessing. At last, Annie has met someone who can handle her."

Before Annie could say anything, Miles replied, "I have no interest in handling Annie. She's a capable woman, and we will always be equal partners in our marriage."

Annie beamed and snapped, "Right answer, Major. You may be easier to train than I'd hoped."

"I probably will be. While my father may be an earl, he married a royal princess who refuses to be subject to anyone. My mother set an excellent example of marriage equality."

Annie nodded in agreement and said, "Your mother sounds like my kind of lady; I can't wait to meet her."

"And, of course, you shall. After we wed, we'll go to England, and she'll insist on introducing you to the court."

"Do you think we'll meet the Queen?"

"The Queen is my mother's favorite cousin. I doubt we can avoid it."

Annie's face lit up, and she replied, "Oh, Miles, how wonderful! Go thrash the French and hurry back."

"Speaking of the French, I'd better get to the *Falcon*. Don't need to miss her sailing."

Martha stood and said, "Miles, have you eaten anything since the chowder?"

Annie laughed and replied, "No, we looked for food at Jonathan's house, but his cupboard was bare. It seems he takes his meals at a nearby widow's home."

"Yes, I helped him make that arrangement. Sarah Carson is a member of Jonathan's congregation and a family friend."

Annie looked at her mother and said, "Jonathan has a congregation?"

"I thought you knew that he's a congregational minister—has been since he was 15."

"Gracious, how does he find the time to farm?"

Martha laughed and said, "Jonathan has the Adams work ethic, and he's a fine farmer. Now, Miles, would you like something to eat before you go?"

"No, thank you. I have one more stop before I return to the ship, so I best be on my way."

"In that case, Josiah and I will allow the two of you a little privacy to say goodbye."

When her parents had left the room, Annie leaped into Miles's arms and kissed him passionately.

"Remember me while you're gone, Miles. I'll be anxious and inconsolable until your return. Now, grab your hat and leave before I am unable to let you go."

Miles pulled away and said, "Annie Adams, I'll be back before you know it. My thoughts of you will be my refuge while I'm away."

"Miles Ransom, take care and return to me quickly. I love you, and I want you to know that you've made me the happiest spinster in the Bay Colony."

Miles replied, "And I'm the happiest man. Now, if you'll turn loose, then I'll try to get out of here while I can."

Disregarding his overwhelming desire, Miles went to

his carriage and instructed Johnny to go to the Dalhousie offices. When they arrived at the office, it was closed, and the blinds were drawn. However, Miles saw a light coming from an upstairs window, and he remembered that Philippe lived above the office. Entering a small alley that ran between the office and the building next door, Miles found a stairway that led to a landing and a door. He motioned to Johnny to wait at the curb and then climbed the stairs.

When Miles rapped gently on the door, he could hear giggles and the sound of hasty movement inside. It took a moment or two before Philippe cracked the door open.

"Have I come at an inconvenient time?"

"No, no, not at all. Give me a minute, and I'll meet you at the office door," Philippe replied and good-naturedly closed the residence door.

By the time Miles had returned to the front door, Philippe was standing in his nightshirt holding it open. He closed the door and said, "I apologize. I'm entertaining a lady this evening, and we weren't expecting company. What can I do for you?"

Embarrassed, Miles replied, "Please excuse the intrusion. I had no idea. I'll write you a letter explaining what I had on my mind, and Johnny can deliver it tomorrow after we sail."

"Don't be silly. Rebecca and I can resume where we left off. Would you like a glass of wine?"

"No, I must get to the *Falcon* before the cutter quits running. I just wanted to let you know that I've asked Annie Adams to marry me, and she has accepted."

"That's excellent news. It seems no one has been able to court the fiery Miss Adams successfully, but you did it in less than a week. This calls for a toast. Give me a minute, and we'll break out a bottle of my best claret."

Before Miles could protest, Philippe raced up the stairs to his rooms and in a moment came down leading a stunning brunette by the hand. Grinning sheepishly, Philippe said, "Miles, I'd like you to meet Rebecca Jackson. Rebecca and I have grown close since the disappearance of her husband, Captain Randall Jackson. Randall was a client and a close friend, but it seems his ship was lost somewhere in the Pacific Ocean. I've been advising Rebecca on her affairs since Randall's misfortune."

Miles bowed slightly. "I'm delighted to meet you, Mrs. Jackson, and I apologize for the late hour."

"No apology needed, Major. Philippe tells me you

will be leaving Boston on the morning tide. I wish you and our entire fleet safe sailing. He also tells me that you have won the hand of Annie Adams."

"Yes, I'm pleased to say that Annie has consented to my proposal. I wanted to let Philippe know that I wish my will changed to bequeath all of my Boston assets to Miss Adams, in the event of my untimely death."

"Well, let us hope that will not soon be the case," Rebecca replied.

Philippe returned with three wine glasses and a bottle of claret. Using a corkscrew, he removed the cork, sniffed the fragrant aroma, and poured a bit into his wine glass. Satisfied, Philippe poured three full glasses and raised his. "To Major and Mrs. Miles Stuart Ransom."

The trio touched their glasses and took a sip of the smooth claret.

Philippe turned to Miles and assured him, "I will take care of the necessary document tomorrow, just as you've instructed."

With that, Miles stood and said, "I best be on my way, and, again, I must apologize for the hour. Mrs. Jackson, I'll look forward to seeing you again on my return."

"Yes, and we will all pray for your safe homecoming."

Miles signaled Johnny to bring the carriage and directed him to the wharf as Miles climbed aboard.

When Miles arrived at the pier, he checked to make sure the *Falcon*'s cutter was still waiting before saying, "Johnny, I'll be gone for an undetermined length of time. While I'm away, I want you to stop by the Henry House each morning and ask Miss Annie if she will need you. If not, then you are free to work as you see fit. If something happens to me, then Philippe Dalhousie will know what to do."

"Aye, Major, and you take care of yourself. Don't volunteer for anything. I learned that on my one sailing adventure on a whaler."

"I'll heed your advice, Johnny, and see you on my return."

Johnny and the carriage rattled up the hill, and Miles walked down the dock to the waiting cutter. He was met by one of the *Falcon*'s midshipmen, who saluted and said, "Major Ransom, are you ready to return to the ship?"

"Aye, Mr. Greene," Miles replied and climbed down into the cutter. "I hope you haven't had to linger for too long."

"No, sir. Lieutenant Vest ordered me to wait until you returned."

When the cutter reached the *Falcon*, Miles climbed to the top of the steps and requested permission to board. The officer of the deck granted permission, so Miles entered through the main hatch and walked to the wardroom. Captain Allen and two of his marine officers were having a cup of tea, and, when Miles ducked through the hatch, they stood and came to attention.

As Miles entered, he motioned for them to return to what they were doing. "At rest, gentlemen." Miles then turned to Allen and asked, "Did the grappling hooks and pikes arrive?"

The officers returned to their seats, and Allen replied, "Aye, sir. They came this afternoon, and I'm pleased to report that they are far better than the regularly issued equipment."

"I'm glad to hear that. Do you have everything prepared?"

"Aye, we just completed the final inspection. With a few minor issues, all is ready."

"Good. We'll be tasked with an on-the-ground reconnaissance of Goat Island. When we land, we'll completely scout the area."

Tom Allen asked, "How many men will we land?"

Miles said, "At this point, I think maybe 20 men to cover our line of retreat, but only you and I will do the actual scouting."

"I don't follow you; why not take the men, in case we find that the island is fortified?"

"Well, think about it, Tom. If the French have placed batteries on the island, then they'll have infantry to support them. Our handful of men would be vastly outnumbered and couldn't possibly pose a threat to the emplacements. If you and I are careful, then we could locate any installations and report them to General Nicholson. He has the proper troops to mount a successful operation."

"Aye, that makes sense. I see what you're saying. Our mission will be to locate any fortifications, not reduce them."

"Exactly — and the fewer men we expose, the less risk we take. The *Falcon* could withstand the loss of you and me, but a company of her marines would cripple her ability to defend herself."

Miles watched as the two junior officers observed this exchange, and he turned to face them. "Gentlemen, do you agree with this strategy?"

Both looked shocked and hesitated, but Miles smiled and said, "Don't be tentative. We value your opinions. You may well see something that we have missed."

The younger of the two officers, Lieutenant James Peterson said, "I agree with your plan, Major, but might I suggest that you consider deploying the landing party inland from the beach? Leave a small crew to guard the cutters and have the rest form a defensive perimeter in the bush. They can better cover a contested withdrawal."

Miles looked intently at Peterson and thought, "That is sound logic. I'll have to keep an eye on this officer."

Miles smiled and replied, "Lieutenant Peterson, I like that idea. I believe you will be the perfect officer to lead the landing party."

Peterson broke out in a wide grin and replied, "I'd be honored to do so, sir."

Miles stood and said, "Keep your seat, gentlemen; I suggest we turn in for the night. Tomorrow, we'll need to be at our best."

Miles left the wardroom and entered his cabin. He slipped into his nightshirt, crawled into his bunk, and tried to dismiss thoughts of Annie so he could focus all his attention on the task ahead.

Thomas R. Lawrence

10 THE QUEEN'S CAPTAIN

Miles was standing near the bowsprit when the *Falcon* raised its anchor and rode the ebbing tide toward the mouth of the Charles estuary. The weather was perfect, and the picket boats guarding Boston Harbor signaled that there was a nine-knot wind from the southwest. Miles may have been assigned to the Royal Marines, but, at heart, he was a sailor.

Miles held the rank of major in the marines, but his permanent rank in the Royal Navy was lieutenant, and he had mastered the art of sailing during his midshipman years. He loved to watch a well-trained crew man the sails. This morning, there was a trailing wind that would allow the ship to sail at its most advantageous angle. Miles did the math and predicted that they could sail directly to Acadia with a speed of 12 knots.

Miles had studied the charts and knew that it was close to 250 nautical miles to the entrance of the Bay of Digby. If the winds held and the seas stayed calm, then they should rendezvous with *HMS Chester* just before dawn on the morning of September 29.

Miles watched as Ron Vest conned the *Falcon* from the estuary to the protected bay. He skillfully tacked the ship between Deer and Long Islands, until she entered the open Atlantic. Vest set a course directly for Acadia, just as Miles had expected. Once the *Falcon* was sailing with the wind, Miles walked aft and climbed to the quarterdeck. "Well done, Ron — a masterful display of seamanship."

"Thank you. If the wind and weather hold, then we'll have clear sailing to Digby. The only problem may be with the fog after we enter the Bay of Fundy."

"I saw the notes on the chart warning about the fog, particularly at this time of year."

"Well, there's no way we can sail at this speed in a fog bank. We'll have to be prepared to slow down to a crawl. Who knows? We may get lucky."

"Will Captain Lowry relieve you tonight?"

"No, he'll take the helm from me after the morning watch and sail until darkness. I'll be here if we hit fog."

"He must have strong faith in your seamanship."

"I suppose he does, but I think it's more a lack of faith in his own."

Miles was shocked that Vest would make such a comment about a senior officer and replied, "Damn, Ron. Don't you think that's a bit harsh?"

"I do, but, nevertheless, it's true. Lowry would rather be in his cabin pouring over charts and reports than actually handling the ship. He's an amazing administrator, but not so much a sailor."

"So you will be at the helm should we meet a French fleet?"

"I would, and I'd relish it. I hate paperwork but love fighting a ship. We make a pretty good team. By the way, according to Nicholson and Reed, the nearest French fleet is south of Hispaniola, and *HMS Endeavor* is tracking it."

"Indeed," Miles replied.

Miles bid Vest good day and returned to his spot near the bowsprit. He climbed into the rigging and enjoyed the gentle roll of the ship's slicing through the calm ocean. After three hours, Miles climbed down and went below to look for food. He found loaves of bread and rounds of cheese on the wardroom table. Miles sat alone and ate while listening to the rhythm of the ship. She held steady on a northeast heading, and the major could feel the miles sliding beneath her hull.

After eating, Miles went to his cabin and lay on his bunk. He picked up an edition of John Milton's *Paradise Lost* and began to read where he'd placed a bookmark. Miles had purchased the epic poem before the *Dragon* sailed from London. It was among the first books to be protected by the newly enacted Statute of Anne. The Queen wanted to make books available to the masses, so she pushed Parliament to pass the law that protected authors and publishers.

When Miles returned to the deck, the ship's bell rang out twice for the afternoon watch. Miles looked at his pocket watch and confirmed the time to be just past one o'clock Boston time. The *Falcon* had been running with the wind for over six hours. If the major's calculations were correct, then they should be approximately 70 miles into their voyage.

Ron Vest was standing over the chart table holding a sextant. He stooped to the graph and made an "X." Miles walked up and looked at it, and he could see that the ship had been running faster than the 12 knots he predicted. Vest saw his reaction and said, "I just shot our position, and we've covered over 85 nautical miles. Not only do we have a favorable wind, but we're also being boosted by the current."

"Will you hold our speed after dark?"

"No. I plan to lower some sails and wait until dawn. If my calculations are accurate, then we'll be at a point 50 miles southwest of the Acadian Peninsula. We'll have to adjust our course to almost due north. Rather than having the wind to our stern, we'll have to quarter back inside, and, although this will cost some speed, we'll still make the entrance to Digby on schedule."

Just then, Captain Lowry climbed to the quarterdeck, and everyone came to attention. He smiled and said, "Stand down, gentlemen. Lieutenant Vest, I have the helm until the dogwatch. I hope you can rest and be quick and spry enough to sail us until dawn."

"Aye aye, sir," Ron replied as he snapped a salute and headed below.

Lowry turned to Miles and said, "Do you have further business on the quarterdeck, Major?"

"No, sir. In fact, I'll go to the bow until it gets too dark to see."

Miles hung in the rigging until the sun was well below the horizon. On the way to his cabin, he grabbed some bread and cheese, and, once again, read Milton until he fell asleep.

Miles awoke with a start. He felt the *Falcon* change its position with relation to the wind and current and figured that they were now on a northerly course for the Bay of Digby. After dressing and completing his usual morning routine, the major stopped by the wardroom, where he found a man dressed in civilian clothes, enjoying a cup of tea.

Miles poured a mug of coffee and addressed him, saying, "Good morning. I'm Miles Ransom, and I'm guessing that you are our surgeon."

"I am indeed," the tall, gray-haired man replied. "I'm Conrad Spencer of Boston."

"Welcome on board. Is this your first time to serve at sea?"

"Yes. I studied medicine at the University of Glasgow and did further studies in Italy before immigrating to the Bay Colony. I've practiced in Boston for the past seven years."

"I'm surprised that you would agree to this posting," Miles replied.

"I was too. Captain Lowry is a friend, and I allowed him to convince me to come. He said that this would be a quiet expedition, but the Army would bear the brunt of the casualties. I might have to do a tooth extraction or treat an injury, but that would be the extent of my duties."

Miles finished his coffee. "Well, Doctor Spencer, I hope you're right. I'm pleased to meet you."

When Miles reached the quarterdeck, he saw that Ron Vest had already resumed command. He felt the ship's rolling beneath his feet and said, "I perceived the change of course. The sea is not as smooth as yesterday."

"No, we're beating north. As soon as the sun gets a little higher, I'll check our position. We should sail into the Bay of Fundy by the midwatch. Then, we'll be in the lee of the land, and we'll be able to pick up some speed."

Miles pulled out two Montoyas and offered one to Ron, who declined. Miles lit his cigar and said, "Think I'll go back to the bow and watch the sunrise. Today should be another easy day."

"I agree, but you never know when you're at sea."

Miles climbed into the rigging near the bow and felt the salty spray on his face. He loved this part of the day at sea, and he took it in with pleasure. Soon, his mind turned to Annie, and he reveled in her until the sun was at a right angle to the hull. After an hour or more of Annie Adams's loveliness running through his head, Miles's reverie was broken when he heard the lookout shout, "Sail to the starboard!"

Miles turned his eyes to the open Atlantic but saw nothing. He climbed higher in the rigging until he could see not one but *five* sails near the horizon. The major climbed down, raced to his cabin, and found the telescope he'd bought in Genoa. When he came back on deck, he could see Ron Vest standing on the rail of the quarterdeck, peering into a glass.

The sails were still not visible from the deck, so Miles scampered into the riggings until he had a clear view. He focused the fine Italian telescope and saw five ships sailing directly at the *Falcon*. He could clearly see the plain white and gold ensigns of the French Navy. Miles studied the larger of the ships and immediately recognized *HMS Elizabeth*. He had served on the *Elizabeth* before she'd been captured by the French.

The *Elizabeth* was a 74-gun ship of the line, and the other four ships appeared to be merchantmen. Miles quickly climbed down and then clambered to the quarterdeck, saying, "Ron, I recognize the man-of-war. She's the former *HMS Elizabeth*. She's carrying 74 guns and appears to be convoying four merchantmen. I suspect they're a supply fleet heading to Port Royal."

Ron asked, "May I use your glass?"

Miles handed the glass to Vest, who climbed to the first level of the main mast and peered to the east. When Ron climbed back on the deck, he handed the glass to Miles and said, "I estimate they are just beyond the sea-level horizon, which, from the deck, is about six miles. Their lookout will have seen our sails about the same time we saw theirs, so we'll not have the element of surprise."

"No, I believe we must assume that they know we're here. What do you plan to do?"

"I plan to engage the *Elizabeth* and prevent the re-supply of Port Royal, but, first, we must convince the captain."

"We? What purpose would I serve?"

"Lowry always seeks a consensus before making a decision. I usually try to bring my own consensus to the meeting. You do agree that we should engage, don't you?"

"Absolutely. This is a classic situation for a battle at sea: two ships of equal armament contesting a strategic issue. I don't think we have any other option."

"Well, let's go below and see if Lowry agrees."

Ron turned the quarterdeck over to Lieutenant Wilson and ordered him to sound the call to battle stations and to plot a course that would intercept the French ships. The drums began to beat as Vest and Miles ducked through the hatch to go below. When they knocked on the captain's hatch, they were met by Lowry, who was pulling on his coat and rushing out. When he saw Vest, he stopped and demanded, "Who the hell ordered battle stations, Lieutenant?"

"I did, Captain. We have spotted a French man-of-war escorting four merchantmen, headed directly toward us. We suspect they are sailing to Port Royal with supplies."

"I see, and are we sure of their colors?"

"Yes. Miles served on *HMS Elizabeth* before she was captured by the French, and he recognized her. She has 74 guns."

"This presents a dilemma. We are under orders to proceed to Digby and reconnoiter Goat Island, but the presence of a 74-gun man-of-war could pose a threat to the entire operation. What do you recommend, Lieutenant?"

"I believe our duty lies in removing the *Elizabeth* as a threat—not to mention preventing supplies from reaching Port Royal. With your permission, I'd like to close with her and destroy her. We can also take the merchantmen as prizes."

Lowry thought for a moment, turned to Miles, and asked, "What say you, Major?"

"I agree with Lieutenant Vest, sir. We must prevent the *Elizabeth* from entering the Bay of Fundy. It would be impossible to carry out the attack with her lurking about."

"Then I suggest that the two of you get about engaging the French. I'll be in my cabin if you need further instructions."

As they made their way back to the deck, Miles said, "I can see that you were accurate in your opinion of Lowry. He's a coward, or he's a fool. Either way, he shouldn't be captain of a fighting ship."

"Miles, I've served with Lowry for a while now, and I can assure you that he is neither a coward nor a fool. He would gladly take part in the hand-to-hand fighting, and he's destined to high rank in the Admiralty. He's staying in his cabin to give me total control during the upcoming engagement."

Miles climbed onto the deck and replied, "I still say that his duty is to be on deck taking responsibility for his men and his ship. No other captain I've ever known would allow subordinates to fight his ship."

Ron Vest climbed to the quarterdeck and took command. He ordered a midshipman to summon all of the officers, and, when everyone had gathered, he said, "Gentlemen, we have a French man-of-war approaching from the east. We are sailing to intercept the man-of-war and the supply ships the vessel is guarding. We should be within firing range in less than an hour, and I intend to engage the warship. We will have the advantage of wind and speed. The man-of-war is beating into the wind and must not outrun the slower charges."

Tom Allen spoke up, asking, "Lieutenant, how do you plan to engage the warship?"

"I plan to close as quickly as I can, turn, and fire broadside until we can get the hooks over and board," Ron said, as he spread a chart across the binnacle and quickly lined it up with magnetic north. He pointed to a spot just south of Seal Island off the southwest tip of Acadia and said, "This is our present position, and plainly we have blocked any attempt by the French to continue on their current course and avoid us."

Ron moved his finger to a point in the open Atlantic and said, "This is their present position. I believe they will turn to the north and make a run for the Bay of Isles on the eastern coast. The French have batteries guarding the bay, and the supplies could be moved overland to Port Royal. I intend to sail between Seal Island and Sable Island and cut them off."

One of the officers asked, "But, sir, wouldn't that course take us across the tip of the shoals?"

"Yes, but we'll have close to half a mile of clearance, and I'm gambling that we can make it. Both ships are equidistant from the Bay of Isles, but we have the advantage of speed. The *Elizabeth* must protect her merchantmen and can only go as fast as the slowest of them. My calculations show that we should intercept them almost 20 miles off the entrance to the bay in about two hours. Gentlemen, man your battle stations."

After most of the officers had gone to see to their charges, Miles moved closer to Vest and asked, "Are you certain about the shoals?"

"Not completely, but, if you are to believe the charts, we have enough draft to clear the shoals. At any rate, it is the only way to intercept them."

"What if they continue west and try to turn to the tip of Acadia?"

"Then we'll engage them earlier, but I don't expect that. They should be making their turn north very soon."

Miles nodded and replied, "I'll climb into the rigging and observe them. I'll let you know the minute they turn."

Miles climbed into the rigging until he reached a spot from which the French fleet was clearly visible. He took his glass and watched them intently. Within 10 minutes, the *Elizabeth* turned north and positioned herself between the English ship and the merchantmen. Miles thought, "That's smart; they can prevent our reaching the merchantmen. They're ready for a fight."

Miles continued to watch as the *Falcon* picked up the prevailing wind and shot forward toward the strait between Seal and Sable Islands. Vest kept the ship as close to the tip of Acadia as he could. He was jockeying for position with the *Elizabeth*. Miles saw that his plan was to reach a point north of the French, wheel to the south, and bring his broadside to bear. The *Elizabeth* was powerless to prevent the maneuver without exposing the merchantmen. There would be a fight, and the English would have the advantage of position.

The enemy ships continued on a collision course for the next hour, until the *Falcon* gained a position between the mainland and the French. The *Falcon* turned due south and approached the *Elizabeth*'s port. Miles could hear the drums beating on the French ship and could see men scrambling into the rigging. He heard Tom Allen shout an order, and the *Falcon*'s marines followed suit.

Miles was deciding where he'd be during the fight when Captain Lowry came on deck in full uniform. He walked up to Ron Vest and said, "Carry on, Lieutenant. I'll stand beside you and observe, if you have no objection."

Vest saluted and replied, "None at all, sir. I'll welcome your assistance."

Lowry looked into the rigging and saw Miles. He turned to Vest and said, "I take it that Major Ransom is serving as your eyes. Am I correct?"

Ron looked up at Miles and said, "Aye, sir, he is."

Miles decided to stay in his position in the rigging and await developments. The ships approached each other, and Miles could now see the golden fleur-de-lis embroidered on the pure, white French battle ensign. The *Elizabeth* was a mighty ship of war, and she would have an experienced crew and able officers. When all was done, Miles felt the fight would go to the boarding parties.

Vest put the *Falcon* on a collision course to intercept the *Elizabeth* and cross her "T." All of the *Falcon*'s starboard cannons could be brought to bear but only the *Elizabeth*'s two forward-bearing carronades. Miles knew that the *Elizabeth* carried only two such weapons, but they were huge 68-pounders, capable of mass destruction at very close range.

Vest ordered a full broadside while still out of range of the carronades. Miles watched as the French ship was raked by the accurate fire from the *Falcon*, and he saw her mizzenmast collapse to the deck.

Vest then turned hard to starboard and aimed his ship directly at the *Elizabeth*. He intended to close with her port to starboard, and Miles heard the order to man the boarding parties.

The ships were only a few hundred feet apart when the two carronades on the *Elizabeth* swept the deck of the *Falcon* with grapeshot. Miles hung in the rigging, and, when the smoke cleared, he realized that the quarterdeck was smashed. No one survived the volley. Miles could see the crumpled bodies of Vest and Lowry lying in pools of blood.

11 THE QUEEN'S CAPTAIN

Miles leapt to the quarterdeck and discovered that he was the only ranking officer left alive. He found one of the junior lieutenants, who was leaning stunned against the mast, and shook him. The young man snapped to attention and said, "Sorry, sir. I lost my focus for a moment."

"I'm Major Ransom, and I am assuming command. I want you to do three things: find Captain Allen of the marines and send him to me, have the bodies of Captain Lowry and Lieutenant Vest taken to the captain's cabin, and go below to assess our damage."

The officer saluted and climbed to the main deck. Miles looked at the helm and saw that, while damaged, it was still operable, so he grabbed a sailor and ordered him to take the helm and stay on course to board the *Elizabeth*.

Tom Allen came running to the deck and reported. Miles told him to take command of the boarding party and close with the French as soon as the ships made contact. Another broadside from both ships made the deck shudder under Miles's feet. Then, the two ships crashed together, and grappling hooks flew from both vessels. The deciding phase of the engagement was about to begin.

Miles ordered the two swivel guns on the bow to be loaded with canister shot and instructed the crew to concentrate their fire on the French quarterdeck until the boarding party had crossed over. The two on the stern were to sweep the rigging of the *Elizabeth* in an attempt to silence her marines who were raining musket fire onto the *Falcon*. As soon as the ships were tangled together, Tom Allen led his boarders over the rail.

Just as the boarders gained the deck of the *Elizabeth*, the lieutenant came running back and reported that, while there was severe damage to the first and second gun decks, the ship was completely seaworthy. Miles ordered him to take the helm and hold the ships together. Then, Miles drew his sword and ran to join the melee taking place on the *Elizabeth*'s deck. Once on board, Miles found Allen directing the fight, so he decided to try to flank the main French resistance.

Miles grabbed a dozen sailors and marines, and they fought their way to the opposite side of the ship. The fighting at this point was hand to hand with cutlass, dagger, and pike. A few shots continued to ring out from the rigging, but the swivel guns had done their job.

Major Ransom could see the French officers directing the defense from the quarterdeck, and he led his men toward them. Miles was a skilled swordsman, and, as he deftly cut his way toward the French officers, he made eye contact with the French captain. What Miles saw was not fear but a steely determination, and he watched as the officer ordered a party of sailors in Miles's direction.

The deck was slippery with blood, and it took an effort to retain one's footing. Miles realized that the men sent by the French captain would overwhelm his party, so he called for a withdrawal in order to regroup. His men fell back to the main deck and formed a defensive perimeter. Tom Allen's attack had lost its momentum, and the battle was swinging to the French. Miles could see the French officers putting together a boarding party to attack the *Falcon*.

Miles commanded his men to return to the *Falcon* to repel the French boarding party. He directed the men to drop back from the rail and to wait for his signal to attack. He sent midshipmen to the bow and the stern with orders to load the swivel guns with grapeshot and to aim them at the French boarding party climbing on the rail.

With a shout, the French ran to board the *Falcon,* and all four swivel guns blasted grapeshot into them. When the smoke cleared, Miles could see bodies strewn across the rails, and he directed his men to attack. Seeing that Tom Allen and his soldiers were fiercely fighting a rearguard action, Miles led his group to their relief, and soon Major Ransom and his men were on the deck, confronting the French captain and his staff. The French put up a noble fight, but, in the end, they collapsed, and their captain, at last, signaled for the fighting to stop.

Some of the Frenchmen were unwilling to relent, and the fighting continued for a few minutes, but, soon, the ship was securely in English hands. The French captain slowly approached Miles, and, offering his sword, he said in heavily accented English, "I am Captain Jean Farrgot, commanding His Majesty's ship the *Concordia,* and I wish to cease the hostilities."

"I am Major Miles Ransom. Are you prepared to strike?"

Nodding his head, Captain Farrgot replied, "Oui," and held out his sword again. Just as Miles reached to take it, he spotted movement above in the rigging of the mizzenmast. As Miles looked up, he saw a French marine sighting down a musket directed right at him. In the split second before Miles could react, the marine fired, and Miles felt the heavy impact of the ball in his upper chest.

Just as Miles turned to the French captain to try to speak, blood began gushing from his mouth, and Miles fell heavily to the deck. Simultaneously, four of the *Falcon*'s marines fired into the rigging, and the Frenchman dropped to the deck. Reacting with urgency, Tom Allen immediately ordered the surrender of the *Concordia* to be turned over to a junior officer. Allen then scooped Miles into his arms and hurriedly carried him across the rails to the deck of the *Falcon*.

With similar quick-wittedness, a midshipman rushed below to the wardroom hatch, where he witnessed Doctor Conrad Spencer's amputating the leg of a seaman who was lying on the wardroom table. The table and deck were running with blood, and there was a pile of limbs in a large wooden bucket. Wounded men were stretched out — writhing in paln — on one side of the compartment, and dead men were lying side by side on the other. The midshipman stepped inside and stammered, "Sir, Major Ransom has been shot! Can you come?"

"Young man, I'm a little busy right now! When I finish attending to this patient, I'll come. In the meantime, have the major moved to the captain's cabin."

"Aye, sir," the midshipman replied and raced topside. Tom Allen and another midshipman were kneeling by Miles, who lay unconscious on the shattered deck, gasping for breath. The boy ran up, skidding on the blood-drenched platform, and breathlessly reported, "The doctor ordered that Major Ransom be moved to the captain's cabin!"

Tom Allen took Miles by the shoulders, and the boy grabbed his feet. Together, they carried Miles below. The captain's cabin had survived the battle intact, so Allen placed Miles across the table and waited for the doctor to come. Tom could hear Miles breathing in shallow gasps, and he saw that the color was completely drained from his face.

Standing over Miles, Tom Allen noticed a flutter of Miles's eyelids. Major Ransom looked up at Allen and mouthed, "Did she strike?"

Tom leaned in close to Miles and whispered, "Aye, she did. Lieutenant Warren has taken command of the *Falcon,* and our marines have secured the *Concordia.* She can still make way, and both ships are returning to Boston. We will probably meet the fleet on their way to Port Royal."

"How bad am I?"

"You took a ball in your chest. The surgeon is completing his work with the crew, but he'll be here as soon as he can."

Miles winced in pain. "Tom, if I don't make it, tell Annie Adams that my last thought was of her. Her father owns the Henry House in Boston."

"I'll tell her if needed, but, for now, you need to rest. We'll be back in Boston before you know it."

Miles muttered, "Thanks, Tom," and his eyes drooped as he drifted off.

In a relatively short time, Conrad Spencer climbed through the hatch, wearing a bloody apron and carrying his medical bag. With one look at Miles, he said sharply, "He's going into shock!" Doctor Spencer hurriedly commenced cutting away the uniform coat and shirt, revealing a small black entry wound in Miles's upper left chest. Spencer began pulling jacket and shirt pieces from the wound so that he could probe. When the surgeon finished cutting away the jacket and shirt, he asked Allen to roll Miles over, exposing his back. Conrad felt along the lower part of the rib cage and found a lump just under the skin.

With a scalpel, the surgeon skillfully, but hastily,

sliced a section of Miles's back and removed a musket ball along with additional fabric pieces. Once Spencer had meticulously cleaned both the entry and exit wounds, he inserted a hollow reed into Miles's chest cavity and allowed air and blood to gush out. He made a shallow incision near the entry wound and carefully sutured the punctured lung, repeating the procedure at the exit wound and then closing it.

When he had bandaged Miles, Doctor Spencer told Allen to place Miles in the captain's bunk. Then, the surgeon wiped his hands on his apron and said wearily, "He has a broken collarbone, a punctured lung, and a cracked rib. I got as much of the fabric as I could, and I made temporary repairs to his lungs. I also inserted a drain in his chest, but he's on his own until we can return to Boston. He's a hearty young man who is in good health, but this will be a battle against infection and pneumonia. The next 48 hours or so will decide his fate, and, even if he survives, he'll still be in danger of infection. Now, I have to return to the wardroom to care for the other men."

Tom Allen assigned one of the midshipmen to sit with Miles, instructing him to let the doctor know if there was any change in Miles's condition. Allen returned to duty. When he reached the deck, he could see the *Falcon* under full sail with the *Concordia* trailing in her wake. Tom climbed to the quarterdeck, where he found Lieutenant Warren at the helm.

Warren was the only senior officer left alive or unwounded, and he had taken command of the *Falcon*. When Allen reported, he said, "Tom, I plan to sail directly to Boston, and there is the possibility that we will meet the fleet on the way. I'd like to have the dead and wounded transferred to the *Concordia* and have the *Falcon* rejoin the fleet. Will you see to the transfer?"

"Aye, sir, and I would like your permission to remain with the *Falcon*."

"I'm sure you would, but I feel you'd be more efficient accompanying the *Concordia*. Ensign Taylor is taking her to Boston, and he could use your support."

"Aye, sir. I'll see to the transfer."

Tom Allen had a squad of marines load the dead and wounded into cutters for transfer to the *Concordia*. He and Doctor Spencer personally oversaw Miles's transfer, and both men boarded the *Concordia*. Later in the day, they met the main body of the British fleet, which *HMS Falcon* joined, and the *Concordia* resumed sailing to Boston.

As they continued toward their destination, Allen went below and sat with Miles, watching his body fight off the shock and possible infection of his wounds. Miles drifted in and out of sleep, but, occasionally, Tom managed to give him a little water. Due to the battle damage and the short-handed crew, the *Concordia* made slow progress, but it finally entered Boston Harbor on the third morning at dawn.

After seeing to the wounded and moving them to the naval infirmary, Allen and Spencer summoned a wagon and loaded Miles into the bed. Allen instructed the driver to take them to the Henry House on Queen Street. It was close to eight o'clock when Allen knocked on the inn's door. It was opened by Annie Adams. As soon as she saw the two naval officers and the wagon, she tearfully exclaimed, "Oh, my God, is he alive?"

Allen took her by the arm and replied, "Yes, but he was shot in the chest two days ago, and he's still fighting shock and infection. Doctor Conrad Spencer removed the bullet and made repairs to his chest and lungs, but I'm afraid he is still in grave danger."

Annie gathered her skirts and bounded down the stoop. She took a quick look at Miles lying in the wagon bed and shouted, "Bring him upstairs! I'll put him in his room, and we'll tend to him there!"

Miles's betrothed raced up the steps and pulled back the bedcovers. Allen and Spencer carried Miles up the flight of stairs and placed him on the bed. Once he was settled, Annie said, "Tell me, Doctor Spencer — what should I do?"

Conrad took Annie by the hand and softly replied, "There's not much that can be done. He's fighting infection and shock, and it's really up to his system's strength. If he regains consciousness, then you can try to get some soup down him, but, for the next couple of days, keeping him comfortable is about all you can do. I'll stop by twice a day to check on him, and, if he goes into crisis, my home and office are close by."

Josiah and Martha Adams met Allen and Spencer as they came down the stairs.

"Gentlemen, I'm Josiah Adams, Annie's father, and Miles's partner. How badly is he injured?"

Conrad shook Adams's hand and replied, "Gravely. He's been shot in the chest, and the ball did severe damage. He's battling for his life, and, if he survives the next few days, he'll still have a lengthy recovery period. This type of wound heals slowly, and he could relapse at any time. Infection and chest complications are our biggest fear."

Martha asked, "Will he need surgery?"

"Hopefully not. I did all I could do on the ship, and any additional surgery would be too risky. Now, we must depend on his will to live and good care. All you can do is keep him as comfortable as possible. I'm going to leave a vial with a mixture of opium and alcohol called laudanum. When I studied in Italy, they used it to control pain. A teaspoon every four hours should help him rest."

"Well, Annie and I will give him the best care, and he's young and hardy, so I guess the rest is in God's hands," Martha said.

"Yes, I believe it is," Conrad replied. "I'll be by to check on him, and you know where my office is."

Tom Allen spoke up and said, "I'll be sailing tomorrow to rejoin the fleet, but I'll be back as soon as we return from Port Royal. Major Ransom took command of the *Falcon* and fought her well. I want him to get full credit for that."

Allen and Spencer left, and Josiah and Martha worriedly climbed the stairs to Miles's room. Annie had gotten him cleaned up and into a fresh nightshirt. She was sitting by the bedside wiping his brow with a damp cloth. When her parents came in, she stood. "He's going to survive this. I plan to see to it. I'll move a cot in here, and I'll stay with him around the clock. He's sleeping fitfully, and I'm afraid he has a low-grade fever. I suspect his body is struggling against infection, and I must keep him calm and quiet. He'll need all of his strength to fight it off."

"Of course—you'll be with him, and your father and I will take care of everything else. Let me know what you need."

By late afternoon, Miles had slipped into a fever-induced coma, and he'd begun to have trouble breathing. Doctor Spencer came by to check on him and told Annie that he was in a battle with the infection, but at least he was still alive — it was going as well as could be expected. Annie sat with Miles through the night, but, near dawn, she feared that he would lose the fight with the oncoming infection in his chest. His breathing had become labored and erratic, and the fever seemed to be getting worse.

But when the sun came up, Miles was still alive. All morning, he remained the same, and Annie never left his side. Conrad Spencer came by to check on him but saw little improvement and promised that he'd be back again in the afternoon. Soon after Conrad left, Philippe Dalhousie came to the inn to find out from Josiah what Miles's condition was. Philippe asked to be notified if there was any change — improvement or decline.

A little after noon, the fever broke, and Miles began to have chills. Annie climbed into the bed and held him close to her until he regained his warmth. She was just lighting the oil lamp on the bedside table when his breathing returned to normal, and he slipped into a deep slumber. It was just after sunrise when Miles's eyes opened, and he saw Annie napping in the bedside chair. He smiled and fell back to sleep. He slept through Conrad's morning visit, and it was midafternoon when Miles awoke again. Annie had just come in carrying fresh linen and was about to bathe him when he said in a weak voice, "I awoke last night, and I thought I was in heaven being attended to by an angel."

Annie nearly dropped the stack of linen. "No, you're in Boston, and you need something to eat."

Annie fetched a bowl of beef broth and fed it to Miles spoon by spoon until he drifted back to sleep. Once again, he slept through Conrad Spencer's visit and well into Friday morning. When Conrad arrived to check on him, he was delighted to find Miles awake and eating a piece of toasted bread. The doctor re-dressed the entry and exit wounds and suggested that a bath might be in order. Miles smiled and replied, "Yes, I believe it might. I'm starting to notice the aroma myself. How long do you think it will be until I've fully recovered?"

"I guess that depends on your definition of full recovery. Your wounds should be completely healed in a couple of weeks, but I have no way of knowing about your lung. It was severely damaged by the ball, and we really can't foresee the long-term effects. When your lung reinflates, I'll remove the drain. You may regain full function, or you may have an ongoing problem. Only time will tell."

"What can I expect if there are long-term problems?"

"You may have difficulty performing physical tasks, and you may tire quickly, but it's not possible to predict the extent of these issues."

"Do you think I'll be fit to serve?"

"We must wait and see; you'll have to make that decision later."

Annie listened to this exchange in silence. She followed Conrad down the stairs and asked him, "How should I care for him?"

"He'll sleep most of the time until the lung heals. Keep his dressing changed and bathe him regularly. I'd like to have him sitting up in the next few days and walking around by this time next week. His appetite should return shortly, so make sure he has good, nutritious food. I'll come back early next week to see how he's doing."

As the doctor predicted, Miles slowly regained his appetite, and he began to spend more time sitting up in the chair by his bed. On Monday, Miles managed to walk a few steps around his rooms, and Annie noticed that his breathing had improved. After

Conrad's visit that afternoon, Josiah helped Miles down the stairs, where he was able to sit in the autumn sun. Annie was seated beside Miles when he said, "Miss Adams, don't you think it is time for us to begin making some plans?"

"I guess you're feeling better. What kinds of plans, my love?"

"I was thinking maybe wedding plans unless you've changed your mind."

"I have not!"

"Good, then I want to pick a time and a place."

"Well, if you've recovered enough, then I've always wanted a Christmas wedding. How about sometime in December?"

"That sounds good, and where would you like to have it?"

"Let's wed at Uncle Jonathan's church in Braintree. I know you're Anglican, but my whole family is Congregationalist, and it's what I would like, if you agree."

"Then December in Braintree it'll be. Why don't you and your mother get to work on the plans? In the meantime, I think I'll just take a little nap here in the sunshine."

12 THE QUEEN'S CAPTAIN

Miles was eating breakfast on Tuesday morning when Josiah handed him a copy of *The Boston Gazette* and said, "Here are the first reports on the battle between the *Falcon* and the *Concordia*. It seems that Captain Allen managed to tell the tale before he returned to the fleet. I thought you might be interested, especially the part about the naval engagement."

Miles thanked him and began to read the report. When he came to the battle with the *Concordia,* he saw that he'd been mentioned for taking command of the *Falcon* and capturing the French ship. The report went on to say that the fleet was in position and planned to attack Port Royal on October 5. Miles set the paper on the table and thought, "It's quite an honor to be mentioned by name in the newspaper, but I'm surprised that I don't seem to much care. My wound must have taken more out of me than I thought. Now that Annie and I are to be married, I'm beginning to think past my career. I've served for over 10 years, and they've been good years, but I'll soon have a family to consider. Oh well—I'll have plenty of time to figure it all out before I'm back to full strength."

Annie came into the kitchen carrying an apron full of apples from the tree in the garden. She dumped them on the counter and said, "Don't forget that Philippe is coming by this morning. He's checked on you every day. Do you feel up to visiting with him?"

"Yes. I'm feeling much better. I thought we might contact Johnny and take a ride in the countryside this afternoon."

"We won't have to contact him; he's parked on the street out front. He stays there all day unless he has a fare—then, he comes right back. He keeps asking about you. If you think you're up to a ride, then I'll tell him, but I don't want you to overdo. You're still quite weak."

"I think I'll be able to go, but let me meet with Philippe, and we'll see how I feel after that."

While Miles finished the *Gazette*, Annie sat at the table preparing the apples for pies to serve in the inn. Miles was reading an article describing Indian raids along the northern borders of the colony. The French seemed to be able to employ the tribes as allies, while most English attempts proved to be costly disasters. Miles decided to try to understand more about the French policy.

As Miles was just finishing the paper, Josiah came in, followed by Philippe Dalhousie. Miles began to stand, but Philippe put his hand on Miles's shoulder and said, "No, Miles. Keep your seat; don't waste your strength on formalities. I'm glad to see you up and feeling better. I've been following your progress through Josiah."

Miles pulled his robe closer and replied, "Yes, Annie has told me of your concern. Thank you for that."

Philippe smiled and pointed at the folded newspaper, saying, "I see you've read the reports. It seems that your action on *HMS Falcon* has made you something of a local hero. Well done, indeed!"

"Thanks, but, actually, all I did was help capture the *Concordia* after her officers were killed in the first broadside."

"You've been credited with commanding a man-of-war in ship-to-ship combat. Apparently, you're one of just a handful of marine officers to do such a thing."

"I appreciate all of the kind words, but, please, tell me

how have you been?"

"Busy. I've been working with all of your managers to integrate your businesses under the Dalhousie umbrella. I'll have to say that we were very lucky to have inherited such outstanding men, and Josiah is the finest."

"Yes, I agree that we have been fortunate. Have you had any problems?"

"None. Everything has gone smoothly so far. Do you have any idea when you'll return to duty?"

"I don't know. The doctor tells me that it may take a while for me to regain my strength. The wound to my lung is a big worry. By the way, Annie and I are going to marry in December in Braintree, and I'd like for you to come."

"Congratulations, Miles! Have you chosen an exact date?"

"Not yet. Annie and Martha are handling all of that. Obviously, I hope you'll attend the ceremony, but I'll have to let you know the date when they tell me," Miles said with a crooked grin.

"Is there any way that I may be of service while you're recovering?"

"I can't think of anything at the moment, but I won't

hesitate to ask if something comes up."

"Please *don't* hesitate. You know where to reach me. Now, I think you need to rest, so I'll say goodbye. I'll check on you later, and, again, congratulations. Annie is an exceptional woman, and I wish the two of you much happiness and good health."

After Philippe's departure, Miles realized how fatigued he was, and so he returned to his room for a nap. When he woke, it was afternoon. After some soup and bread, Annie and Johnny helped Miles into the cab, and Johnny took them for a long ride in the country. When they returned, Miles was exhausted, and he asked Annie to help him back to his bed, where he was soon in a sound sleep.

The following days slipped by, and, with each one, Miles grew a little stronger. He was able to get up and down the stairs without help. On Tuesday morning, October 14, the *Gazette* featured the latest dispatches from the fleet. Port Royal had fallen, and the French had surrendered all of Acadia to the British. The flagship carrying Nicholson and his staff would be back in Boston by the following Monday.

The next week, a midshipman from *HMS Dragon* came to the inn and inquired as to the health of Major Ransom. The midshipman asked if it would be possible for Miles to receive a visit from Sir William Darcy and Captain Lloyd Sparks in the early afternoon. When Annie went up to Miles's room and presented him with the request, Miles assured her that he was not only up to it, but he would also welcome it.

Miles considered trying to put on his uniform for the visit but finally decided that his recovery was not that far along, so he settled for a bath, a shave, and a clean robe. He was sitting in the fresh air and sunshine when Annie came out and announced that his visitors were arriving. She escorted Sir William and Lloyd Sparks to the garden, where Miles introduced her as his intended and issued an invitation to them to attend the wedding celebration. After receiving heartfelt congratulations, Annie withdrew to the kitchen.

Sir William took a seat on the garden bench opposite Miles and said, "Major Ransom, I can only tell you of my personal pride in your recent actions while commanding *HMS Falcon*. I can assure you that your bravery and initiative were noted by every naval officer in the fleet. I've written a report to the Admiralty—I informed them that your quick thinking and decisive action prevented the *Falcon* from falling into enemy hands and put a stop to the *Concordia*'s attempts to disrupt our operations."

Miles thought for a moment and then replied, "I have not written my account of the action between the *Falcon* and the *Elizabeth*, but I want Captain Tom Allen to receive credit for his part in the battle. Tom executed his duties in a manner deserving of notice."

Lloyd Sparks smiled and said, "I am confident that you'll have the opportunity to mention him when you meet with Nicholson and his staff. I talked to Captain Reed, and he and Nicholson are planning to pay you a visit."

"I see, and when do you think they'll be coming?"

"Soon, I expect. Dixon asked me to report on your condition after our visit. Are you up to receiving them this week?"

"I think I am. I tire quickly, but I should be able to see them."

Sir William spoke up and added, "Miles, you are still under my command, so I'm ordering you to remain on convalescent leave until after January 1, 1711. The *Dragon* has been assigned to the Atlantic Squadron, and it will be based here in Boston. Lloyd and I would be honored to attend your marriage to Miss Adams, so please let us know the place and time."

"Aye, sir. As soon as Miss Adams informs me of the

date," Miles said smiling, "I'll send you a message. We'll be honored to have both of you there."

Sir William stood and said, "As you noted, you still tire quickly, so Captain Sparks and I will bid you goodbye. It's good to see you're recovering, but please allow us to extend any assistance you may require."

Both officers shook Miles's hand and then withdrew from the garden. Miles sat back on his bench and thought, "It would seem that Sir William and Nicholson have reached a working agreement and have put the past behind them. That's good; success appears to have a soothing effect on personal relationships. I remember my father saying, 'Victory has many fathers, but defeat is an orphan.' The Port Royal operation seems to have glory enough for all involved, even a small slice for me."

On Thursday morning, a message arrived from Nicholson requesting permission for a party of officers to visit on Friday morning. Miles replied that he would welcome the general and his entourage at ten o'clock. On Friday morning, Miles arose early, and Annie helped him into a new uniform. He was sitting at a table in the inn when the general and his party came through the door.

Miles stood and saluted the general. "Welcome, General. I'm honored that you came to visit me."

Nicholson refused Miles's outstretched hand but said, "Major Ransom, I believe you know Captain Dixon and Lieutenant Colonel Holmes."

"Yes, it's good to see all of you. Congratulations on the fall of Port Royal."

Nicholson ignored the compliment and continued, "Major, I have never in my career seen such a blatant and disgusting display of self-promotion as you have instigated."

Stunned, Miles stood silently in shock. Nicholson continued, "I have no intention of allowing you to take credit for defeating the *Concordia*. My report to London will place the credit where it belongs, to the senior surviving naval officer, Lieutenant Cary Warren."

Miles looked at Reed and Holmes, but both men diverted their eyes. He turned to Nicholson and said, "General, I take great offense at your accusations of self-promotion. I have been bedridden since my wounding. I have no idea why you are accusing me in this manner, but, rest assured, you have made an enemy today, one who will never forgive your behavior."

"Major, you are still on active duty and subject to my command, so I suggest that you keep a civil tongue.

As for having you as an enemy, you are of no consequence. Now, if you'll excuse me, then I'll leave you to your recovery."

Miles turned to Reed and Holmes, saying, "Again, gentlemen, you have my congratulations on the victory."

Reed bowed slightly and replied, "Thank you, Ransom. Holmes and I are pleased to have been involved."

Nicholson turned on his heels and left the inn with Holmes and Reed close behind.

When Nicholson and his staff were gone, Miles sat fuming over Nicholson's accusations and general hostility. It made no sense to Miles, and, further, he knew that this would not be the end of it all.

On a beautiful afternoon in late October, Annie asked Miles to take a cab ride into the countryside. When they were out of the city, she took his hand and said, "Miles, Mother and I have decided to move the wedding to Saturday, November 15."

"I see. Is there any particular reason to move it up?"

"Yes," Annie said bashfully. "It seems that I am with child."

Speechless, Miles sat quietly holding Annie's hand for

a few moments.

In what felt like a lifetime to Annie, Miles responded, "Annie, you've made me the happiest man in New England! How long have you known?"

"I've suspected it for over a month, but Doctor Spencer confirmed it yesterday."

"Did he say when?"

"He didn't have to—since we've only made love that night in September, we can expect the baby in mid-June. I'm so glad and relieved that you're pleased."

"Of course I'm pleased! I'm more than pleased; in fact, I'm delighted that we're moving the date! Annie, you and I need to discuss our future, and this makes it all the more important. Nicholson's outlandish behavior had already prompted me to consider this, but, in light of this surprising news, I don't believe I'll be happy continuing to serve on active duty. I'll want to be with you and our child."

Annie looked directly into his eyes. "Miles, I knew you were a marine officer when I decided to come into your bed. I'm content to keep a home and raise our children while you are at sea."

"I thank you for that, but I'm not willing to be gone for months at a time while our child is growing up.

It'll be best for me to allow my commission to go dormant so that you and I can start a new life. In fact, I've been weighing Philippe's suggestion that we give some consideration to moving to the Carolina Colony."

Annie turned to him and said, "I assumed that we would stay here in Boston. You've got a substantial investment in local businesses, so it just seemed logical."

"Yes, that does make sense, but I'm not sure it's what I want to do. We have a significant investment in Boston, but it represents just a small portion of our wealth. We have ample capital to do whatever we decide. The Dalhousie firm can manage our Boston investments just like it handles the balance of our holdings."

Annie looked at him with an expression of surprise. "Miles, we've never discussed your business affairs, but I'm beginning to suspect that you are far wealthier than I thought."

"Well, yes, we're certainly well off. My father gave me my inheritance when I joined the Navy, and the Dalhousies have managed it well. We're in a position to do whatever we please, wherever we choose."

Annie sat in silence for a few minutes and then said, "I feel like I just woke up in a fairy tale. You're going to have to give me time to adjust to all of this."

"You've got the rest of your life to adapt, but the first thing to do is to go on with the wedding. After the wedding, I think I'd like us to visit England so that you can meet my family. If you approve of that plan, then I'll book passage for the week after the wedding. That way, we can miss crossing the Atlantic in the dead of winter. With luck, we can be at my home for Christmas."

"Miles, I don't know what to say. I'll take care of the wedding, but I'm leaving everything else to you. As Ruth said in the Bible, 'Where you go, I will go, and where you stay, I will stay. Your people will be my people and your God my God. Where you die, I will die, and there I will be buried. May the Lord deal with me, be it ever so severely, if even death separates you and me.'"

Miles looked adoringly at her and held her close until the cab returned to the inn.

The next month centered on finalizing the wedding plans, and all of the activity gave Miles a chance to recover further. He met with Philippe Dalhousie and booked passage on an express mail packet that was set to sail for London on November 20. When Miles was certain that everything was in place, he wrote to his father informing him of his wedding plans and his scheduled arrival in Southampton the week of December 18.

In early November, Miles had Johnny take him to Philippe's office to discuss the opportunities for settlement in the Southern Colonies.

Philippe received Miles in his office, and the two of them sat around the fire, where Miles asked about farming in the South. "Tell me, Philippe. What appeals to you about locating in the South?"

"I think the main attraction is the opportunity to buy large acreages at very low prices. Most of the prime land is found in the coastal plain of the Southern Colonies but has already been acquired in Maryland and Virginia. There are still large tracts to be had in Carolina."

"How does one manage the cultivation of crops on such large tracts of land?"

"It requires impressive amounts of labor. The large operations are called plantations, and most utilize black slaves from the Islands of the Caribbean, though some still employ indentured servants. In Maryland and Virginia, most planters grow tobacco as their cash crop, but Carolina is suited to rice cultivation."

"Philippe, I'm morally opposed to human slavery. If I were to attempt to grow tobacco or rice, then I would insist on using paid labor."

"I agree with you in principle — slavery is an abomination — but no one has successfully grown a commercial crop without using slaves. There are large plantations whose owners are in London. Managers and overseers run their holdings, and they return handsome profits."

"I want Annie to meet my family, so I plan to go back to England directly after our marriage. I want to use the time to determine my future. If I decide to consider the Southern Colonies seriously, then I'd like to visit with some of the plantation owners before I make a final decision. Could you arrange introductions?"

"I'd be pleased to do so. Let me know when you are certain of your plans."

Miles opened his bag and took out a box of the Montoya cigars and passed them to Philippe.

"Soon, you'll be able to buy these at Seymour's, but this should hold you until they come in."

Thomas R. Lawrence

13 THE QUEEN'S CAPTAIN

As the final days before the wedding approached, Miles worried about leaving Johnny Cochrane behind. Finally, he asked Johnny to join him in the inn, where they sat by the fire and shared a pint. Miles could sense that Johnny was uneasy, so Miles said, "Johnny, I believe you to be unmarried. Am I right?"

"Aye, sir. I just never met the right lass."

"So you have nothing binding you to Boston?"

"Not really. I've worked on a merchant ship and a whaler, but I don't find a sailor's life much to my liking. I've been able to wring out a living with my cab."

"Have you been pleased with our current arrangement?"

"Oh, yes, sir. I've never done so well."

"Well, I want to suggest expanding our agreement. Mrs. Ransom and I will be sailing to my home in England as soon as we're married, and I'd like you to come with us as my 'gentleman's man.' Do you have an interest?"

"Major, I've never served as a gentleman's man. What would my duties be?"

"On the voyage over, I'd expect you to be responsible for all of our baggage and belongings. Once we arrive at my father's home in Hampshire, I'll arrange for you to train under his man."

"Will you and Mrs. Ransom live in England?"

"I don't know what precisely we'll ultimately do, but, whatever we do and wherever we go, I would want you to be with us. I can promise you a good income and a safe retirement when it comes."

"I'd have to sell my cab and horse, but I believe I know just the fellow who would buy it," he said excitedly. "If you want me, then I'll be glad to take the position."

"Fine, consider it done. I'll book passage for you on our ship. Be prepared to sail on the Thursday following the wedding."

When Miles told Annie of his arrangement with Johnny, she seemed puzzled.

"Annie, what's troubling you?"

"Nothing, I guess. I just never dreamed that we would have servants. I've always tended to things myself."

"Well, all of that is going to change when we sail, and the first item on that list is a lady's maid for you."

Annie looked at him in total disbelief. "Miles, what in the world would a maid, lady's or otherwise, do for me?"

"She would be responsible for maintaining your wardrobe and assisting you in your personal life."

"Miles, I have exactly four dresses — three for daily use and one for Sunday. I hardly need help maintaining them, and just exactly what sort of personal things would she be helping with?"

"She would attend to your bath and your hair, and any other things that you might need."

"What's wrong with my hair? Don't you like it?"

"I love it, but, in England, you'll want to adopt the latest fashion."

"Miles Ransom, I've been bathing myself since I can remember, and I'll decide when I want to change my hair style. I will not be dictated to by a bunch of toffs in London."

"Annie, I've got some news for you. When we marry, you'll become a toff."

"We'll just see about that!"

"You will be expected to have a lady's maid, so try to get used to the idea."

"Exactly where do you imagine me to find a lady's maid in Boston?"

"I think I know just where to look. Let me talk to Philippe and see if he can help."

"If I've got to share my personal life with someone, why can't I choose?"

"Of course you can—I'm just trying to help."

"Well, I'd like to run this by my cousin Temperance. She's a couple of years older than I am and still unmarried. She might be interested."

"That's a fine idea, but talk to her soon; you'll need to purchase a maternity wardrobe that will carry you to the baby's birth. Once the child is born, you can buy whatever you want in London. When can you speak with Temperance?"

"Johnny is taking Mother and me to Braintree this afternoon. I'll ask Mother on the way. If she is agreeable, then I'll talk to Temperance when we're there."

While Annie and Martha visited in Braintree, Miles walked to Philippe Dalhousie's office and tapped on the door. The customary young man answered and said, "Major Ransom, come in. Mr. Dalhousie is expected back at any moment. Please have a seat. May I get you tea?"

"No, thank you. I'll be fine."

Miles was leafing through the *Gazette* when Philippe came through the door and saw him waiting. A smile crossed his face, and he said, "Miles, I didn't see Johnny outside. How did you get here?"

"I walked, and I enjoyed it very much. The exercise and fresh air felt good. I hope this is not an inconvenient time."

"No, not at all—in fact, I'm glad you came. We have some business to discuss."

"I suspected that we did," Miles replied.

Miles stood, followed Philippe into his office, and took a seat by the fire. Philippe poured two glasses of claret and joined him. They sipped the wine, and

Philippe said, "I've completed the transition of your business interests here in Boston. All of the managers will report to this office, and we will provide you with annual updates. Unless you instruct otherwise, all profits from these businesses will remain in your Boston account. You may draw against these funds as you see fit."

"That's just what I want. You may add to my holdings in New England if you see a particularly attractive opportunity. Annie and I are sailing to London to visit my family the Thursday following the wedding, which brings up another favor that I need from you."

"Of course—how can I help?"

"Do you remember my somewhat poorly timed visit just before the fleet sailed?"

"Yes, but that certainly was no cause for concern on your part."

"Good. You introduced your friend as Mrs. Jackson—Rebecca, as I recall."

"That is correct, and she has asked about your recovery on several occasions."

"Do you think she would be amenable to assisting Annie in the purchase of a maternity wardrobe for our voyage?"

"I'm sure Rebecca would be delighted. How would you want to proceed?"

"Any way that won't set Annie off on a tirade about toffs and the gentry. Maybe the two of you can join us for dinner tomorrow at the Henry House. That will give me a day to lay the groundwork."

"I'll have to ask Rebecca if she is available. May I send you a note later today?"

"Of course, and please give Mrs. Jackson my warmest regards."

The men sat for a while sharing wine and cigars until Miles noticed the lengthening shadow through the office window. He said goodbye and, in the fading sunlight and the growing chill, Miles walked the blocks back to the inn. When he arrived, he saw Johnny's cab sitting at the curb. Johnny touched his hat with his whip, and Miles went into the inn.

There was a lively crowd standing at the bar, and Josiah was serving ale and pig's feet as fast as he could draw the pints. Miles spoke to him and then went into the kitchen where Annie and her mother were preparing the evening meal. Miles poured a cup of coffee and sat at the table, watching them scurry about. Finally, he saw an opening and asked, "How did your trip to Braintree work out?"

"Very well," Annie replied. "The wedding plans are complete; all we have to do is show up at the church on time."

"What did you decide about your cousin Temperance?"

"She thought it would be great fun. She has already begun to pack for the trip. Do you have a berth booked for her?"

"I'll see to it first thing in the morning. I've invited Philippe Dalhousie and his lady friend to join us for dinner here tomorrow. I hope you don't mind."

"Not at all. I believe he's seeing Rebecca Jackson, who is a lovely woman."

"I'm glad you think so because I've suggested to Philippe that she might assist you in buying a wardrobe for the voyage."

"I'm pleased to have her help. She is a lady of taste and refinement, and I do need all the guidance that I can get when it comes to choosing clothes."

Miles felt a sigh of relief slip out, and he breathed a little more easily. He chatted for a few minutes and excused himself to prepare for dinner.

Dinner the next evening went far better than Miles dared hope. Annie and Rebecca hit it off well and made plans to go shopping on Friday. Annie was in the early stages of pregnancy, so her regular clothes still fit. With Rebecca's help, she was able to buy outfits that would carry her through delivery. When they returned, Annie had to ask Johnny to secure four more trunks to transport it all.

The next week flew by in a blur of last-minute details. Miles visited with Sir William and told him about his decision to request an indefinite leave of absence. Sir William prepared orders extending Miles's recovery leave until March 1, 1711, to give him time to visit with the Admiralty in London and make it official.

Miles decided to mention the visit from Nicholson and related it all to Sir William, who listened intently. He then said, "Miles, Nicholson is a petty politician. He sees every situation in the light of his own self-interest. He has promoted Reed to rear admiral without consulting the Admiralty, and I suspect he is overreaching his authority. As far as the battle with the *Concordia* goes, I have written my report to the Admiralty, and you have been given full credit for the victory. That will be the official record."

"Thank you, Sir William. I am never inclined to claim something that's not mine, and I'm sure you gave Captain Allen his fair share of the action."

"I did. He's mentioned by name in my report."

On the day before the wedding, Temperance came to the inn, along with all of her belongings, and began her duties as Annie's lady's maid. Miles asked Philippe to be his best man, and Annie chose Temperance as her maid of honor. On the morning of the wedding, Johnny drove them to Braintree.

Annie was radiant in her wedding gown, and Miles wore the full dress uniform of the Royal Marines. After the ceremony, the couple left the church under a bridge of swords held by the ranking officers in attendance. Then, there was a reception at the Adams family home. Miles and Annie danced until five in the afternoon, when Johnny drove them to a seaside cottage for their first night as husband and wife.

On Sunday morning, Johnny returned and drove Miles and Annie back to Boston, where, on Wednesday evening, they enjoyed a farewell family dinner at the inn. The next day, the cabby who had bought Johnny's rig took the couple, along with their attendants, to the pier, and the four of them boarded the *Mary Celeste*. Miles and Annie had a spacious cabin with a large bed, and Johnny and Temperance both had private cabins. The *Mary Celeste* sailed on the morning tide, and soon they were clear of Boston Harbor and in the open Atlantic.

Shortly after departure, Annie became a little queasy

and asked to go to their cabin. Miles strolled over to the quarterdeck and requested permission to climb up. The young officer commanding the deck introduced himself as Lieutenant Roger Blankenship. Blankenship was second in command.

"Major Ransom, it's an honor to have you and Mrs. Ransom on board. I followed the reports from the fleet, and I want you to know how much I admired your action with the French man-of-war."

"Thank you, Lieutenant. I appreciate your kind words. If I may, I'd like to ask you a question."

"Of course — please do."

"Last fall, I made the crossing of the Atlantic on board *HMS Dragon*. We had fair weather for the entire voyage, but it took us 52 days to make it to Boston. We are scheduled to dock in Southampton in less than 30 days. Is the *Mary Celeste* that much faster than a Royal Navy ship?"

"No, sir. The prevailing winds in the North Atlantic are called the westerlies, and they are constant from west to east. When sailing from Europe to North America, a ship must beat against the prevailing winds. While going from North America back to Europe, we sail with the wind. This, coupled with the favorable seas provided by the Gulf Stream currents, cuts our sailing time by close to half."

"Thank you, Lieutenant. I suspected that to be the case."

"Will you and Mrs. Ransom be joining us for meals in the wardroom?"

"No, Mrs. Ransom is not feeling well, so we'll have our meals in our cabin."

Miles spent almost the entirety of every day in the rigging of the *Mary Celeste*. Within a week, Annie had gained her sea legs, and she and Temperance enjoyed sitting in chairs on deck. Miles would join them and explain the operations of the ship. Johnny soon found the crew to be good fellows, and he fit right in with them. They were blessed with decent weather, and, with the one exception of a line of squalls lasting for just one day, the voyage passed without incident.

On Monday morning, December 15, the *Mary Celeste* rounded the Isle of Wight, entered the Solent, and docked in Southampton just after noon. Miles left Johnny to deal with the baggage and went ashore to arrange for a coach for the four of them and a dray wagon to haul the mountain of luggage. Miles engaged a coachman, who agreed to take them to Conway Hall, Miles's family home near North Waltham. With the coach and wagon in tow, Miles returned to the ship and oversaw Johnny as he loaded the dray.

The trip from Southampton to Conway Hall was close to 40 miles and took them through the old Roman city of Winchester. The clouds had come in from the sea, bringing a steady rain when they began their journey. The coach was well suspended, and the roads were good, so their trip took less than six hours. It was well after dark when the coach pulled through the gates of Conway Hall, and the large, three-story home of the Earl of Conway gleamed in the winter rain. Lights could be seen in every window.

The coach pulled beneath a covered porte-cochere, and it was met by a crowd of people. Miles could see his father and mother leading the delegation of relatives and servants. A young man in full livery opened the coach door and placed a stepping stool for the ladies. Miles helped Annie and Temperance to the ground, and the fact that Miles assisted Temperance was not lost on the assembled servants. Miles took Annie by the hand and led her up the stairs to his parents. He smiled broadly and said, "Mother, Father—this is my wife, Annie."

Lady Conway took Annie's hand in both of hers and said, "Welcome, my dear. We are delighted to have you and Miles home for the holidays."

Lord Conway took Annie's hand, gave it a gentle kiss, and said, "Welcome home. We have been looking forward to this since Miles's letter came."

Miles spoke to old familiar faces in the assembled staff, and he noticed some new younger ones, as well. While everyone moved inside, Miles pulled Geoffrey Collins, the head butler, aside and said, "Geoffrey, this young lady is Annie's cousin *and* her lady's maid. She is new to the position, and I'd like you to introduce her to Molly, Mother's maid. I'm hoping Molly can give her some guidance."

"Of course, Master Miles. I'm sure Molly will be happy to assist the young lady."

Miles then turned to Johnny and continued, "This is Johnny Cochrane, my man. I would also like you and Henry to take him under your wing and show him his duties."

"Again, we'll be happy to help him learn the ropes. I just want to say how happy we all are to have you home, Master Miles. We are so proud of your recent action while commanding *HMS Falcon*."

"Thank you, Geoffrey. I'm sure my role has been blown out of proportion."

"All I know is that your father and brother have been bursting their buttons with pride. We will be serving a small family dinner in your honor."

Miles entered the hall to find it resplendent in holiday decorations. There were wreaths in the windows and a large evergreen — glowing with candles and ribbons — in the entranceway. Miles followed his father and brother into what was known as the small dining room. The room was paneled in walnut, and a table set for over a dozen ran the length. There was a crackling fire in the large fireplace.

After visiting with his father for a moment, Miles found his brother and his brother's wife, Isabelle, taking a glass of wine from a waiter. Miles approached them and said, "Good to see you, David. You're looking well."

David, who was six years older than Miles, had begun to show the first signs of middle-aged spread. As heir to the earldom, David lived in London, where he tended to the family's commercial interests. One day, David would inherit his father's seat in the House of Lords, but, for now, he was a merchant prince. Miles had grown up with Isabelle, so he took her hand and said, "You are as pretty as I remember. How can David have aged so much, but you retain all of your youth?"

"I see your years at sea have sharpened your wit, if

not your eyesight. We're pleased to see that you have recovered from your wounds."

"Not entirely, but I'm making progress. I have a favor to ask of you."

"Oh, and what might that be?"

"Annie is not familiar with the ways of our society. She is quick and intelligent, and she has a kind nature—if you would take her under your wing, then I will be forever grateful."

"Don't you think that might be your Mother's prerogative?"

"Mother is the granddaughter of a king and the cousin of our reigning monarch. She'd have no patience with a girl like Annie. You, however, are one of the kindest people I've ever known. Please do this for me."

"Of course—I'll make it my mission to help her become comfortable with all of us."

Geoffrey Collins came into the crowded room and announced, "Your Lordship and my Lady, dinner is prepared."

Miles and Annie were seated at the head of the table on the left side of Lord and Lady Conway, and David and Isabelle were sitting to their right. When everyone was in his or her place, Lord Conway stood, and all of the men stood with him. He raised his glass and said, "To my prodigal son, Miles, hero of the Port Royal campaign, and his beautiful new wife, Annie."

The toast was acclaimed around the table; then, the footman began serving the meal. As they dined, Lady Conway made small talk with Annie, asking about her life in Boston, and Annie joined in, holding her own. After dinner, the ladies withdrew to the parlor, and the men joined Lord Conway in the library for brandy and cigars. Once everyone had a snifter of brandy and a smoke, Lord Conway turned to Miles and said, "Now, Miles, you must tell us all about the battle between the *Falcon* and the *Concordia*."

Miles, realizing the futility of arguing, retold the story, with the principal credit being given to the role played by Tom Allen and his boarding party. When Miles finished, his brother stood and said, "To Miles, a credit to the Ransom family."

There was a hearty round of "Hear! Hear!" Miles decided to change the subject and asked his father about the recent union between England and Scotland, decreed by Queen Anne. This led to a lively discussion of the nature of the newly formed Kingdom of Great Britain and how the union would affect all aspects of life in the realm.

The clock in the hallway struck ten. Miles stood and said, "I'm afraid it's time for me to call it a day. Annie and I have completed a long journey, and we should retire."

Miles went to the parlor and told everyone present that, unfortunately, he and Annie were exhausted and required sleep, at which point, his mother stood, took him by the arm, and whispered, "I agree — Annie needs her rest. After all, she is carrying your child."

Miles looked at his mother in total shock. His face confirmed his mother's comment, and she gave him a pat on the arm and a conspiratorial smile. Annie and Miles left the room and climbed the stairs to the second floor, where Temperance met them in the hall and showed them their rooms. Temperance helped Annie into her nightgown, while Miles changed in his closet.

When they were both tucked in for the night, Annie turned to Miles and said, "I love your mother. She's very kind."

"Yes. Kind and perceptive. She's guessed that you're with child."

"Oh, she didn't guess. I told her. She would notice the morning sickness, so why wait?"

14 THE QUEEN'S CAPTAIN

The week before Christmas was filled with holiday activities. On Sunday, the family attended church at St. Alban's in the nearby village. Annie, in keeping with her pledge to Miles, accepted the Anglican liturgy and took Communion with the family. On Monday, Miles's sister in law, Isabelle, suggested that Annie spend each day with her, learning the customs and mores of the English upper class. Annie called it toff's school and tried to seem interested. Johnny and Temperance embarked on their apprenticeships, as well.

Miles spent the week visiting with his father and brother. They roamed the estate, riding and hunting pheasant. Miles had always looked up to his older brother and found the time with David both pleasurable and interesting. David's business affairs kept him at the forefront of British commerce, and he worked with the worldwide network of Dalhousie offices. David, in turn, found Miles's dealings with Philippe in Boston intriguing.

The closer it got to Christmas, Miles noticed a marked increase in the household activities. Decorations were refreshed, and it seemed that the kitchen operated around the clock. The day before Christmas Eve, Johnny drove Major Ransom the 20 miles from Conway Hall to the market city of Winchester. Miles scoured the vast market and bought gifts for everyone. Henry, Lord Conway's man, provided Johnny with a list of the uniforms and clothing he would need, and they visited a local tailor, who took Johnny's measurements and promised to have it all ready by New Year's.

On Christmas Eve, the entire household attended a special Christmas Eucharist at St. Alban's and then returned to Conway Hall for a buffet dinner. After dinner, everyone gathered by the tree in the main hall. Presents were opened and carols sung. Miles gave his father and brother cases of the Montoya cigars, and he gave his mother a silver mirror made by the Boston silversmith, John Coney. Miles presented Annie with a delicate strand of perfectly matched pearls, and her first gift to him was a silver cigar cutter. It was close to midnight when the fire began to die, and everyone started excusing themselves for bed.

On Christmas morning, they all met for a hunt breakfast, in preparation for the annual holiday hunt. Isabelle had managed to find a riding outfit for Annie. The large satin dress had pantaloons that made it possible to ride either sidesaddle or astride. When Annie came down, she asked Miles, "Well, what do you think?"

"Very elegant. You look like you were born to the hunt. How are you planning to ride?"

"You know I want to ride astride. It allows a greater margin of safety when jumping."

"You mean it makes it easier for you to ride hellbent for election."

"Yes, there's that, as well."

Lady Louise, overhearing the conversation, stepped between them and scolded, "I hope you don't intend to ride to the fox this morning. Need I remind you that you are carrying my grandchild?"

"I promise to be careful; I'm just looking for a nice ride on a crisp winter morning."

"Well, good. You can travel with the rest of the ladies

as we follow the hunt from a safe distance."

After breakfast, the horn sounded, and the hunt was on. Miles chose not to ride hard and held back, keeping Annie in sight. She rode in the middle of the pack of ladies and kept her promise. After the hunt, the grooms took the horses, and everyone enjoyed a buffet meal in the main dining hall. Annie decided to retire and take an afternoon nap, while Miles visited with their neighbors and friends.

Major Ransom was chatting with an old chum when his father approached him. "Miles, may I see you for a moment?"

Miles excused himself and followed Lord Conway into the library. His father closed the door, moved in front of the open fire, and turned to Miles. "I've just received word that Francis Nicholson's report to the Army downplays your role in the battle. What is this about?"

Miles told Lord Conway the whole incident, including the preamble involving Nicholson's treatment of Sir William Darcy. When Miles had finished, his father thought for a few moments and then replied, "I suspect that I am to blame for Nicholson's actions. I have opposed his rise to power at every point possible. I believe him to be completely without ethics and a self-serving scoundrel. He is well aware of my feelings and probably took this opportunity to strike back."

"Well, there's nothing to worry about, although I was offended by his attitude and told him so. He replied that my offense was inconsequential to him, and we left it at that. I would never serve under the man again, but, since I may be leaving the service anyway, that is not likely to come up."

"He has very much offended the Admiralty by promoting one of his lackeys to rear admiral, and offending the Admiralty is not inconsequential. Your career is still viable if you choose to remain on active duty. William Darcy's report was glowing, and, believe me, he has much more influence at the Admiralty than does Nicholson."

"I'm pleased that Sir William feels that my actions were appropriate. I value his goodwill and professional opinion. That is far greater than what Francis Nicholson chooses to believe."

The family was invited to a New Year's Eve ball at the Duke of Hampshire's home, Litchfield Castle. The duke and duchess were the ranking nobles in Hampshire, and the duchess was Lady Conway's older sister, Evelyn. It was a day's coach ride from Conway Hall to Litchfield, and everyone was expected to spend the New Year as guests of the duke and duchess.

Temperance and Johnny were nervous about the whole thing, but they had both been in intensive training and were assured by Henry and Molly that they were ready. Annie seemed completely at ease and told Miles that she was looking forward to the ball. She forced him to practice the latest dances for an hour each evening. Lady Conway had her seamstress alter one of her ball gowns for Annie, and it fit perfectly.

As the family arrived at Litchfield, they wound through the oaks lining the long circular drive, and, at last, came in view of the castle, which was looming on the crest of a hill. Litchfield had originally been a Norman hill fort, and the duke's family, the Patillos, had been given their title by William the Conqueror shortly after Hastings. As the group arrived at the castle entrance, they were greeted by a small army of servants and were shown to their rooms by one of the duchess's ladies. They were told that there would be a welcoming reception before dinner, but they would have a couple of hours to rest and dress for the evening.

The suite of rooms assigned to Miles and Annie included dressing areas for them both, and Johnny and Temperance began unpacking the several trunks containing their clothing. Miles opened the large

French doors that led out onto a balcony overlooking the estate, and he and Annie walked into the cold, gray afternoon.

Miles took off his jacket and wrapped it around Annie's shoulders and said, "This will be your introduction to my parents' social circle, and you seem amazingly serene about it."

"Why wouldn't I be? After all, Miles, we colonists are not complete boors. Your mother and Isabelle have carefully drilled me in English etiquette, and I even know which fork to use. I also understand the pecking order. The only people I have to curtsy to are the Duke and Duchess of Hampshire. The Ransoms will outrank everyone else."

Miles pulled her closer and replied, "I forget just how much all of this means. The military certainly has rank and privilege, but, for the most part, it's based on merit, not the fortunes of one's birth."

"Oh? Then the vanquisher of the *Concordia* would still be the youngest major in the Royal Marines, even if he'd been a farmer's son?"

"Probably not, but I've seen men who started as powder monkeys rise to command fleets of Her Majesty's warships."

"Speaking of Her Majesty, Isabelle tells me that we'll be invited to a private audience with Queen Anne after the New Year."

"Yes, the Queen invites all of the Stuarts to dinner and a musical each February. It's usually a dreary affair, but, as you can imagine, it's a command performance."

"Dreary affair? Miles, we're talking about the Queen of England. How many Boston girls would ever get to meet her?"

"I guess it's a pretty big deal, but I always dreaded a visit to the palace. We had to mind our manners and be on our best behavior. I wanted to spend my time with the horse guards."

"I can believe that. All men are still boys at heart. Tell me about the Duke and Duchess of Hampshire."

"The first duke came over with William in 1066. He was instrumental in subduing the Anglo-Saxon population and establishing William's rule. The Patillos have been loyal subjects to every monarch and were staunch Royalists during the Civil War. Cromwell wanted the duke's head on a pike but never managed to catch him. When the restoration came, the Patillo family recovered all of their titles and lands. The current duke married into the Stuart family and sealed the deal."

"I've been told that the duchess is your mother's older sister, so she must also be a cousin of the Queen. Where does that put you in succession to the throne?"

"Somewhere along with Johnny Cochrane and Temperance, I would guess. There is no direct Stuart heir to Queen Anne, but I'm sure the crown will pass to some distant relative. The Ransoms won't be in that hunt."

Annie smiled, took his hand, and placed it on her belly.

"I guess this little guy will never make me Queen Mother, huh?"

"Nor will he ever be Earl of Conway. He'll have to find his own way in this world of ours, and, by the way, what makes you so sure he's a *he*?"

"Mothers know. Don't you want a son?"

"What I want is a fully equipped baby, and a girl will be just fine."

"Maybe next time, but this one is a baby boy."

The couple came back into the suite, shivering from the cold, and Miles took Annie over to the open fire and held her close. He heard the clock in the hall chime four times and said, "We have a few minutes before we have to dress; let's spend the time together in this big feather bed."

There was a hunt the following morning, but both Miles and Annie declined. Instead, they rode around the duke's vast estate and shared a picnic lunch at a small glen by the river. The next day, after a special church service at the castle chapel, everyone retired to dress for the ball. Temperance assisted Annie, while Johnny expertly laid out Miles's formal dress uniform.

When they were ready, Miles stood with Annie and looked at their images in the large mirror in the suite. Reflected was a beautiful young woman on the arm of a dashing officer of the Royal Marines.

The ball would be held on the third floor of the castle, which contained a full-size dining area with a table set for over 50 guests, and an adjacent ballroom with a 10-person orchestra, already playing on a raised platform. As each couple entered the hall, they were announced by a deep-voiced man in full livery. As Miles and Annie approached, he shouted, "Major and Mrs. Miles Stuart Ransom."

A light scattering of applause grew into a full-scale ovation. Miles's reputation as the victor of the battle with the *Concordia* was met with noticeable appreciation and admiration. He acknowledged the tribute with a slight bow, and he and Annie faded into the gathering crowd. Miles recognized boyhood friends and distant relatives, and proudly introduced Annie to them all.

At the conclusion of a magnificent dinner, the Duke of Hampshire stood, tapped his wine glass, and raised a toast: "To Her Majesty, Queen Anne."

The men stood and shouted, "Hear! Hear!" The orchestra broke into a spirited rendition of "God Save the Queen." The duke and duchess led everyone into the ballroom and began waltzing to the music. After a respectful amount of time had passed, everyone joined them on the floor. Annie and Miles cut a handsome figure, and he reveled in dancing with his elegant bride.

Annie danced with almost every man in attendance, and Miles had to relate the action with the *Concordia* over and over again. The evening ended with a German breakfast, and the sun was rising when the couple finally got to bed. The following morning, nearly everyone slept in, and Miles and Annie were no exception. The next day, Johnny loaded all of their trunks into their coach, and, after a huge breakfast, they began their return journey to Conway Hall.

With the festive holiday season concluded, the Ransom family fell back into a comfortable routine.

Lord Conway spent most of his days tending to the running of his large estate, and David returned to his London office to oversee the family's business interests. Miles soon grew bored with merely sitting around, so he decided to go to London to meet with the Admiralty. He discussed his plans with his father, who served on the House of Lords Committee of the Admiralty. When Miles mentioned his intention to ask for an extended leave of absence, his father commented, "Miles, as you know, I have tried to allow you the freedom of making your own decisions since the day I took you to enlist, and I won't try to tell you what to do now, but I will share my opinion with you."

"Yes, please do. You know I value your counsel," Miles replied.

"As I see it, you are at a critical juncture in your military career. Not only are you the youngest major in the Royal Marines, but you have also attracted much favorable notice since the engagement with the *Concordia*. William Darcy has been particularly vocal on your behalf, and, as you know, your mother has been whispering in the Queen's ear. I believe you can rise to high rank, but not in the Royal Marines."

"I'm not at all certain that I want to pursue a military career, but I do understand that rank above lieutenant colonel is impossible as a marine officer."

"Indeed — so it would be in your best interest to request a transfer to the Royal Navy and to do it while your reputation is at its current level."

"As I said, I'm not certain that I want to continue on active duty in either service. I have a wife, and we have a child on the way. I don't want the long absences that will be necessary as a serving officer."

"What alternatives are you considering?"

"Philippe Dalhousie has suggested that I consider buying land in one of the southern colonies and becoming a farmer. That would be a big adjustment, and I'm still undecided, but I know that I want at least a two-year leave from active duty. Annie will deliver in June, and I would like to take an extended tour of the continent after the child is weaned."

"I hope you don't intend to take the child with you. Your mother and I will be delighted to care for it, and we can always find a wet nurse so that you don't have to wait until weaning."

"I'll discuss it with Annie and see what she thinks, but I suspect we'll avail ourselves of your offer."

"Are you seriously considering farming?"

"As much as anything else. Thanks to you, I have no financial worries, so I can pretty much do as I please."

"I was intrigued that you made substantial investments in Boston. You must feel that the colonies will continue to grow and prosper."

"I do. The interesting thing to me is that they remain as 'English' as they do. Love of the mother country runs strong throughout New England, and I believe this will persist as long as the royal authorities continue to treat them fairly."

"I have a front-row position in the House of Lords, and support for our colonies in North America runs strongly throughout the House," replied Lord Conway.

"I honestly believe this is in the best interest of the Crown. Our colonies can be major trading partners and form a defensive barrier against France and Spain."

Lord Conway paused for a moment and then replied, "Miles, if you want to be a farmer, then have you considered buying an estate here or in Scotland?"

"I certainly haven't ruled it out and would give serious thought to such a proposal. After we return from our tour of Europe, I'll have time to decide exactly what we're to do."

"I'll support you in anything you choose; it might be advantageous to have a branch of the Ransom family in the New World. The Dalhousies have made a significant commitment in that direction, and it seems to be working out well for them."

"I agree. My recent dealings with Philippe Dalhousie have convinced me that they know their way around the colonial economy."

"Speaking of colonial products, where did you get these excellent cigars?"

"Unfortunately, they came from a rival colony. I bought them from a privateer while we docked in Kingston, Jamaica. If you'd like, I'll include you in any future purchases."

"Yes, please do, and include David, as well. He'll end up smoking mine if I allow it."

The two men lit another cigar, poured a glass of claret, and talked of affairs of state and the English economy.

In late January, Miles had Johnny hitch up a carriage, and the two of them drove the 40-odd miles to London, where they were guests in David's home in Kensington Gardens. Miles had requested, and been granted, a meeting with the proper office in the Admiralty. He made his visit to the Admiralty, where he officially requested a two-year leave in order to completely recover from his wounds. The leave was granted, and Miles then shared his plans with David.

With David's help, Miles located a nearby town house, which he purchased, and, once again, he asked Isabelle to work with Annie to help get the house furnished and staffed. When Miles returned to Conway Hall and told Annie of his purchase, she just shook her head but agreed to accept Isabelle's assistance in overseeing the furnishing and staffing.

Isabelle suggested that they employ the services of a young man who was establishing himself as a leader of the modern approach to design. With his help, they chose to buy a new style of furniture that was just coming into fashion. It featured the use of walnut and mahogany rather than English oak, as well as sleek cabriole legs and padded feet. This new style also made it possible to use lighter rugs and window treatments.

The work on the town house continued into late February, when everything was suspended and preparations began for the Queen's dinner. Miles and Annie were guests of David and Isabelle, while Lord and Lady Conway took up residence in their London home. Annie was just beginning to show signs of her pregnancy, and Isabelle helped her find a suitable dress for the evening. Miles chose to wear his dress uniform.

The dinner was scheduled for February 19 and would be held at the Queen's residence at Kensington Palace. The invitation noted that there would be a musical preview of George Frideric Handel's new opera, *Rinaldo,* which was due to premiere on February 24 at the Queen's Theatre in Haymarket. Handel would direct the orchestra himself, and the cast would sing the arias. Annie had never been to an opera, and she was ecstatic at the prospect. Miles would have preferred to undergo a dental procedure but smiled and encouraged Annie.

On the appointed evening, the Ransoms were transported to the palace by coach and were announced along with several dozen extended members of the Stuart clan. Queen Anne was seated on a small throne on a platform, and each couple or person was introduced. Miles and Annie were in the middle of the crowd, and, when their names were called, they advanced to the throne, where Miles bowed and Annie curtsied.

The Queen acknowledged them and then held up her hand to stop the music. She clapped her hands, and a courtier appeared, carrying a sword on a satin pillow. She instructed Miles to approach the throne. "Miles Stuart Ransom, I am pleased to present you with a small indication of our esteem." She took the sword from the young man and withdrew the blade. She allowed Miles to kneel at her feet, whereupon she tapped him on the shoulder and said, "Miles Stuart Ransom, I dub thee Sir Miles, in reward for your victorious defense of our realm. Please rise, Sir Miles, and accept this emblem of your knighthood."

Miles rose and took the sword from the Queen, retreated several steps, and bowed. "Your Majesty, I am honored by your notice and remain your loyal subject."

The Queen smiled and said, "Before the evening ends, I would like to hear about the *Concordia*, firsthand."

"As you wish, Your Majesty."

Miles and Annie moved on and joined the family, who were beaming from ear to ear. Miles walked up to his father and asked, "Were you aware of this?"

"Yes, Sir Miles. I have to admit that I was. The Queen wanted it to be a surprise, so we all kept it quiet. Congratulations!"

"Thank you, Father. From all of the accolades being heaped on me, you'd think that the *Concordia* was the first enemy ship ever to have been taken."

"Not the only one, just the most recent—your fame will subside sooner rather than later. May I see your sword?"

Miles handed the sword to his father. Lord Conway withdrew it from its sheath and read the engraving: **"Presented to Sir Miles Stuart Ransom in recognition of his faithful service to our realm. February 19, 1711. Anne Regina."**

Miles's father turned the sword over and said, "Miles, we are so proud of you. You are a credit to the Ransom family."

"Thank you, Father. Now, I best be finding Annie."

Miles found Annie at the center of a group of women. She was being introduced to a host of Stuart family members. When he saw an opening, Miles took her hand and pulled her away. He smiled and said, "Well, what do think so far?"

Annie's eyes gleamed, and she replied, "Miles, my mother isn't going to believe it! Her daughter, the wife of a knight! I can't wait to write her and tell her all about this fairy-tale evening!"

"The evening is young yet. Let's find our places for dinner."

Annie was the first to see the place card that read, "Sir Miles and Lady Ann Ransom."

The dinner was filled with good food and conversation, and Annie was enthralled by Handel's opera. She made Miles promise that they'd see more opera during their upcoming tour. The Queen summoned Miles to tell her about the action with the *Concordia,* and the Ransoms were among the last to leave the palace. When they reached David's home, both Annie and Isabelle were exhausted and went straight to bed. David and Miles had a brandy and a cigar before retiring after such an exhilarating evening.

15 THE QUEEN'S CAPTAIN

The weeks following the Queen's dinner were filled with furnishing the town house in London. Miles and Annie moved in the first week of May, and Isabelle made arrangements for a midwife to attend to Annie's forthcoming delivery. Their new home had servants' quarters in the basement, and soon Johnny and Temperance were joined by Lawton Carson, a butler, who set about hiring the necessary staff. All were in place, when, on June 19, Stuart Percy Ransom was born.

The baby's birth had been uncomplicated, and Annie and Miles welcomed him into the family with joy. They decided to call him Stuart, and soon their lives settled into a comfortable routine. They employed a nanny to care for the child's needs, even though Annie continued to breast-feed him.

The summer of 1711 was spent at Conway Hall in order to escape the oppressive London heat, and Lady Conway soon became a doting grandmother. Miles worked with his father on the estate, carefully observing the relationship between Lord Conway and his tenants. One afternoon in August, Miles asked, "I've noticed that we don't grow a cash crop. Why is that?"

His father thought for a moment and replied, "To cultivate such a crop in our climate is almost impossible, and those that will grow are too labor-intensive. We do plant corn and wheat for our own use, but we depend on the sale of beef, poultry, and dairy products to generate cash."

"I noticed that we have an extensive orchard with apples, pears, and walnuts. Do we sell these?"

"We do, but most are used here on the estate."

"How are the tenants compensated for their labor?"

"We provide housing and small garden areas, and the tenants share in the sale of the products they produce. We take a serious interest in our workers and their families."

"Do you make a profit from the estate?"

"Not as such. We're able to maintain the estate and Conway Hall with the proceeds, but anything above that is spent on tenant and staff welfare. The family businesses make a handsome amount, enough to support our lifestyle."

"I would like to visit with some of the men who own plantations in the Southern Colonies. Do you happen to know someone like this?"

"I'm sure I do. What do you wish to discuss with such a person?"

"I'm interested in the operations of a plantation. I think that I'd like to buy some land in Carolina when Annie and I return to North America."

"I am acquainted with Baron Baltimore, Charles Calvert, whose father founded Maryland. I'm sure he would agree to see you."

"Does he live nearby?"

"He lives in St. Pancras in London, not too far from your home in Kensington Gardens. I'll write to him and request an audience for you this fall."

"Thank you. Let me know when and where."

In early September, Miles, Annie, and the baby moved back to their home in London, and Miles and Annie were soon caught up in the city's social whirl. They attended parties and balls on a regular basis and found time to indulge Annie's newfound appreciation of opera and the stage. Miles had just returned from a visit to David's office, when Lawton, the butler, brought him a letter from Philippe Dalhousie. Miles went to his study, opened it, and read:

July 23, 1711

Dear Miles,

I hope this finds you, Annie, and young Stuart in good health. Josiah gave me the happy news of Stuart's birth, and he and Martha are proud grandparents. I wanted to be the first to tell you of my own good news. Rebecca and I are to be married in October. I wish you could be here.

I have included with this letter an accounting of your holdings and the results of the businesses you own. As you can see, you have a cash balance with us of £22,456. The value of your holdings based here in Boston, including all business interests, is £2,400. I hope you are content with our results so far.

I just received a statement of your total holdings that are under management by our firm, and they total cash of £187,479 and property valued at £4,804.

I would like to offer my congratulations on your recent knighthood. The news reached Boston in late March and received widespread coverage in the local press. I can't wait to see the sword that was presented to you by the Queen.

Josiah tells me that Annie and you intend to take an

extended tour of the continent as soon as Stuart is old enough. The Dalhousie offices will be notified and stand ready to assist you in any way. Please allow us to serve you as you travel.

Rebecca and I will look forward to your return to Boston. Please let us know of your plans. Take care and enjoy your travels.

Your servant,

Philippe Dalhousie

Miles put the letter down. He realized how much he missed Boston, and his friends and Annie's family. He sat at his desk and began to write a return letter.

September 16, 1711

Dear Philippe,

I was pleased to receive your letter of July 23. It was good to hear from you, and I want to offer my congratulations on your upcoming marriage to Rebecca. Annie will be particularly pleased. I also appreciate the accounting of my holdings, and, yes, I'm very content with the results of your management of my affairs. Annie and I purchased and furnished a home in the Kensington Gardens area of London, and Annie has become quite the social butterfly. She seems to be adjusting to being a "toff" quite well.

We plan to remain in either London or Conway Hall until Stuart has been weaned, or is at least in the hands of a wet nurse. My parents have offered to care for him while we travel, and I hope we can start our trip in the early summer of next year. As you know, I have homes in Paris and Bordeaux, as well as in Rome. Due to the current state of war between Great Britain and France, I'll be unable to visit France, but we will go to the Netherlands and Italy. My younger brother, William, is studying in Rome, and I haven't seen him for some time.

I am giving serious consideration to returning to North America and purchasing a plantation in one of the southern colonies when we complete our tour. I intend to follow your suggestion that I look into Carolina. I believe you *mentioned a new office in Charlestown, and maybe you can introduce me to the manager there. If we can start our tour in June of 1712, I believe we can return to Boston in the spring of 1713.*

Please keep in touch, and, again, congratulations on your marriage to Rebecca.

Your faithful friend,

Miles Ransom, KB

Miles sealed the envelope and summoned Lawton to see that it was posted. Lawton brought a note from Lord Conway telling Miles that Baron Baltimore had agreed to see him at his home at ten on the morning of September 27. Miles made a notation of the date on his desk calendar and then took Annie the news of Philippe's engagement to Rebecca.

On the morning of the 27th, Miles had an early breakfast and then dressed in his best civilian suit. His coach dropped him at the entrance to Baron Baltimore's home, where Miles was met by the baron's butler, who guided Miles to a study overlooking the extensive grounds of the home. When the baron entered the room, Miles stood and said,

"Baron, it was kind of you to agree to see me."

Baron Baltimore extended his hand and said, "The honor is all mine, Sir Miles. I've wanted to meet and congratulate the victor of the Battle of Mahone Bay."

The term "Battle of Mahone Bay" caught Miles by surprise, and he realized that the Admiralty had officially named the action with the *Concordia*. Miles caught himself and said, "Baron, I can assure you that my role in that effort has been totally blown out of reality."

"Possibly so, but that's how our heroes are chosen. I suspect the honors were well deserved. Lord Conway tells me that you're considering settling in one of our southern colonies."

"Yes, sir. I married a Boston girl, and we already have property in New England. It has been suggested that I buy land for a plantation in Carolina."

"As I'm sure you know, my father, Cecil Calvert, Second Baron Baltimore, founded the colony of Maryland as a refuge for Catholics, and I had the honor of serving as governor there until 1684. Are you considering Maryland as an option?"

"No, sir. I want to find uncleared land to carve out a working plantation, and almost all of Maryland has been settled. Carolina seems to be more open to development. My interest in visiting with you is related to the actual management of a plantation."

"I see. Well, we certainly own extensive land in Maryland, and all of it is under cultivation. We grow tobacco and indigo as our cash crops, and corn, wheat, and barley to support our slaves."

"The slaves are one of my main concerns. I'd prefer not to own slaves, and I hope I can follow the tenant-farmer system used by my father and other landowners here in England."

"Few, if any, of the men who have plantations in North America personally approve of human slavery, but we all accept the fact that significant amounts of cash crops cannot be raised otherwise. Our holdings represent our primary source of income, and we depend on them."

"I have no quarrel with slave labor used by others, but, if possible, I would do everything I could to avoid its use on my property. If Annie and I were to settle there, then we would be satisfied with the plantation paying for itself. We are fortunate to have independent income sufficient to allow us that luxury."

"I admire your position on slavery — in fact, I very much share it. However, the institution of slavery has become entrenched in the plantations of the Southern Colonies, and I'd suggest you not openly oppose it."

"I can see that and will keep my own counsel. Do you have any other advice for me?"

"Yes, both Carolina and Maryland are proprietary colonies and are governed by owners here in Britain. As one of these proprietors, I believe we are more sensitive to the interests of large landholders than either a Royal Colony or Charter Colonies. We serve as a buffer between the interests of the large landowners and the ambitions of the lower classes."

"Isn't that bound to be a bone of contention within the colony?"

"It is, and, at present, the colony is in the hands of Protestant rebels, but my grandson, Charles, is contesting the seizure, and we expect him to prevail."

"Was this a popular uprising by the commoners?"

"Not at all. It was purely religious. My family is no longer Catholic, and Charles is in the process of publicly proclaiming his Protestant beliefs."

"Baron Baltimore, I sincerely appreciate your time and counsel. If I may, I would hope to be able to talk with you again."

"By all means — you're always welcome in my home,

Sir Miles. Call at any time."

"Thank you, sir. I wish your grandson success in his endeavors to regain the title to Maryland."

Miles left the baron. On the ride back home, Miles mused, "I suppose it's hard for a man like Baron Baltimore to see it, but there is a basic disconnect between the colonial system and the long-term prosperity of the colonies. I suspect this will be a much grander problem in the future. I'm willing to bet that a large landholder will have to decide if he's willing to side with local sentiments, or try to stand aloof and keep milking the system for his own use."

The more Miles thought about it, the clearer it became. There would come a day, maybe in the distant future, when such a man would have to take sides. The ability of the British government to retain control of its colonies depended on Parliament's assuring equal protection under British Common Law for its colonial subjects. This was something to consider when Miles decided what to do with the rest of his life.

Miles and Annie spent Christmas at Conway Hall, attended the Duke of Hampshire's ball and hunt for New Year's, and enjoyed Queen Anne's dinner in February. Miles was pleased that the hero of Mahone

Bay had slipped into history, and he enjoyed quietly visiting with relatives. On the way home from the dinner, Annie asked if Miles had noticed the decline in the Queen's health. Miles agreed that she was clearly in discomfort and looked way beyond her 47 years.

Miles realized that he would soon no longer have the protection of his military position and decided to take measures to arm both him and Johnny. He owned the matched set of pistols from Italy given to him by his father, but they were too large and heavy for everyday concealment. Miles decided to visit with the London gunsmith, Joshua Langston, and see just what was available.

Langston welcomed Miles, and, after hearing his travel plans, made several recommendations. First, Langston suggested two flintlock pocket pistols, specially designed to allow the owner to conceal them on his person. The guns were fitted with a powder pan that had a cover connected to the trigger mechanism. The cover receded when the trigger was pulled, and the flint spark hit a full pan of powder.

In addition to the pistols, Langston suggested a short double-barreled shotgun. The shotgun was rigged with straps that allowed it to be hidden beneath a thick traveling coat. He also suggested a walking cane that concealed a rapier-like blade of high-quality steel. Miles bought four of the pistols for Johnny and him, the shotgun for Johnny, and the walking cane for himself. Langston also gave him two sets of brass knuckles and a folding knife that opened with the flick of a spring-loaded button.

In June of 1712, Annie and Miles left the London house to the care of Lawton Carson and the staff, and moved Stuart to Conway Hall. Before Annie and Miles left on their trip, the family celebrated Stuart's first birthday with a party on the lawn. He was doted on by everyone at Conway Hall, and Annie and Miles felt comfortable leaving him there while they traveled.

On the morning of June 20, with Johnny and Temperance in tow, Miles and Annie boarded the *Anne Regina,* which sailed between Southampton and Rotterdam. They were blessed with perfect summer weather, and Miles felt glad to be back at sea. Annie and Temperance sat on the deck, and Miles, climbing into the rigging, took up his favorite spot.

The *Anne Regina* passed through the narrowest part of the channel during the night and anchored off the entrance to the Rhine river delta until the tides changed early on a Tuesday morning. Shortly after noon, the ship moored in Rotterdam's harbor, and the Ransom party was met by a young man from the local

Dalhousie office. He secured transportation to the DeBeers House.

The Dalhousies had arranged a suite for Miles and Annie and single rooms for Johnny and Temperance. Miles only intended to spend two nights in Rotterdam and then continue to Portugal on a Dutch ship. On Wednesday, Annie and Temperance made plans to visit the city's international market area, and Miles had been invited to have lunch with Louis Dalhousie, the firm's manager in the Netherlands. Johnny made arrangements for a carriage for Annie and Temperance, and a coach came to take Miles.

Rotterdam was known as the gateway to Europe. It was the continent's largest port and sat astride the Rhine, Meuse, and Scheldt river systems, which led into the heartland of Europe. Miles was taken to a private club in the financial center, and, when he entered, he was led to a table. A young man dressed in the latest fashion introduced himself as Louis Dalhousie and said, "Ah, Sir Miles, I am delighted that you could join me. Philippe has written to expect you and to offer any assistance that you might need. I hope you found the DeBeers House comfortable."

Miles shook the outstretched hand and replied, "Indeed, we are very comfortable; I thank you for finding it for us. How are you and Philippe related?"

"We are cousins. In fact, we grew up together in

Bordeaux. I understand he is doing a skillful job running our Boston office."

"I can vouch for that. Philippe has handled my affairs in North America splendidly."

"I'm glad to hear it. The club offers a variety of dishes, and I suggest that we order."

Miles picked up the handwritten menu and chose soup along with a braised rib of beef. After the meal had been served, he and Louis talked about the ongoing war between England and France and its effect on world trade. Near the end of the meal, Miles caught the eye of a man sitting two tables away. The man nodded and then diverted his eyes. Miles leaned across the table and asked, "Louis, have you noticed the man sitting two tables to your left?"

Louis took a discreet peek and replied, "That is Albert Macon; he works in the French consulate here in Rotterdam. Why do you ask?"

"Nothing. He just seemed to recognize me. Probably thought I was someone else."

"I wouldn't be concerned. I know Albert, and he is harmless. Being a French firm, we often have dealings with the consulate."

The conversation continued into the afternoon, and

Miles returned to the DeBeers House. As he left the coach, he noticed Albert Macon, the man from the club, ride by in a carriage. When Macon saw Miles looking at him, he, again, diverted his eyes. Miles had just changed into more comfortable clothes when Annie and Temperance came bursting through the door, Johnny following with an armload of bags and boxes. Miles smiled and said, "Well, Annie, you seem to be getting the hang of shopping. Might I assume your trip was a success?"

"Indeed, you might. The market is filled with the latest fashions from the capitals of Europe, and I actually showed great restraint. I did splurge on something, and I hope you like it as much as I do."

Annie picked up a rectangular package, wrapped in white paper, and began to open it carefully. She pulled a small oil painting out of the paper and turned it so that Miles could see it clearly. It was a painting of a young girl wearing a pearl earring, sitting facing a mirror, an open window to her back. The light from the window made her reflection in the mirror shimmer in a luminescent glow.

Miles looked at the painting for almost a minute and then said, "I love it. Where did you buy it?"

"I found it in one of the stalls in the marketplace. It's over 50 years old, and it was painted by a young artist from Delft. His name was Johannes Vermeer, and he died in 1675. The dealer had another of his paintings of the same girl, with the same earrings, only facing the other way, looking out the window. I liked this one better."

"It's wonderful. What did you have to pay for it?"

"Well, that's the bad news. I'm afraid I spent too much."

"Oh? How much?"

Annie sighed and sheepishly replied, "£350. I hope you're not angry."

"Not at all. You probably should have bought them both."

"Oh, Miles, I was so worried that you'd be vexed with me. Thank you for being pleased."

He took her into his arms and kissed the top of her head.

"Annie, you will never vex me by purchasing beautiful things."

Thomas R. Lawrence

16 THE QUEEN'S CAPTAIN

On a Thursday, Annie and Miles arose early, and, after a quick cup of coffee and a hard roll, they packed their trunks. Johnny loaded them on board the Swedish ship *Hendricka,* which was to sail on the noon tide to Lisbon, Portugal. Miles chose not to sail on an English ship in wartime. Everyone was on board by ten in the morning. The *Hendricka* sailed down the Rhine estuary into the North Sea and turned south back through the channel.

Miles and Annie were invited to sup with the *Hendricka*'s captain, Olaf Andersson. In spite of the language barrier, they enjoyed a pleasant meal. Annie returned to their cabin, and Miles went on deck to enjoy the last cigar of the day. It was a clear and calm night, with a blanket of stars glimmering overhead. Miles spoke to the officer of the deck, and, with his permission, Miles took his usual spot in the rigging. When Miles returned to their cabin, Annie was fast asleep, and he soon joined her.

Miles awoke when he felt the *Hendricka* come to a stop, and he heard a boarding party embarking. He looked out the small porthole and saw pitch darkness. Miles decided that they had probably taken on a pilot to guide them through the narrows between Dover and Calais, so he rolled over and went back to sleep. He'd just dozed off when there was a gentle tapping on the cabin's hatch. He eased out of bed and found one of the *Hendricka*'s officers holding a lantern.

When Miles cracked the hatch, the young man said in heavily accented English, "Sir Miles, the captain requests your company in his cabin, if you please."

"Of course — give me a minute to get dressed," Miles replied.

Miles tiptoed to get his clothes and put on his boots, but Annie stirred and sleepily asked, "Miles, is it morning?"

"No, my dear. I have been requested to join the captain. For some reason, we have visitors."

"Oh my, I hope there isn't any danger."

"I'm sure not. If there were danger, then the drums would have sounded. I'll be right back and fill you in.

Try to go back to sleep."

Annie reached up and kissed him. She then rolled on her side and snuggled back under the quilt. Miles slipped into the passageway and followed the officer aft. He tapped on the captain's hatch, and a deep voice said, "Enter."

The officer stood aside, and Miles ducked through the hatch to find the captain standing behind his desk and two men standing to the side. When Miles looked at the men, he was stunned to see that one of them was the Frenchman, Albert Macon, and the other seemed slightly familiar, as well, but Miles couldn't place his face in the lantern light.

Miles looked into the eyes of Macon and said, "Well, monsieur, we finally meet. How may I be of service?"

Macon bowed slightly and replied, "Indeed, we do, Sir Miles. I'd like to present a recent adversary of yours, Captain Jean Farrgot, currently commanding our ship of the line *La Courone*, and formerly captain of the *Concordia*. I believe the two of you have met."

When Macon held the lantern closer to the other man, Miles recognized the French officer who had surrendered his sword just before the musket ball hit Miles's chest. Miles smiled and said, "Captain Farrgot, I'm pleased to see that you have been exchanged. Have you come to strike your colors again?"

"Happily no, Major Ransom, but it is truly an honor to finally meet the hero of Mahone Bay. I've read the English accounts of the battle and wondered if I was involved in the same action. I'm glad to see you've recovered from your injury."

"I, too, sometimes wonder the same thing when I read them. Blood and gore sell newspapers it seems, and, yes, I've regained my health. What may I do for you that would warrant the boarding of a neutral ship?"

"A gentleman from Paris wishes to have a word with you, and I've been ordered to invite you aboard *La Courone*. I can assure your safe return to Lisbon in time for the arrival of the *Hendricka*."

"And if I refuse?"

"If we have not returned to *La Courone* by the end of the midwatch, a boarding party will come to escort us back. If you choose to come peacefully, then I will allow the *Hendricka* to continue to Lisbon and not alarm Lady Ransom."

"Well, Captain, you seem to have the advantage this time. Shall I surrender my sword?"

"No, that will not be necessary, as much as I'd love to own a sword presented by Queen Anne herself.

Besides, if the press got wind of this meeting, then you'd probably be made a duke."

"Unfortunately, I'm on extended leave, so you must take a civilian into your custody. May I inform my wife and servants of our change of plans?"

"Of course, and bring any personal items you may need. But, please, leave your walking cane behind. Don't tarry, as we shouldn't want the boarding party to become anxious."

Miles returned to their cabin and found Annie awake and fully clothed. Temperance and Johnny were standing by the hatch. Johnny had on a long traveling coat, and Miles suspected that the shotgun was hanging by its straps. He stepped in and said, "It seems that I will be sailing to Lisbon aboard a French man-of-war. The *Hendricka* will continue to Lisbon, where I will meet you at the pier. There is no call for alarm. I have the French captain's word that I will be completely safe. It seems that someone from Paris wants to visit with me."

Annie looked at her husband and asked, "Miles, I know you don't want us to worry, but are you sure of your safety?"

"As certain as you can be of anything in a time of war. Johnny, I expect you to care for the ladies until we meet in Lisbon, and don't even think about using that shotgun. If we resist, then we put the crew and passengers of the *Hendricka* in danger. Now, please prepare me an overnight bag, and don't include any weapons. I'll be leaving my cane, as well."

"Are you sure, sir? I checked, and there are only two men and a four-man boat crew. I'll take care of all of them if you give the word."

"You may well take the two men, but there's a 74-gun warship within hailing distance. If we resist, then we place this ship, her crew, and the passengers in danger. Best we comply."

Johnny packed the bag, and Miles held Annie and said, "Try not to worry; I'm confident that I'll meet you in Lisbon."

"Miles, I don't worry about things that I can't influence, but you might mention to these Frenchmen that if harm befalls you, then they will never again enjoy a peaceful night's sleep."

"I may keep that to myself, but I like the thought."

Miles scooped Annie into his arms and kissed her. He then took the bag from Johnny and made his way to the captain's cabin. When Miles came through the hatch, he saw the two men seated at the captain's desk, sipping on steaming cups of coffee. They rose to their feet, and Macon said, "Captain Andersson, let me thank you for your cooperation and hospitality. I'm glad we were able to avoid an international incident tonight."

Andersson smiled and replied, "It was a simple mathematical decision. 74 is bigger than none. I will have to file a report with my owners, but I'll downplay the matter. I don't want to place Sir Miles in jeopardy."

Macon returned the smile and said, "I can assure you that Major Ransom is in no danger and will be awaiting your arrival in Lisbon."

The Frenchman nodded to the hatch and indicated that Miles should lead the way on deck. When Miles gained the main deck, he could see *La Courone* riding within 200 yards, lights ablaze and making no attempt at concealment. Miles tossed his bag to one of the French sailors manning the small cutter and climbed down the netting. There was a slight breeze coming from the French coast, and scattered clouds passed across the gleaming moon.

When the cutter drew alongside *La Courone*, Miles could see the gangway had been lowered into position, and their party was invited aboard. Once on the main deck, Captain Farrgot stood stiffly and said,

"I must bid you adieu for the moment. I have a ship to command, and the meeting you are about to attend is far above my pay grade. I hope your time on *La Courone* is pleasant, and I'll look forward to seeing you in the morning."

Farrgot turned to his officer of the deck and said, "Make full speed to Calais."

Miles felt the wind catch in the sails and felt the ship surge forward, leaving the *Hendricka* falling behind them. Macon called out to a midshipman and ordered him to take Miles's bag to the captain's cabin. He then turned to Miles and said, "Now, if you will follow me, there is someone who is anxious to meet you."

Miles followed Macon below, and they stopped in front of the hatchway leading to the captain's cabin. Macon rapped on the hatch, and a pleasant voice replied, "Entrez."

Macon stepped inside the cabin, and Miles followed. Sitting at a desk was a sallow-faced man of about 40 years, simply dressed, and showing no indication of rank. His face bore the signs of exposure to the weather, and Miles guessed him to be a military man. Macon stood aside and said, "Your Highness, may I present Sir Miles Ransom, the English gentleman you wished to meet."

The man behind the desk stood and extended his

hand. Miles shook it, and the man turned to Macon and said in flawless English, "Thank you, Albert. You may leave us now. I'll send for you later."

Miles was stunned by the title "Your Highness." Astonished and confused, Miles was almost sure that this plain man was not Louis XIV, the Sun King. He was far too young—but he must be of the royal family of France to warrant that title.

Sensing Miles's confusion, he smiled and said, "No, Sir Miles, you are right. I am not Louis. I am Charles d'Orleans, Duke of Chartres. The king is my cousin, so I am granted the right to be addressed as 'Your Highness.' However, I am comfortable with Charles, if I may call you Miles."

"Of course—I'm familiar with your military operations and your standing in Versailles. I'm honored to meet you, even though our countries are at war."

"Miles, I, too, am familiar with your victory at Mahone Bay, and our work here tonight may change the state of war between our countries."

"Well, I feel that my part in the battle has been blown out of proportion. Captain Farrgot and his crew fought honorably. I have nothing but admiration for him."

"So noted. Now, I am afraid we must get down to business. *La Courone* will take me back to Calais before dawn, and you will continue your journey to Lisbon. However, right now I have chosen to entrust you with highly sensitive information that mustn't fall into the wrong hands. I presume my choice will be a sound one."

"I'll feel more comfortable addressing you as 'Your Lordship,' as I would address a duke at home, but, please, use Miles. If I understand you, then you wish me to transmit secrets of state. To whom do you want me to take them?"

"I'll leave the final choice to you, but we know that you are a Stuart, that the Queen holds you in personal esteem, and that you have her ear. We also know that your father is a leader in the House of Lords and that your Admiralty respects you. I'm sure you will find the right person."

"Why me? I'm a junior officer in the Royal Marines and still in my twenties. Surely you have back channels to my government more appropriate than I."

"Of course, there are such back channels, as you call them, but none that I would trust with this information. Not only are you well placed and come highly regarded by one of our major financial houses, but also, quite by chance, you've made yourself available. In diplomacy, like life, timing can be everything. Now, let me make our proposal. I will share very private information that you may use if you need to explain why we chose you as our messenger.

"Our king's health is not good. He is, for the most part, bedridden, and suffers pain in his feet and lower leg. He realizes that at 69 years of age, his rule is nearing the end, and he wishes to settle the issue of succession to the throne. He knows that he must end this war about Spanish succession in order to address our own. Therefore, I have been instructed to inform your government of our proposed terms."

The duke took an envelope from his coat, handed it to Miles, and continued, "This document outlines our terms. Read it carefully, commit it to memory, and destroy it. When you return to England or, as your country is now known, the United Kingdom, take this information to Queen Anne or a person near her."

Miles accepted the letter and said, "Your Lordship, just as your king is nearing the end of his days, our queen is also in failing health. I visited with her in February and found her to be in great discomfort. I believe it would be better to choose another avenue."

"Yes, we've heard rumors of her illness, which is why you are free to decide to whom the terms should be presented."

A knock came at the hatch. Macon stuck his head in and said, "Your Highness, we are approaching the dock in Calais. Your carriage to Paris is waiting."

"Thank you, Macon. I'll be there in a moment."

Macon shut the hatch, and the duke said, "It seems that I must go. I need to hurry back to Paris. I'm glad to have had the pleasure of meeting you. You are an outstanding young man, and I hope your mission will lead to the end of this useless war. Please visit if you are ever in Paris. I understand you own a home there."

"Yes, I have a home on Rue St. Simon. I will do my best to see that your information reaches the appropriate ear. I am flattered by your confidence, and I hope that our paths will cross again. Have a safe journey to Paris."

"I hate to interrupt your travels, but I hope you will proceed to London with haste."

"I'll book the first ship leaving Lisbon."

"I believe Macon has taken the liberty of booking you and your party on a ship sailing on the evening tide. Apologize to Lady Ransom for me."

"I'm sure she will understand."

"Good, then come on deck and bid me farewell."

The duke and Macon descended to the dock without fanfare and boarded the waiting coach. Miles felt a presence at his side, and Jean Farrgot said, "I'm glad to see the duke sail away. Now, I can deliver you and your party to Lisbon and resume my efforts to redeem my naval career."

Miles turned and said, "I suspect that the duke's visit may aid you in that. I gave you and the crew of the *Concordia* a good review."

"I thank you. The duke is fourth in line for the Crown and will surely be appointed regent, awaiting the maturity of the prince. Now, let me get us on our way to Lisbon."

Farrgot gave the orders to sail and said, "Major, I realize that your repose was interrupted. Would you like to take a rest?"

"No, I got a couple of hours before you came, and I'm too agitated to sleep."

"Good, then shall we go to the wardroom to see if we can get some coffee? Or would you prefer tea?"

"I'd much prefer coffee, thank you."

When they entered the wardroom, everyone came to

their feet. Farrgot told them to return to their seats and asked a steward to bring brioche and coffee. He and Miles sat, and both ate one of the hot, fresh rolls. Farrgot asked, "May I call you Miles?"

"Yes, and may I use Jean?"

"Of course," Farrgot replied.

Miles asked, "Do you intend to remain in the Navy when the war ends?"

"The wars between our countries never actually end. There are just pauses between battles, so I will remain in the service. What do you plan to do?"

"I'm not certain—if peace does come, as I suspect it will, then I plan to return to North America and decide then what to do."

Farrgot nodded and replied, "My family has sugar plantations on the Island of Hispaniola, so I've had occasion to visit the Caribbean, but I have never been to the continent."

"I thought Hispaniola to be a Spanish colony. How did a French family acquire plantations?"

"My mother is Spanish, and my father took over her family's holdings. I was actually born in Marseilles during a visit to my father's family, so I have French citizenship."

Miles heard the bell sound and said, "Jean, I thank you for your hospitality and hope that we might meet again. When will we reach Lisbon?"

"We should be there before nightfall. I believe your ship will leave for England as soon as you and Lady Ransom are on board. Now, I must attend to my duties. Feel free to nap in my cabin, or you may roam the ship."

"I'll try to catch a little rest. Later, if I have your permission, I'd like to climb into the fore rigging and watch the sea."

"As you wish—summon me if you need anything."

Farrgot rose and left the wardroom, and Miles managed to get several hours sleep before they reached Lisbon.

The sun was sinking below the western horizon when Miles met the *Hendricka,* tying up to the pier. He could see Annie, Johnny, and Temperance standing at the rail waving to him. He and Johnny loaded their trunks on a waiting carriage, and Miles sat down next to Annie. She looked at him and said, "I see that you were right about the level of danger. When we get to our lodgings, I want to hear all about it."

"I'm afraid that we will be boarding a ship for

London. We must return home at once. I'll explain it when we are under way."

Annie sighed and said, "Miles Ransom, you never cease to amaze me. You seamlessly move from one adventure to another."

The couple boarded a Portuguese ship, the *Santa Gloria,* and sailed on the evening tide. Once they were in the Atlantic, Miles explained the night's meeting in detail. Annie shook her head and replied, "Miles, in the short time we've been married, I've met the Queen of England and several dukes and earls. Now, you've met the future Regent of France. Mother is just not going to believe it. I'm glad we are returning to London. I'm missing Stuart terribly. Come to bed, and let me help you get some sleep."

17 THE QUEEN'S CAPTAIN

The *Santa Gloria* entered the Thames Estuary just after sunrise and curled around the Isle of Dogs. They slipped past the gleaming white Tower and docked at the Tower Pier, with all the church bells in London ringing. Miles rounded up a carriage, while Johnny dealt with the trunks. It was close to two o'clock when the four travelers arrived at 1315 High Street in Kensington, and they were met at the door by Mr. Carson and the staff.

Miles assisted with the unloading. He then asked Johnny to hitch up the carriage to take Annie and him to Conway Hall. It was nearly dark when they arrived, and Annie went straight to the nursery, with Lady Conway in tow. Miles found his father sitting at his desk in the study. When Miles walked in, Lord Conway looked up and said, "Didn't you just leave for a three-month tour of the continent?"

"I did, but I've had to cut it short."

"Well, I guess I can see that. Is something wrong?"

"No, but I need your advice on a matter of some importance."

Miles spent the next 15 minutes telling Lord Conway the details of his meeting with the Duke of Chartres. When Miles finished, he said, "I'd like your thoughts on where I go from here."

Miles's father sat holding his chin in his hand for several minutes and then replied, "Are you certain that the man you met was Charles d'Orleans?"

"I had never met the man before, but I doubt an imposter could have commandeered a French man-of-war. Jean Farrgot seemed sure of his identity."

"Well, I suppose we'll let someone in Whitehall decide if this is a legitimate peace offering. All you can do is pass it on."

"Yes, but the question is to whom?"

"I agree that the Queen's health suggests that we don't involve the Palace. I have a good relationship with Robert Harley — Earl of Oxford, Earl Mortimer, and Lord High Treasurer. He has the ear of the Queen and is Her Majesty's chief minister. I suggest that we travel to London and have a chat with Harley."

"When should we leave?"

"I'll send a dispatch rider to Harley tonight asking for an audience as soon as possible. I'll tell him that we can be reached at your home in Kensington. We'll leave at first light. Now, I suggest that you find your wife and child before you're missed."

Miles thanked his father and bounded up the stairs to the nursery. He found Annie holding the baby, Annie and Lady Conway both cooing to Stuart with baby talk. Miles kissed his wife and mother and told them of the plans to leave for London at dawn. Miles took Stuart from Annie, put him on his shoulders, and raced around the nursery making horse sounds. He played with Stuart until the child began to get cranky. Annie took Stuart back and said, "I think we need to change his nappy and let him have some milk."

Miles left the nursery and found Johnny sitting at the kitchen table with a steaming cup of tea. He told Johnny to have the carriage ready for the morning trip. Miles caught the aroma of food on the stove and realized he hadn't eaten since leaving the ship

Mrs. Lattimore, the family's longtime cook, caught this out of the corner of her eye and said, "Have a seat, and I'll sneak you a quick supper. Little boys never change."

Miles obediently took a place next to Johnny and devoured the food, just as he had done so many times before he'd left for the Navy.

Annie had insisted that Stuart's bed be moved from the nursery to their bedroom. The next morning, Miles managed to slip out of bed, while it was still dark, without making a sound. Both baby and mother were still asleep when Miles eased down the stairs and joined his father for a quick breakfast. When they left for London, the sun was just peeking over the eastern horizon.

Miles and Lord Conway arrived at 1315 High Street just after noon, and Carson met them at the stable door with a message for Lord Conway. The earl quickly read the letter and said, "There will not be time to tarry. Lord Mortimer will see us at his office in the Banqueting House in Whitehall at two o'clock today."

Miles instructed Carson to have their overnight bags placed in their rooms and told Johnny to take them to Whitehall. The carriage stopped on Horse Guards Road, opposite the front entrance to the building. Banqueting House was the only structure of Whitehall Palace that survived the fire in 1691. Designed almost a hundred years before by Inigo Jones, the building had been entirely restored. Miles and Lord Conway were met by a footman, who instructed Johnny to move the carriage to the stable area and escorted Miles and his father up a flight of stairs to the Lord High Treasurer's suite of offices.

The father and son were met by a handsome young man, dressed in the height of London fashion. He told them that he was Martin Barclay, secretary to Lord Mortimer, and that the lord would join them soon. They took seats in an antechamber with high vaulted ceilings. Oil portraits of Queen Anne and her predecessors, dating back to William, lined the walls. Miles noted the absence of any paintings from the Cromwell period and thought, "The victors always write history."

Within minutes, a door on the far wall opened, and Robert Harley — Earl of Oxford, Earl Mortimer, and Lord High Treasurer — walked in and said, "Conway, it's been too long. How are you and Lady Louise?"

"Fine, Robert. She sends her regards." Lord Conway nodded toward Miles and added, "This is my son, Major Miles Ransom, and, as I said in my note, Miles has a message from the French government that I thought you'd want to hear."

The elegantly dressed man turned to Miles and, with a smile, said, "Sir Miles and his exploits at Mahone

Bay are well-known to those of us in the Queen's service, but I was not aware of any diplomatic post held by our young hero. Let us sit and hear what Sir Miles has to say."

Harley led them into his private office and suggested that they take a seat at a sturdy oak table looking out over the Horse Guards' barracks and the grounds of St. James's Palace. Harley noticed Miles admiring the view and said, "Yes, Sir Miles, it is quite a panorama. I consider it the most pleasant part of this position. Now, tell me what Charles d'Orleans had to say."

Miles carefully related the conversation held on *La Courone,* trying to leave nothing out. When he finished, Mortimer sat quietly for a moment and then asked, "Did the duke say explicitly that Louis XIV would relinquish any claim to the Spanish throne?"

"Yes, and he had me commit the other terms of his offer to memory."

"I see, and, of course, I'll want to hear them, but the French claim to the throne of Spain is the core issue that brought about the current war, and you say the French are willing to give it up?"

"The duke was quite emphatic on that point."

"Well, let's hear the rest of their terms. Anything beyond the succession will be, as they say, icing on the cake."

Miles related the terms from memory, including the French acquiescence to recognize Britain's claim to Acadia, or, as it was now known, Nova Scotia. When Miles had finished, Mortimer replied, "The French terms are more than we'd ever hoped. I'm not surprised to hear that they are willing to surrender their claim to Nova Scotia. I suspect General Nicholson's occupation of Port Royal might have made that inevitable. Nicholson has been appointed Governor of Nova Scotia and has moved to impose British rule quickly."

"Yes, sir, I've read about it in the papers. It's good that we don't have to withdraw after so much blood has been spilt."

"I'm sure you are pleased, Sir Miles, since part of the blood spilt was your own. Have you completely recovered from your chest wound?"

"I have, sir. Thank you for asking."

Harley pulled a velvet rope, and the young man who had met them came into the room. Mortimer smiled and said, "Martin, would you be so kind as to have tea brought in to us?"

When the tea had been served, Harley talked about

politics with Lord Conway and then turned to Miles, asking, "Well, Sir Miles, I understand Orleans interrupted your visit to Portugal and Italy. Do you plan to continue your tour?"

"I'm not certain. Lady Ransom and I may choose to return to Boston. Her parents have never seen young Stuart, and I know she misses her mother. Besides, I'm considering purchasing some land in the Carolinas and settling there."

"Do you plan to resign your commission in the Navy?"

"I'd prefer not to, but I may have no choice in the matter. I'd like to keep my commission and be on extended leave."

"Do you think you'd have an interest in joining our diplomatic efforts? You seem to have the trust of the man who will most likely be Regent of France in the near future."

"No, sir. I've no formal education and speak no other languages. My talents, if any, lie in the military."

"Well, think it over. I'm sure we could work something out if you change your mind. Often, there is more to diplomacy than tact and protocol. We would like to have officers who can be more active, if need be." Harley stood and said, "Conway, you should be very proud of Sir Miles. He has made a name for himself in the highest circles of our government. Please, keep me informed of his plans. I want to thank both of you for bringing me this good news. Maybe we can end this wasteful war."

Lord Conway and Miles stood and shook Harley's hand, and young Barclay appeared, as if by magic, and escorted them to where Johnny and the carriage stood waiting.

The carriage pulled on to Horse Guards Road, and Lord Conway said, "Miles, don't you think you should consider the earl's offer of a position?"

"Not really. I don't want to spend the rest of my life dealing with intrigue and diplomatic obtuseness. I will always respond to a call to service, but, as I told the earl, I'm better suited to direct action."

"You mentioned going back to Boston. Is that your plan?"

"I'll want to discuss it with Annie, but I'm leaning in that direction."

"If you decide to go, then when would you leave?"

"If we're to go this year, then I'd want to sail before winter hits the North Atlantic. I'd like to pay a visit to Carolina while we're in North America, and next spring would be a perfect time."

The men returned to Miles's home and agreed to have dinner at Lord Conway's club, but each retired to his room to rest and dress for dinner. Miles took a short nap and then put on his formal uniform. He found his father sitting in the library, nursing a glass of whiskey. Lord Conway was dressed formally, complete with his best wig. He raised his glass and said, "We have time for a wee bit of single malt before we leave. Come, join me."

The two sat and chatted for a while. Then Miles asked, "Tell me about your club."

Lord Conway took a sip and replied, "White's, as our club is known, was formed in 1693 by a group of prominent men in government, the military, and the church. I was included as a founding member. We purchased a building on St. James, Piccadilly, and converted it to include quiet seating and fine dining. We also have well-appointed rooms for members visiting London."

"Do you use it often?"

"Yes, especially when the House is in session. Your brother, David, lives nearby, so it gives us a place to meet while I'm in London."

Miles and Lord Conway arrived at the elegant

building just before eight o'clock. They were ushered in by a footman and led by a butler to Lord Conway's seating. Lord Conway ordered whiskey, looked around the room, and said, "Miles, the most influential men in the realm are members here. That's the Earl of Pembroke, who was Lord High Admiral until 1709, and he is sitting with Thomas Tenison, the Archbishop of Canterbury. It is not unusual to see members of the royal family either."

Father and son finished their whiskeys and moved to the elegantly appointed dining room. They ate their meals and talked about the meeting with Harley. They were having a last glass of wine when the butler handed Lord Conway a folded note. The earl read it and said, "Inform Lord Cooper that we'll be pleased to join him."

Lord Conway turned to Miles and explained, "Anthony Cooper, Earl of Shaftesbury, has invited us to join him in the smoker for brandy and cigars. I'm surprised that he is here. He's been gravely ill for over a year. I have always respected Lord Cooper. He and I served on the Admiralty committee in the House."

The men stood, and Miles followed his father to a room in the back of the club that appeared to be an extensive library. Bookshelves lined the walls, which were hung with portraits of deceased members. There was an elderly gentleman, sitting alone, with a brandy snifter and a freshly lit cigar. When he saw Miles and Lord Conway, he nodded that they were to join him.

Lord Conway insisted that the man keep his seat, grasped his outstretched hand, shook it, and said, "Anthony, this is my son, Major Miles Ransom of Her Majesty's Royal Marines."

Cooper indicated that they should have a seat and replied, "This young man needs very little introduction. I spoke to Harley earlier today, and he tells me that we owe a debt of gratitude to Major Ransom. Not only does he excel in war, but it seems he has helped in peacemaking, as well. Quite an accomplishment for one so young."

Miles took Cooper's hand and replied, "Thank you, Lord Cooper. I've only done my duty in both cases, but I am grateful for the kind words."

The trio took a seat, and a footman brought two brandies and a box of Spanish cigars. Miles bit the end of his cigar and lit his father's before he lit his own. Everyone took a sip of the brandy, and Miles thought that both the brandy and cigars were of top quality. Lord Conway looked at Lord Cooper and said, "Anthony, I know you have been ill as of late, and it is good to see that you're improving."

"I'm not at all certain that I am improving, but, after Harley told me that you and your son were here in London for the evening, I took a chance that I might find you here. I wanted to meet the victor of Mahone Bay."

"Yes, we're staying the night at Miles's home in Kensington and will return to Conway Hall in the morning. I wish you had joined us for dinner."

"Meals no longer hold any interest for me. Nothing I eat agrees with me, and I'm living on porridge and potatoes. But, I can still enjoy a glass of brandy and a good smoke, so I looked forward to this evening."

Lord Cooper's attention seemed to drift away for a moment, but he quickly recovered and picked up the conversation.

"Harley believes, and I agree, that the Crown owes young Miles a debt of gratitude, and he has asked me to help find a suitable method of payment. Harley mentioned that Miles might be interested in securing land suitable for farming in our colony of Carolina. Is this true, Miles?"

"Yes, sir. The firm that tends to my assets suggested that I might do this and felt that Carolina offered the best opportunity to find new land."

"I'm sure that my position as one of the proprietors of Carolina was the reason that Harley called on me. He suggested that I aid Sir Miles in securing a suitable tract of land, if he chooses to settle there."

"I've never been south of Boston, so I know nothing of the Southern Colonies. If Lady Ransom agrees, then we'll sail to Boston for Christmas. After the holiday season, I would plan a trip to Charlestown to begin looking into purchasing some land."

"I see, and when would you leave for Boston?"

"If we are to arrive this year, then we must go soon. Because I'm traveling with Annie and the baby, I don't want to be in the mid-Atlantic in winter."

Lord Cooper thought for a moment and then replied, "I'd like a chance to visit with the other proprietors before you sail. Will you be here in London?"

"If we are to sail before winter, then we must leave by September 1. It will take close to 60 days to make the voyage. We will probably move to Conway Hall and sail from Southampton. I'll close the London house as soon as possible."

"Yes, you will not have the currents and winds to aid your voyage. I've crossed to Carolina a total of three times, and I agree that you want to avoid winter in the North Atlantic. I will confer with the other owners and be back in touch with you before you sail."

Miles thanked Lord Cooper for any help he could provide as he and Annie sought a future home. Lord Conway looked at his pocket watch and suggested that they finish their brandies and allow Lord Cooper to retire for the evening. Cooper was visibly relieved. He soon stood and shuffled away. Lord Conway and Miles stood as he left, and then Miles's father suggested that they have a last brandy. When the drink was served, he turned to Miles and said, "It seems that you've made quite an impression among highly placed men. I suspect you will have considerable assistance when you get to Charlestown, and I'm confident that you will go as soon as you can."

"Yes, I agree. Annie will be thrilled at the prospect, and I need to get about figuring out what to do with the rest of my life. Now, let's get a good night's sleep; it's been a busy day."

Johnny and the carriage were waiting, and soon they were back in Miles's home. Lord Conway went straight to bed, and Miles told Johnny to be prepared to return to Conway Hall in the morning. Miles asked Mr. Carson to come into the study and informed him of their plans to close the London home. Carson asked, "Sir Miles, do you want me to dismiss the staff?"

"No, Carson. I'd prefer to keep things as they are. You may grant each member time off, with pay, as you see fit. I have no idea when we will return, but I want you to maintain the status quo. If you have any problems, then my brother David will be nearby to aid you. Do you have any questions?"

"No, sir. I hope you, Lady Ransom, and the young master have a safe voyage to America, and you may be sure that all will be in order when you return."

Miles and his father left early the next morning and were back at Conway Hall just after noon. Miles allowed Johnny to tend to his bags and ran off to find Annie.

18 THE QUEEN'S CAPTAIN

Miles found Annie in the nursery playing with Stuart. He kissed both of them and said, "If you've got a moment, there's something we need to discuss."

"Oh dear! I hope you haven't gotten into more mischief in London."

"No, actually the visit with the Lord High Treasurer went very well. I told him what Charles d'Orleans requested, and it's now in the hands of the powers that be. I got a pat on the head and a job offer."

"What sort of job offer?"

"Harley offered me a diplomatic position."

"And?"

"I thanked him but turned it down. I told him that we

had other plans."

"We do?"

"Yes, I thought we might go to Boston for Christmas. I know you are caught up in the Lady Ransom saga, but I'd kind of like to see your parents if you think you can work it into your social calendar."

Annie jumped into his arms, hugged him tightly, and cried, "Oh, Miles, are you serious? Could we really get back to Boston in time for Christmas?"

"Yes, I'm serious, and we can be there if we leave before September."

"I'll tell Temperance to start packing right away. I've missed my folks so much."

"I'll try to book passage on the *Mary Celeste* for her return to Boston."

"Miles, I can't tell you how happy this makes me. What will we do after Christmas — return to England?"

"No, the weather will be too bad until spring, and, besides, I want us to pay a visit to the Carolina Colony. I've been thinking we might buy some land and settle there. How would you feel about that?"

"It sounds exciting! I've loved London, and being Lady Ransom has been fun. However, I will never really be part of all of this, and life in the country sounds beautiful."

"Well, we'll go to Charlestown in the spring and see what we can find. We should start to pack. We may have to charter a ship just to haul your wardrobe."

Miles and Johnny began making the necessary arrangements to sail at the end of the month. Miles was able to book passage on the *Mary Celeste,* which was scheduled to sail on August 29. He broke the news to his parents over dinner and was pleased and relieved to see that both of them were supportive of his plans. He and Johnny drove to London, where they picked up all the items that they planned to take on the voyage.

While in London, Miles spent an evening with David and Isabelle and told them of his plans. David offered to help in any way he could, and Isabelle said she would go to Conway Hall right away to help Annie with last-minute details. Miles asked David to keep in touch with Carson and help him with the house on High Street. David treated Miles to dinner at White's that evening.

The week before they were scheduled to sail was filled with unexpected but manageable problems, and both Miles and Annie were kept busy. On the morning of August 26, a dispatch rider came with a packet addressed to Miles. He took it into his father's study and found Lord Conway reading the latest edition of *The London Review*. When Miles came through the door, the earl looked up and asked, "Did I hear a rider out front?"

"Yes, it was a dispatch rider from Robert Harley with a packet addressed to me."

Miles held the leather-bound package up so that his father could see it, and Lord Conway said, "Well, open it and let's see what Robert has to say."

Miles untied the fastened buckle and discovered two sealed envelopes inside—each addressed to him. He broke the seal on the first and unfolded an official communication from the Admiralty that proclaimed the following:

By the Commissioners for Executing the Office of Lord High Admiral of the United Kingdom:

Miles Stuart Ransom, KC, is hereby appointed a Captain in Her Majesty's Fleet.

By the Power of Authority given us by Her Majesty's Letters Patent under the Great Seal, we do hereby constitute and appoint you a Captain in Her Majesty's

Fleet. Charging and commanding you in that rank or in any higher rank to which you may be promoted to observe and execute the Queen's Regulations and Admiralty Instructions for the Government of Her Majesty's Naval Service and all such orders and instructions as you shall from time to time receive from us or your superior officers for Her Majesty's Service. And likewise charging and commanding all officers and men subordinate to you according to the regulations, instructions or orders to behave themselves with all due respect and obedience to you their superior officer. Given under our hands and the Seal of the Office of Admiralty this 17th day of August in the tenth year of Her Majesty's Reign.

By Command,

With Seniority of Lord High Admiral, Thomas Wentworth, Earl of Stafford

There was a note attached to the commission. Miles read it and then handed both documents to his father. The note was from Robert Harley:

**The Office of Lord High Treasurer
Robert Harley, Earl of Oxford
By Appointment of Anne Regina**

August 21, 1712

Miles Stuart Ransom, KC

Sir Miles,

It is with great pleasure that I present you with a regular commission in Her Majesty's Royal Navy. The Lord High Admiral felt that your recent service deserved recognition and that a rank in the Royal Navy would be appropriate. You have been removed from active duty until called upon by the Sovereign. You may go to America and follow your fate knowing that you will always be able to return to active service.

Your Faithful Servant,

Robert Harley, Earl of Oxford

Lord Conway read the note and document. He then said, "It appears that Harley was able to address your concerns about retaining your commission. I suspect you are among the youngest captains in the Royal Navy. I couldn't help but notice that there is another document. Better take a look."

Miles untied the ribbon on the second document and read it with utter surprise. When he'd finished, he passed it to his father and said, "You are not going to believe this." Lord Conway perused the following document:

We the proprietors of Her Majesty's Colony of Carolina on this the 18ᵗʰ day of August in the tenth year of the reign of Her Majesty, Queen Anne, do proclaim and grant title to Miles Stuart Ransom, a tract of land in the Colony described as follows:

From the center of the northernmost point on the southern bank of the Edisto River at Latitude 33° 09N, and extending one mile from said point in both directions to a point four miles south. Approximately 5,120 English acres.

Said land is granted to Miles Stuart Ransom in grateful appreciation for his service to Her Majesty, Queen Anne. Free simple title to this tract is given to Sir Miles Stuart Ransom and his descendants for perpetuity as proscribed by the Law of Primogeniture.

Signed and sealed this 18ᵗʰ day of August, 1712.

Anthony Ashley Cooper Esq.

Anthony Ashley Cooper, Earl Shaftesbury

Lord Conway smiled and said, "Looks like our

brandy and cigars at White's have paid a big dividend. I'd say that the Queen has been most generous in rewarding your service. I congratulate you, Miles. I'm very proud."

Miles replaced the documents into the packet and replied, "I doubt that any single action at sea has been so rewarded. There's a lot to be said for being at the right place at the right time."

"Yes, and doing the right thing when there. Now, best you find Lady Ransom and give her the news."

Miles thanked his father and left to find Annie. She was with Temperance, who was cradling Stuart in the gazebo down by the river. Miles trotted over and said, "Well, Annie, I hope you've enjoyed being the wife of a major because all of that has changed."

"Oh, Miles! What have you done now?"

"It seems that I have been promoted to the rank of captain in the Royal Navy and given a large grant of land in the Carolina Colony."

"How will all of this alter our lives?"

"About the same as being Lady Ransom did, and none of this will make much difference when we get to Carolina. We'll just be simple farmers."

"It sounds like you've made up your mind about

settling in Carolina."

"Yes, probably so. Unless our land is a swamp, I think I'd like to give it a try."

Miles sat and played with Stuart, who had taken his first shaky steps the week before. After a while, Miles told Annie that he would see her when she came in, and he hurried across the lawn.

On Saturday morning, Johnny loaded all of their baggage onto a large dray hitched to two Clydesdales and hauled it all to Southampton to be taken aboard the *Mary Celeste*. Miles's parents invited a few friends and neighbors for an informal farewell dinner on Sunday evening, and, on Monday morning, Miles's parents accompanied them to the dock in Southampton. After a teary goodbye on the quay, the five boarded the ship and began to ride the ebbing tide to the open Atlantic.

After several days at sea, Miles noted that Annie was experiencing nausea every morning and asked the ship's doctor to look in on her. When the doctor finished his examination, he met Miles in the galley. With a broad smile, he said, "Sir Miles, I'd say Lady Ransom is with child. You are going to be a father again."

Miles thought for a moment and then asked, "Can

you determine when the child will be born?"

"Not for certain, but, from what Lady Ransom tells me, I think you're looking at some time after the first of the year, probably in early January."

"Is there any particular caution we should observe during the voyage?"

"Not really. I suspect she will be over the morning sickness in a week or so, and then she should feel fine, unless something happens — then we'll do what we can to aid her."

Miles thanked the doctor and went immediately to their cabin to tell Annie the good news. He scooped her in his arms and said, "We're going to have another baby!"

"Don't you think I've known that?"

"Really? Why didn't you tell me?"

"I wanted to be sure I could carry the child to term, but the doctor said that I should have no problems. I hope you're pleased."

"You know I am. In fact, I couldn't be happier. The doctor estimated the birth to be in January."

"Yes, and I should be fully recovered in time for our trip to Carolina."

"We'll have to see about that when the time comes. Now, you need to take care."

The voyage took two months, but the weather was sunny, calm, and warm. They docked in Boston, and, as the ship tied up, Miles, Annie, and Stuart stood by the rail, waving at Annie's parents who were waiting on the pier. Annie smiled and held up Stuart. Her mother virtually jumped up and down with anticipation.

When the gangway had been placed, Miles picked up Stuart and followed Annie to her parents. She hugged her father, and she and her mother held a long tearful embrace. When Miles put Stuart down, he ran and leaped into his grandfather's outstretched arms.

Once everyone had hugged and kissed, Miles saw a smiling Philippe Dalhousie standing by a large dray wagon. Philippe walked over, shook Miles's hand, and said, "Welcome back, Sir Miles. You've had quite a busy time. You left as a marine major and return a Royal Navy captain. Not a bad year, I'd say. I can't wait for a full report."

"The promotion was just announced the week before we sailed. How did you know?"

"We have our own mail service, and we keep close track of our clients. The news reached me within five weeks."

"Is this service available to clients?"

"Normally it is not, but, in your case, I'm willing to include anything in our weekly sailing."

"Weekly? You must have your own fleet of ships."

"We do. Each week, a ship sails from Bordeaux and picks up mail for all of our offices worldwide. One of these ships arrives in Boston each week. It usually takes 40 to 50 days to get the latest news."

"Does your Charlestown office receive the same service?"

"It does, and you will be authorized to use it. It's good to have you back, Miles."

"One of the nicest things about coming to Boston is that I will be here for your wedding. What date have you set?"

"Well, about that. We originally planned a November wedding, but certain events changed those plans. We were married in early June."

"What made you decide to move the date?"

"Mainly the prospect of a baby due in January, but I wanted an earlier wedding, and the baby drove Rebecca to agree."

"That's excellent news! Congratulations! As it turns out, Annie is expecting another baby, also due in January. She and Rebecca can share the experience."

"Rebecca will be thrilled. Now, let me fill you in on what I've done. Since Rebecca has moved out of her house, we have held it for you and Annie to use during your stay in Boston, for a reasonable rent. I also had Nelson's Livery send over this dray to help Johnny with your baggage. I'm sure a knight and his lady don't travel light."

"Thanks, Philippe. The rental of Rebecca's house sounds perfect, and you're certainly right about a lady's not traveling light. Annie's wardrobe will fill this wagon, while I have the same baggage I had when I arrived. I appreciate the use of Rebecca's home. Also, you and I need to talk as soon as Annie, Stuart, and I get settled in."

"You'd better go now with your family. I'll be available anytime. Just let me know when you want to meet."

Milos rejoined the welcoming party, and, on the trip back to the Henry House, he shared the news of Rebecca's home. Martha frowned and said, "Oh, I was expecting you to use your rooms at the inn."

"I thought that we might do that, but we'll need more

space for Stuart and Lady Ransom's wardrobe, not to mention the new baby."

"I still can't believe that my daughter is a knight's lady who has met the Queen; my family will be so impressed!"

"Annie fit in with all the toffs like a hand in a glove, and my family loves her, as well."

Josiah spoke up and asked, "Is a knight a hereditary title?"

"No, I'm afraid it's not. It will die upon my death."

"I never thought I'd be the father of a knight's lady. The Adams family has always been unconcerned with titles, but it's different when it's one of your children."

"Quite so," Miles replied, as the carriage stopped in front of the Henry House. They entered the inn, and Miles told the driver to come back in two hours. Annie and her mother started to prepare the noon meal. Josiah and Miles got a cup of coffee and sat in the empty tavern. Miles offered a cigar and lit it for Josiah. Miles then said, "How has our business been?"

"Remarkably good. We've cultivated our reputation for good food and drink, and our revenue has seen a healthy increase."

"That's good to hear, and I have some more good news. I've been granted title to 5,000 acres of land in the Carolina Colony. Annie and I are thinking about settling there and becoming farmers."

"Granted title? Why?"

"I recently had the opportunity to relay a diplomatic matter to Robert Harley, the Lord High Treasurer, and I suspect this was his way of showing the Crown's appreciation."

Miles spent the next half hour retelling the events aboard *La Courone* and the details of his meeting with Charles d'Orleans. When Miles finished, Josiah shook his head and replied, "Not only have you met the Queen, but you've also met the most powerful man in France. You and Annie have been busy."

"Yes, we have, and we're both looking forward to having a quiet holiday season as your guests so that we can decompress."

Annie came in, wearing an apron, and her hair was wrapped in a scarf. She looked exactly as she did the first time Miles met her, and his chest ached with love. She said that the food was ready in the kitchen, and the men obediently followed her.

Thomas R. Lawrence

19 THE QUEEN'S CAPTAIN

When the two couples had finished their meal, the four of them sat around the table talking about Conway Hall and London. Josiah and Martha wanted to hear all about the home in Kensington, and, of course, meeting the Queen. Annie told them how gracious Lady Conway and Isabelle had been as she learned to be a lady. Miles shared that he had discovered that afternoon about the marriage between Philippe and Rebecca and the baby they were expecting. Annie was thrilled — she couldn't wait to see Rebecca.

Stuart woke up from his nap, just as Johnny announced the arrival of the carriage they had requested to take them to Rebecca's home. Her lovely, three-story brick town house at 116 Unity Street sat just across from the North Church. It had been built in 1689 by Rebecca's seafaring husband, and, after his death at sea, she had remained there until her recent marriage to Philippe. All of the furnishings had been left intact. Miles and Annie loved it at first sight.

The Ransoms spent their first two days moving, but Philippe had requested a meeting on Friday morning, so Miles and Philippe agreed to convene at the Dalhousie building at ten o'clock. Miles arrived with perfect punctuality and was ushered into Philippe's office. Philippe immediately rose from his desk, grasped Miles by the hand, and said, "Have a seat, and I'll have coffee served. Then, you've got to tell me all about your conquest of London."

The friends spent the next two hours sipping coffee, while Miles related the details of everything that had occurred since he left Boston. When he finished, Philippe smiled. "Is that all that happened? I can't believe you're only a knight."

Miles laughed. "Sorry to disappoint you; I'll try to do better next time. Is there any news from here?"

"Nothing that you wouldn't already know. Francis Nicholson was appointed Governor of Nova Scotia and has moved rapidly to expel the French leaders and establish British rule."

"Has he gone to Port Royal?"

"No, he continues to keep his office here in Boston.

His treatment of the French colonists has been especially brutal."

"I have to say that I'm not surprised. He is without a doubt the most arrogant and egotistical man I've ever met."

"When do you plan to travel to Charlestown?"

"It will be in the spring of next year."

"Will you take Annie with you?"

"No, and she won't like it, but I need to see our land before I drag her and the children into the unknown wilderness."

"I agree. There are still problems with the natives, not to mention last year's rebellion by Quaker dissenters. I understand that Royal Marines were sent from Virginia to deal with it. I hear from our Charlestown office that order has been restored, but the resentment remains."

"I don't want to end up in the middle of a religious war. The Queen has the ultimate authority in our colonies, and I'm a staunch Royalist and Anglican."

"Also, the European settlers are fighting the Tuscarora tribe over land rights. I don't know if your area would be involved, but it's possible. The natives attacked a settlement on the Pamlico River earlier this year and massacred several hundred people."

"That sounds like its far north of my grant, but you can't be sure. Maps of the area are sketchy, at best."

"How would you like company on your trip? I need to visit our Charlestown office, and it would be the perfect time to introduce you to our manager there."

"I would welcome the company. Annie and Rebecca will have given birth by then, and we could sail in March or April."

"I'll get dispatches off to Bordeaux and Charlestown, advising them of our intentions. We can set you up with our Charlestown office while we're there. I'll be sure there is a current account of your assets when we arrive."

"That sounds ideal. Now, I have a question for you. What do you and Rebecca plan to do with her house?"

"We've been debating whether to sell it or keep it for rental property. Why, are you interested?"

"I may be. Annie seems to love it, and we'll need a home for return trips to Boston."

"Allow me to talk to Rebecca, and I'll let you know."

The men sat for another half hour. Then, Miles

returned to Unity Street and spent the balance of the day with Annie and Stuart. At breakfast the next day, Annie asked Miles to step into the garden. When they were alone, she said, "There's something I need to tell you."

"Yes?"

"Temperance and Johnny plan to be married."

"Oh, I think that's just fine! I had no idea they were involved, did you?"

"Of course! She and I share everything."

"I see — and when is this wedding to take place?"

"Next week, in Braintree, and we're standing with them."

"I'll be delighted, but what's the rush?"

"There will be yet another baby in January."

"You have to wonder just what happened last April. Must have been a particularly romantic month."

"Don't be flip. Our baby will have at least two playmates now!"

"Oh well — the more, the merrier, I always say."

"You might want to say something to Johnny; he's in

a daze since Temperance told him."

"I will, and we'll have to find a special gift for them. Do you think they'll want to keep their positions?"

"Temperance assures me that they do, and I can't tell you how relieved I am. I depend heavily on her."

Johnny and Temperance were married by Jonathan Adams, and Miles and Annie gave them the gift of a week at an inn on Cape Cod. The holidays arrived, and the entire family gathered at the Henry House for the harvest feast. Christmas was spent in Braintree. Annie, Temperance, and Rebecca were all in the latter stages of their terms, and, shortly after the New Year's celebrations, Rebecca gave birth to a healthy baby boy. Miles sat with Philippe during the delivery and took him to the inn while the midwife tended to Rebecca. The men sat at a table near the fire, and, after offering Philippe a cigar, Miles said, "Congratulations! You have a son."

"It seems almost impossible to believe that Rebecca and I made that little creature. I don't think men will ever understand motherhood."

"You're right about that, and, for my part, I'm glad it works the way it does. Men would never endure the pain of delivery voluntarily."

Philippe nodded in agreement and then said, "I've

wanted to talk to you about the house on Unity Street, but things have been so frantic that I've not had a chance. Rebecca and I would love for you and Annie to make it your home in Boston, and we'll either give you a long-term lease or, if you prefer, you may buy it."

"I've been reluctant to broach the subject — Annie and I love the house, and we would be grateful for the opportunity to own it."

"You can consider it yours, with one caveat. Rebecca would insist that you retain the staff. They have been with her since childhood, and she wants them always to be cared for."

"That won't be a problem. We think they're special, and, besides, if we settle in Carolina, then you'll be managing it anyway. Just draw up the papers and make sure you price it to give Rebecca a fair sale."

"I'll have the papers ready next week."

"Good. Now, I need to get you back to your wife and baby."

Miles and Annie stood as godparents at the christening of Jean-Maurice Dalhousie, and, just a week later, Temperance gave birth to a little girl. The new mother was recovering a few days later, when

Annie woke Miles in the middle of the night and said, "My water just broke. Would you get Mother and the midwife as soon as you can? The pains are already starting."

Miles leapt out from under the covers and knocked on Johnny's bedroom door. When Johnny opened it, Miles told him to fetch the midwife. Miles lit the wood stove and placed a large pan of water on the top. He wasn't certain why, but those had been the midwife's instructions. Miles returned to Annie. Martha had cleaned the bed and done her best to make Annie as comfortable as possible.

When Martha and the midwife came rushing into the room, they chased Miles out, with instructions to remain calm. Following their advice, Miles went into the kitchen, where he found Johnny and Josiah sitting at the table drinking coffee. The expectant father poured himself a cup and joined them. They heard Annie cry out with the onset of the labor pains, and Johnny smiled, saying, "It won't be long now."

Annie's screaming continued for what seemed like forever, and Miles noticed the first hints of dawn reflecting off the icicles hanging from the eaves. The men had just made their second pot of coffee, when Martha came in and said, "Miles, Annie is having too much trouble. The baby is turned wrong, and the midwife thinks we should call Doctor Spencer."

Miles said urgently, "Johnny and I will go immediately!"

Miles and Johnny rapidly made the short ride to Conrad's home, where they found the doctor awake and in his clinic. Miles explained the situation. Conrad grabbed his bag and hurried with them out to the carriage. On the way back to Unity Street, the doctor remarked, "From what the midwife said, I suspect we have what we call a breeched baby. While this is not uncommon, it is worrisome that the midwife has not been able to turn the baby."

Miles desperately asked, "How serious is this?"

"It will depend on turning the child into the proper position in the birth canal. If I can do that, then your wife can continue with a standard delivery."

"And if you can't?"

"Then the only option is a Cesarean delivery. Again, it's not an uncommon procedure — but riskier to the mother and the child."

When Doctor Spencer had rushed upstairs, Miles retreated to the kitchen and joined Josiah. He explained what the doctor had said, and Josiah replied, "I know it's hard to do, but try not to worry. Annie is young, healthy, and quite a fighter. She'll pull through this."

Miles nodded and said, "I'm sure she will, but I hate the pain she's enduring. If you don't mind, I'd like to step into the garden for a few moments. Call me if there's news."

Miles put on his thick woolen coat and walked into the garden behind the kitchen. He hardly noticed the freezing air. Silently, he pleaded, "God, you know I'm not a praying man, but, if you are there, please be with my Annie and help her through this terrible ordeal."

Miles walked up and down the garden in deep thought and prayer, as the sun rose above the rooftops. He was lost in his thoughts when Josiah came to get him.

"Miles, the doctor has been unable to turn the baby, and he has decided to do the Cesarean procedure. He told me that it is his experience that both mother and child survive. It seems he has a formula that he used in Italy. He called it 'ether,' and he said it would put Annie to sleep while he takes the baby. The doctor did say that, in the event of having to make a choice, he would always choose the mother's life over the child's."

"Of course! Annie and I can have other children! I'd be devastated to lose the child, but, if it has to be, then it must be done."

Miles and Josiah returned to the kitchen and started on the third pot of coffee. Martha came down to get the pan of simmering water and said, "Doctor Spencer has prepared Annie for the surgery. He tells me that it won't be long now."

No more than 15 minutes had passed, when they heard a long, moaning scream. Miles winced and said, "I hope that's a good sign."

Josiah looked pale and stricken. He slowly said, "Miles, that wasn't Annie; it was Martha."

Miles leapt to his feet and met Doctor Spencer as he was coming down the stairs.

"Miles, I'm afraid I have terrible news. I lost both your wife and the baby girl due to massive hemorrhaging. There was nothing I could do to save them. I think you'd better wait a bit before you go up."

Miles pushed Spencer aside and bounded up the stairs, three at a time. Miles raced into the bedroom and saw Annie's body covered in blood, the lifeless form of a baby girl lying beside her. He knelt, took his wife's hand, and held it to his chest. Miles rocked back and forth with a low sob coming from deep inside him. Martha, her face streaked with tears, put her hand on his shoulder and said, "Miles, you must leave now. I should clean Annie, and the doctor needs to close the incision."

Miles stumbled as he tried to stand and nodded in agreement. He took one more look at Annie and the baby and then slowly descended to the kitchen. Miles and Josiah sat in silence, each in his thoughts, both in quiet desperation. As he was leaving, Doctor Spencer stopped in to offer his condolences, but both men, grief-stricken and in shock, could only silently nod in response to his kind words. Shortly, Martha came down to tell Miles and Josiah that they could come up. When they entered the room, Annie and her baby lay together on the freshly made bed, both peaceful, as if asleep.

Miles stood and stared at his beautiful, spirited, wonderful wife and their tiny infant daughter for the last time. He could not bring himself to walk away until, finally, Martha put her arm around him. Resignedly, Miles uttered, "I will see to the funerals. I believe Annie would want to be buried in the churchyard in Braintree. I'll ride now to let Jonathan know."

Martha nodded in agreement and replied, "If you and Jonathan will make the burial arrangements, then Josiah and I will prepare Annie and the baby. We'll bring them later this afternoon."

"I'd like to name the baby Louise Adams Ransom, to honor both my mother and the two of you, if you have no objection."

"Of course not—we'll meet you at Jonathan's house before sundown."

Miles had Johnny fetch a horse from the livery stable, and Miles rode with calm deliberation toward Braintree. When he came to the point in the road where he and Annie had met the bandits, he turned off and galloped over the fields, remembering their wild ride to safety so long ago. The memory of Annie burned a hole in his chest, and tears streaked his face. Miles found Jonathan at the church, and, though he could hardly get the words to form, Miles gave Jonathan the wretched news of the deaths of his beloved Annie and their baby daughter. Solemnly, Jonathan agreed to have the burials the next morning as requested, but he asked Miles to please join him in the church to pray together. Miles allowed himself to be led into the small, quiet sanctuary.

When Josiah and Martha arrived with their dear Annie and their baby granddaughter, the bodies— both dressed in simple, white gowns—were placed in plain, pine coffins. A wake was held in Jonathan's parlor, and, in the early morning, mother and child were buried, side by side, in the churchyard. Stoically, Miles stood beside the open graves and said goodbye to his true love and a little girl he would never know. He could only go through the motions of receiving the family members and his good friend, Philippe Dalhousie.

When the simple burial service was finished, Miles insisted on covering the caskets himself. When he had completed the mounds of fresh dirt, Miles found Annie's father and said, "Josiah, I need to have some time to myself. Could you and Martha take responsibility for Stuart while I'm away?"

"Of course. How long will you be gone, Miles?"

"I don't know — until I think I can go on without Annie."

"Do what you need to do, and know that Stuart will be well cared for. Is there anything else we can do to help you?"

"Just let Philippe know that I still want the house on Unity Street, and I'll see him when I return."

Miles embraced Josiah, mounted his horse, and rode off alone. He went back to Unity Street and changed into warm, everyday clothing and a rain slicker. He then rode his horse to the warehouse on Battery

Wharf. Miles asked the manager to find him a one-man skiff and to return the horse to Nelson's Livery.

The manager found a skiff, per Miles's instructions, and loaded camping gear and dried food aboard. When all was ready, Miles climbed into the small boat, raised the sails, and headed toward the open ocean. He sailed between Deer Island and Long Island and then headed east. Miles passed just to the north of Lovell Island, continued to Calf Island, and, finally, reached Outer Brewster Island, the last land before the open Atlantic.

Miles sailed into a protected cove on the northeastern end of the island and pulled the skiff above the high-tide line. When Miles had loaded his gear on his back, he climbed from the beach to the headland. When he found a copse of trees on a hill overlooking the Atlantic, he made a rustic camp. Miles had just finished his canvas lean-to, when the leading edge of a winter storm came crashing ashore.

Miles endured the snow, sleet, and icy rain of January and February, while sitting by his fire, staring out to sea. He thought of Annie and wept bitterly day after day, and he allowed his grief to wrap around him like a dark cloak. Winter morphed into early spring without his notice.

One morning in mid-March, Miles realized that the days were beginning to warm up, and the first signs of spring were poking their heads up in the meadows. He gathered his gear, made his way back to the skiff, and returned to Boston.

Philippe was sitting at his desk, when his clerk ushered in a shaggy-haired man with an unkempt beard. His face was weathered and brown, and, at first, Philippe did not recognize him. After a moment, Philippe smiled and said, "Miles, I take it you have returned to the living."

"Yes. Are you ready to go to Charlestown?"

"I *can* be by early April, which should give you time to get a bath and shave. You need to do both as soon as possible. By the way, where did you go? The last anyone heard, you were seen in a one-man skiff, headed out to sea."

"I camped on Outer Brewster Island."

"Did you accomplish your purpose?"

"I think so. I've put the memory of Annie in a special place in my heart, but I need to get on with my life. I've still got Stuart to think about."

"I took the liberty of sending a letter to your father, telling him of Annie's death. I hope you don't have any objection."

"Of course not — I should have written him myself before I left."

"Miles, you were fortunate to be able to function at that time. Now, clean up before you go to the inn to see Stuart, Josiah, and Martha; you look a fright right now. Rebecca and I will want to have you to dinner soon, but, for now, go see your son."

Miles walked to the house on Unity Street, where he was met at the door by Johnny. He took one look at Miles and yelled out, "Temperance, draw a hot bath! Sir Miles is home!"

Miles sank deep into the scalding hot water and let the aches and pains begin to dissolve. He lathered his face and removed the beard. After wrapping himself in a robe, Miles allowed Temperance to trim his unruly head of hair. In late afternoon, Johnny brought the carriage around, and, dressed in clothes that hung on his gaunt body, Miles rode to the Henry House.

When Miles entered the inn, Josiah was standing by the bar and barely glanced at the stranger coming in. He took another look and shouted, "Miles Ransom, what has happened to you?"

Josiah grabbed Miles and lifted him off his feet. As Annie's father set Miles down, he called out to the kitchen, "Martha, Miles is home, and he looks like he needs a meal!"

Martha walked through the door, holding Stuart by the hand, and, when the boy saw Miles, he ran into his arms, crying, "Da Da!" Miles picked him up and kissed the top of his head. He knew that, finally, he was able to be back home.

20 THE QUEEN'S CAPTAIN

Miles held Stuart close and realized that this child was his only connection to Annie. He fought back the tears and then held Martha in a long embrace. She pulled away, looked at him, and said, "Miles Ransom, you sit down right now, and I'm going to fix you a decent meal. You look terrible."

"That seems to be the consensus. I have to admit that I'm ravenous."

Martha began warming things on the stove, and Josiah poured Miles a hot cup of coffee. They sat as the food was being prepared, and Josiah asked, "What are your plans?"

"Philippe Dalhousie and I are going to sail for Charlestown as soon as passage can be arranged. I want to carry out the plan that Annie and I had dreamed of making a reality. I hope you and Martha will continue to care for Stuart until I've had a chance to see my land. Once I know what I have, I'll begin clearing and building a home there. Johnny will be going with me, and it would be nice if Temperance could move into my rooms here in the inn."

Martha set a steaming bowl of clam chowder in front of him and said, "Of course, Temperance will be most welcome. She's family, and I can help her with Alice."

Josiah asked, "How long do you think you'll be gone?"

"It depends on the situation when I get there, but I would expect to return in the fall of this year. I hate to miss Stuart's second birthday, but I need to move on with our plans."

Miles was on his second bowl of chowder when Philippe pushed through the kitchen door. Philippe took a look at him and said, "Well, you certainly smell much better than the last time I saw you, and I hope Martha can put some meat on your bones."

Josiah poured another cup of coffee for Philippe, and Martha offered him a bowl of chowder, which he declined.

Josiah said, "Miles tells us you'll be going to Charlestown with him."

"Yes, I need to visit our office there, and, to that end,

I've arranged for the two of us to travel on the next Dalhousie courier ship, which is due to sail on April 11."

Miles looked up from his chowder and said, "Johnny will be coming with me; will there be room on board for him?"

"Not a problem," Philippe replied.

"Good," Miles said. "This will give me a few weeks to prepare for the voyage."

"Rebecca has instructed me to invite the three of you to our house on April 8, for a departure dinner."

Martha replied, "That will be delightful, Philippe. I should have Miles back in shape by then."

Miles agreed and added, "Do you think we'll need to buy supplies here before we sail?"

"No, Charlestown is a thriving port, and everything you'll need will be available."

Early in the morning of the next day, Miles walked to Nelson's Livery, where he saddled a horse and rode to Braintree. He dismounted at the church and tied the horse to the fence. Then, he walked to Annie's and Louise's graves. The dirt was still bare, but Josiah and Martha had placed marble markers on their graves.

Miles stood with his hat in his hand and read.

LADY ANN ADAMS RANSOM

ANNIE

Loving Daughter, Wife, and Mother

1694–1713

Rest with the Angels

Miles stood in silence. Then, he looked at his daughter's grave.

LOUISE ADAMS RANSOM

Daughter of Miles and Ann Ransom

1713

Miles stood by the graves dry-eyed but filled with overwhelming pain and sadness. He had cried himself out during his stay on Brewster, but, this morning, he acknowledged an empty place in his chest that he knew could never be filled. Miles saw the open space beside his wife and daughter and realized it was being saved for him. Silently, he promised Annie that he would always take care of Stuart and that he would do his best to fulfill their dream of settling in the south. Miles stood staring at the graves for a few minutes more, and then he remounted his horse and rode back to Boston.

Several days before they were scheduled to sail for Charlestown, Miles dressed in his naval captain's uniform and had Johnny take him to the pier where *HMS Dragon* was moored. Miles requested permission to embark and was piped aboard by a young ensign he didn't recognize.

Miles introduced himself and asked to see Commander Sparks. The young man saluted and replied, "You must mean Captain Sparks. If you'll follow me, I'll take you to his cabin."

"That won't be necessary, son. I know the way."

Miles descended below deck and made his way to the captain's cabin. He rapped on the hatch, and a deep voice said, "Come in."

Miles found Lloyd Sparks standing in his shirtsleeves, bent over his chart table. Miles smiled and said, "You seem to have made yourself at home in Sir William's cabin."

A wide grin broke across Sparks' face, and he rushed around the table, grabbed Miles by the shoulder, embraced him, and said, "Damn, Miles. I was worried that I'd never see you again. I heard the awful news about Annie and your daughter, and, God, I hate it for you."

"Thank you, Lloyd."

"How are you?"

"Well, I've got a son to care for, so I'm trying to go on with my life. I assume you're now captain of the *Dragon*. Where is Sir William?"

"He was promoted to rear admiral and recalled to London to serve on the Admiralty staff."

Miles nodded and then replied, "I'm pleased to see that you were promoted to captain. You deserve it. Is Bob Gaines still on board?"

"No, Bob was transferred by your Colonel Holmes to duty in Asia. Holmes, Reed, and Nicholson tried everything they could to ruin Sir William, but, in the end, they failed. I notice you're out of marine major's uniform, and you're impersonating a Royal Navy captain."

"Actually, I'm on an extended leave, but, yes, Sir William isn't the only one with friends in the Admiralty."

"A knighthood AND a naval commission. That must have been some action at Mahone Bay."

"Yeah, and a grant of 5,000 acres in Carolina to boot. Fate works in strange ways."

Sparks insisted that Miles stay and have a glass of

brandy and a cigar. They talked about the *Dragon* and old times until Miles had to return to shore. He rode a cab to Unity Street, took off his uniform, and carefully stored it away. His official duties as a naval officer were over, unless he was recalled to duty. On Saturday evening, Miles and the Adams couple dined with Rebecca and Philippe. While the evening was subdued, everyone seemed to enjoy the food and fellowship.

Early Tuesday morning, everyone gathered at the pier to send Philippe, Johnny, and Miles on their way. The trio boarded the Dalhousie packet ship, *Aquitaine*, and sailed into the Atlantic. The *Aquitaine* made her way into the open Atlantic but kept in close to shore to evade the Gulf Stream, as its warm currents surged to the north.

The chosen route posed some risk of running aground, particularly along the coast of Northern Carolina, but the vessel managed to avoid the graveyard of ships just off Cape Hatteras. Philippe spent most of his time in the owner's cabin, suffering from mal de mer, while Miles took his usual spot in the rigging, where he admired the expert seamanship of the *Aquitaine*'s captain. The voyage took just over two weeks. They rounded the headland of Sullivan's Island and docked in Charlestown before noon on April 28, 1713.

There was a carriage waiting for the travelers, and the driver helped Johnny load their belongings. They were driven to the Dalhousie office on the corner of King and Market streets. The men were met at the door by a handsome young man with sandy, almost red hair, who was at least six feet tall. He was broad-shouldered and muscular. When he saw Philippe, he broke into a wide smile and shouted, "Cousin Pepe! I'm glad to see you made it!"

Miles rolled his eyes and muttered, "Pepe?"

Philippe laughed and replied, "Miles Ransom, this is my cousin Henri. He is my Uncle Claude's son, and we grew up together in Bordeaux. I'm sure you've noticed his hair and blue eyes; we suspect that there was a Viking somewhere in our family tree. Henri, this is my good friend, and our client, Sir Miles Ransom."

Henri extended his hand and said, "Sir Miles, we've been expecting you. Our deepest condolences on the loss of your wife and daughter."

"Thank you, Henri, and I'd prefer to be addressed as Miles, if you don't mind."

"Of course, if that is your preference. At any rate, we've prepared a report on your holdings, which, if I understand, Philippe will be managing from our office here in Charlestown."

"That depends on what I find when I visit the land recently granted to me."

Henri led them into the lobby of the firm's offices, and Miles could see Philippe taking it all in. Henri stopped by a young man's desk and said, "Jean, this is Philippe Dalhousie, the manager of our offices in the British North American colonies, and the other gentleman is one of our clients, Miles Ransom. We'll be in my office for a while, but, later, please show Philippe to his office."

Once they were seated and coffee and wine had been served, Henri reached into a drawer and removed a thick file. When he untied the ribbon, he reached out and handed it to Miles.

"We took the liberty of preparing a report on your property. I hope it will aid you in your due diligence."

Miles opened the file and read it. The report confirmed the location of the land grant and gave a brief summary of the current situation regarding the fighting between the Europeans and the Tuscarora tribe. The report concluded that after the Carolina Militia had defeated the Tuscarora chief, Hancock, at the battle of Fort Neoheroka, the threat had been removed. When he finished the report, Miles asked,

"What will happen to the Tuscarora now?"

"More than 900 were killed during the fighting; many more were captured and sold into slavery in the Caribbean; and most of the survivors have immigrated to New York and joined their cousins in the Iroquois Confederation. Those that remain in Carolina will be dealt with after a treaty is signed."

"Do you feel it's safe to bring women and children to the area of my land grant?"

"As far as the natives go, I believe it is, but, first, I'd suggest that you clear the ground and build an infrastructure to support civilized life."

Miles thought for a moment. He then asked, "Have you received my accounts?"

"Yes, and Philippe has given me the latest reports from Boston," Henri replied and handed Miles another stack of papers.

Miles found the composite financial report and saw that, as of April 1713, he had £259,396 in cash, and real property valued at £5,025.

Miles asked Philippe, "Can I draw against these funds here in Charlestown?"

"Of course—Henri is authorized to advance any sums that you may require. Now, I suggest we allow Henri to show us to our rooms so that we can get settled in. You and I will be Henri's guests for dinner this evening at Dunlap's Tavern on Bay Street, where he tells me the food is excellent."

The next morning, Miles instructed Johnny to purchase four horses and four pack mules, along with all of the tack needed to journey to the land grant. After a light breakfast at Dunlap's, Philippe went to his office, and Miles decided to pay a courtesy visit to Thomas Craven, the governor. Miles walked the short distance to the governor's office and approached a young man sitting at a desk, just inside.

"Good morning—my name is Miles Ransom," he said. "I'd like to speak with Governor Craven."

"Do you have an appointment, Mr. Ransom?"

"No, but I'm hoping he might see me anyway."

"If you'll wait for a few minutes, then I'll see if he can meet with you this morning."

The young man went up the staircase but soon returned, led by a stern-looking man in the uniform of a Royal Navy lieutenant. The officer walked up to Miles and said, "I'm James Merriweather, military attaché to Governor Craven. You can't just walk in here and demand to see His Excellency. You must first make an appointment."

Miles eyed the man and then said, "I have not demanded anything; I only asked if I could pay my respects to the governor. If it's an inconvenient time, then I can come back."

"I suggest that you submit a request to me in writing, stating the nature of your meeting, and I'll decide if the governor will see you."

Miles replied, with some irritation, "Exactly who are you again?"

"I'm Sir James Merriweather, an officer in Her Majesty's Royal Navy, and I don't have time to waste."

"Well, Sir James, I certainly don't want to waste your time. I'd appreciate it if you would tell the governor that Sir Miles Ransom, captain in the Royal Navy, attempted to pay his respects."

Miles turned on his heels and walked out of the building, steaming. He walked to Dunlap's, ordered a brandy, and lit a cigar. He was just finishing his second drink when Johnny came in.

"I hoped I'd find you here. A naval officer came to the Dalhousie office looking for you, and he seemed rather agitated."

"Oh? Well, let's allow the little fop to stew in his own juice. We can carry on with our business without the approval of the governor or his lap dog. Did you find our horses and mules?"

"Yes, sir. They're waiting at the livery stable."

"While I change and pack for the trip, go see to provisions for us and the animals. I'll meet you at the livery stable in an hour."

Miles returned to the office and found Philippe sitting behind his desk. Miles stuck his head in and said, "Just wanted to say goodbye. Johnny and I are leaving now to inspect my new land. Will you be here when we return?"

"That depends on how long you're gone. I plan to go back to Boston on the next company packet, which is scheduled to sail on May 15."

"I doubt we'll be back by then, so thank you again for your help in getting me set up with Henri."

"Glad to be of service, Miles. Henri will see that all of your needs are met. Don't hesitate to ask him for anything."

"I won't, thank you. Please tell Josiah, Martha, and Temperance that we'll return to Boston before winter sets in."

"Don't forget—you have carte blanche to sail on our packets. Henri will make those arrangements when you're ready."

The friends shook hands, and Philippe patted Miles on the back. Miles carried his handbag and walked to meet Johnny at the livery. Johnny had saddled two of the horses and tied the pack mules and other horses together. The mules were loaded with their gear, and, just after noon, Miles and Johnny rode west on the road to Parkers Ferry on the Edisto River. They made camp before dark and rode to the ferry the next morning.

The men crossed the Edisto just after dawn, and, as soon as the sun was fully up, Miles pulled out his instruments and map to determine their position. According to the map, they needed to head north along the western bank of the Edisto for some 60 miles or so until they reached a big bend in the river.

Miles and Johnny tried to keep the river in sight as they worked their way through a dense forest of virgin oaks and other hardwood trees. The Edisto's waters were black and flowed languidly toward the Atlantic. It was slow going, and they camped two nights before reaching the large bend in the river. The land on the western side of the river rose almost a hundred feet to a bluff. Miles shot another position and found that they were at 33° 09N. They had found his land.

Miles and Johnny made a campsite on the bluff and spent the next two weeks roaming across the grant. They located a spring about a quarter of a mile from the edge of the bluff and lined it with rocks, creating a pool of fresh, cool water. Every night, they sat by the fire, and Miles told Johnny about his plans to carve a working farm out of this dense wilderness and his idea of doing it without slave labor. The land was not suitable for indigo or tobacco, so they would have to rely on lumber and animals to provide their crops. One night, Johnny was listening to Miles talk about the future, and he asked, "What will we call this place?"

Miles thought for a moment and replied, "I think we'll call it River's Bend Plantation at Annie's Landing."

ABOUT THE AUTHOR

Photograph: Tim Patton

A son of the Mississippi Delta, Thomas R. Lawrence is a retired venture capitalist and self-proclaimed serial entrepreneur. He is a graduate of Mississippi State University and remains an avid Mississippi State University Bulldog fan. Tom founded *Front Porch Press, LLC* (to provide an outlet for new Southern writers) and *Porchscene: Exploring Southern Culture*, www.porchscene.com, an online blog. He currently resides in Opelika, Alabama.

Other books by Tom Lawrence are available at www.amazon.com, www.barnesandnoble.com and www.frontporchpressllc.com.

Made in the USA
Lexington, KY
06 May 2017